A Sugarloaf Secret

ROSEMARY WHITTAKER

A Sugarloaf Secret

Rosemary Whittaker

Also by Rosemary Whittaker

A Sugarloaf Valentine
A Sugarloaf Mix-Up
A Sugarloaf Surprise
A Sugarloaf Christmas
A Sugarloaf Easter
A Tale of Two Christmases
A Boxful of Christmas
The Cinnamon Snail
Sunshine State
The Wattle Birds
The Feijoa Tree

 Stopwatch Publications

First printing, 2024

ISBN-13: 978-1-922651-48-8

This book is a work of fiction. Names, characters, places, and incidents are the product of the author's imagination or are used fictitiously. Any resemblance to actual events, locales, or persons, living or dead, is coincidental.

Published by Rosemary Whittaker
www.rosemarywhittaker.com

For Sharon and Ian - Bernie's much-loved grandparents.

Thank you for making my recent trip to Melbourne such a delight.

Chapter One

'Meghan!' shouts a familiar voice, and I turn to see Isabella pushing her way towards me through the crowd of people.

She's wearing a vivid red dress and the highest heels I've ever seen. I can't imagine how she plans to get through the evening.

'You look lovely!' she says, dodging around a server and nearly making him drop his silver tray.

'So do you,' I say. 'And so does Lily.'

Lily is standing near the stage talking to a man I don't know. She's wearing a pale blue and silver mid-length dress that sets off her delicate fair colouring to perfection.

'Doesn't she?' agrees Isabella. 'I helped her choose that dress. She wanted to wear the same one she wore to Ethan's christening, but I refused to allow it. This is a huge night for us, and we're going all out for it. She took some persuading, but she finally agreed as long as I allowed her to leave the label in and return the dress if we didn't win. I told her not to be such a pessimist. How could anyone refuse to give The Sugarloaf Bakery a prize?'

'Let's hope the judges agree,' I say. 'Do you know who they are?'

She shakes her head. 'I have no idea, and no one will tell me. It isn't fair. The judges ought to wear some sort of costumes that make it easier to recognise them. All the women are in full length gowns, and the all men are wearing black tie. It makes it impossible to know whom we should butter up.'

'That's a good thing,' I say. 'No one wants to win an award because they've been ingratiating themselves with the judges.'

'I wouldn't mind,' she says wistfully. 'But I doubt I'll get the opportunity if I don't know who any of them are. I don't expect the judges to wear full costume, but how much trouble could it be for them to wear a powdered wig or carry a gavel?'

'You'll have to rely on merit,' I say, and she sighs.

'I suppose so, but it doesn't seem right. Anyway, I'm starving. I'm off to check out the food. Lily says she's too nervous to eat, which makes no sense. If you're nervous, you should do something relaxing. And what could be more relaxing than eating your way through an entire buffet? Would you like to join me?'

'In a minute. I want to say hello to Lily first.'

'You object to me politely greeting the judges,' says Isabella. 'But you don't mind sucking up to your boss?'

'I only want to wish her good luck. That isn't sucking up. And you're my boss too.'

'You'd never think it,' she says. 'You haven't mentioned I'm the most amazing person here tonight, and my dress would grace a state banquet.'

'It's lovely,' I say sincerely. 'I wish I could carry off something like that. But I'm slightly concerned about those shoes. Didn't you like your feet the shape they were?'

She glances down. 'They are a bit extreme, but they go well with this dress. You wouldn't believe how long it took me to find them. I had to search absolutely everywhere.'

'Where did you finally find them?'

'At the back of Georgia's wardrobe, under a pile of sweaters. If I didn't know better, I'd have thought she was hiding them from me. But I'm sure she would never have done anything so unhelpful, especially as she knew this was the exact shade of red I was looking for. I've left some old sneakers wrapped in tissue paper in their place in case she suddenly gets suspicious and goes upstairs to check on them.'

'Do you think she'll burst in halfway through the ceremony to get them back?' I ask.

'I wouldn't put it past her. She's capable of anything. The only thing in my favour is that she's the laziest person I've ever met. She'd have to drive over here and find us first, which might mean missing her dinner. I think I'm safe for the evening. You don't have a sister, do you?'

'I'm an only child. I have no siblings to steal my things.'

'You're welcome to mine,' she offers. 'Don't laugh. I'm serious. Say the word, and I'll deliver her to your door. I'll even throw in a free pair of shoes.'

'I doubt Eleanor would be too keen. She's a great landlady, and I want to keep living with her.'

Isabella's shoulders sag. 'I was afraid you'd say that. It's what everyone says when I offer to sign Georgia over to them. If you ever change your mind, let me know.'

'I will,' I promise. 'I don't want to worry you unduly, but that buffet is disappearing fast.'

Isabella looks horrified. 'Why didn't you tell me instead of keeping me hanging around here talking about shoes?'

She heads towards the food, leaving me to look for Lily, who seems to have disappeared. I decide to join Isabella and get myself something to eat before the award ceremony starts.

I start to make my way through the crowd. Two large men in tuxedos stop to greet each other, blocking my way.

'Excuse me,' I say, but neither of them hears me.

'Hello?' I say more loudly.

One of the men turns to look at me. 'What is it?'

I hesitate, not wanting to tell them they're in my way. They may think I'm making an unfavourable comment about their size. And with my luck, they'll both be on the judging panel. Isabella was right. It would be a lot easier if the judges were wearing wigs.

'I'm a bit trapped,' I say with a pleasant smile

An odd expression crosses his face. 'Trapped in what sense?'

I gesture to them both. 'You're slightly … taller than me.'

'Were you intending to climb over us?' he asks with a frown.

'Climb over you?' I catch his meaning and flush. 'Oh, no! I was trying to get around you, but I can't. It's like going on a bear hunt, isn't it?'

His frown deepens. 'A what?'

'We're going on a bear hunt,' I say. 'We can't get over it, we can't go under it. Oh, no! We've got to go through it!'

I stop abruptly. 'Not that I'm comparing you to a bear. I only meant …'

The two men give each other bemused looks before stepping aside for me to pass.

'Thanks,' I say. 'Well, it was nice to have …'

I make my escape and head towards the buffet. I hope they weren't really judges. If they were, I've certainly scuppered the bakery's chances of winning an award tonight.

I relax as I remember they don't know who I am. It works both ways. The judges don't identify themselves to us, but nor do we identify ourselves to them. I should be all right as long as they don't see me talking to Lily and Isabella. Maybe I should sit far away from them during the ceremony, just to be on the safe side. I know the winners have already been chosen and their names sealed inside gilt-edged envelopes, but I don't want to take any chances. These awards seem so important to Lily and Isabella. I mustn't be the one who destroys their chance of success.

I duck my head in embarrassment as I weave through the crowd. Going on a bear hunt! What was I thinking? Why couldn't I have politely asked them to move so I could get past? Some of Lily's nervousness about these awards must be rubbing off on me. I'm only working at The Sugarloaf Bakery for six months until Abby, their regular pastry chef, gets back. But it's a great place to work, and I already feel invested in its success.

I'm so busy thinking about the buffet that I forget to watch where I'm walking. As I navigate the maze of tables adorned with marzipan sculptures and intricately crafted sugar flowers, my heel catches on a piece of loose carpet. I may not be wearing skyscraper shoes like Isabella, but my heels are higher than I'm used to. This, combined with my speed, spells disaster.

I lose my balance and topple forward. To my horror, I see a chocolate fountain right ahead of me. As though in slow motion, I feel myself crashing towards it. I have a vision of being fished out of it, encased in chocolate, with the eyes of everyone here upon me, including those two men.

'First she muttered something about a bear hunt,' I can hear them saying. 'And then she dived headfirst into a chocolate fountain. They should be more careful about the type of people they allow into this type of event.'

I close my eyes and brace myself for impact just as an arm wraps around my waist and pulls me back. With a gasp of relief, I find myself standing upright, spared the humiliation of a chocolate-coated catastrophe.

Chapter Two

'Steady on!' says a man's voice. 'No swimming allowed here.'

My face flames as I turn to look at my rescuer. He's tall and dark, and he's wearing an impeccably tailored tuxedo. There's a subtle hint of stubble on his jaw. His eyes are a deep blue and, right now, shimmering with amusement.

'Thank you,' I mutter. I don't mean to sound ungracious, but I'm aware the people around us are staring at me and giggling.

'My pleasure,' he says, releasing me. 'I wasn't sure whether it was deliberate. I didn't have time to ask you, so I took a chance.'

'It wasn't deliberate,' I say. 'You have great reflexes.'

'Thanks. I used to play fly half at school. I've caught many a ball at exactly that angle. The balls weren't heading for a chocolate fountain, but the principle is the same. I'm Ben, by the way.'

'Meghan,' I manage.

'I almost dived in myself when I arrived,' he says. 'That's why I was in two minds about stopping you. It might have been deliberate.'

'I spent half a day shopping for this dress,' I tell him. 'And more than half my wages. I didn't do this on purpose. I can't afford to have it dry cleaned after wearing it for only an hour.'

'You could stand out in the rain for a while,' he suggests. 'That's what I intend to do at the end of the evening to make sure this tux is clean and ready to return to the rental place. Anyway, I was heading in the general direction of the buffet before I took this detour to prevent you from becoming the world's first living chocolate sculpture. Were you doing the same thing?'

'I was,' I say. 'It's a good idea to fuel up before events like this. In my experience, they're always interminable. No one cares about any category except the one for which they've been nominated, but they have to pretend to be fascinated by everything the presenters say. Which is difficult because the presenters are always so full of themselves and their own importance. Why can't they understand that no one wants to listen to them waffling on? All we want is for them to say, "Hi, everyone. Here are the nominees. This one has been chosen. It was almost certainly rigged, but there's nothing I can do about that. So, I'll present it with as few words as possible and allow you to get on with your evening."'

'It sounds as though you're speaking from experience,' he says. 'Have you attended many of these events?'

'Not too many. But I've watched the Oscars and the Golden Globes. It's beyond me how everyone can sit there for hours looking interested. I suppose it's because they're actors.'

He looks amused. 'I expect you're right. And how about you? Will you be sitting there bored out of your mind tonight, or do you have a vested interest? Have you been nominated for something?'

'No. I'm only here –'

The lights dim and soft music starts to play.

'Ladies and Gentlemen!' says a voice. 'We would like to let you know the fifteenth annual Local Spoon Awards ceremony is starting in five minutes. Please take your places as quickly as possible.'

'Too late,' Ben says ruefully. 'I knew I should have left you to fall in and focused on getting myself something to eat.'

'You'll have to wait until after the ceremony,' I tell him.

'There's a McDonalds a couple of miles away. If need be, I can stop in there on my way home.'

I raise an eyebrow. 'Don't let anyone hear you say that. Everyone here tonight is a total foodie.'

'Not everyone,' he says. 'Some of them will have come along to support their partners.'

'I doubt it. Would you attend an event like this unless you absolutely had to?'

'It would depend on how good the food was,' he says.

'I'm sorry I stopped you from finding out.'

'I'm not,' he says. 'You spent half a day searching for that dress, and I can see why. It's stunning. I couldn't have lived with myself if I hadn't saved it from a cocoa-butter-based tragedy.'

I laugh, and he smiles back at me, his eyes crinkling. For a rugby player, he's extremely attractive. Not a broken nose in sight. Not even a squashed ear.

The music grows louder, and he sighs. 'Time to find our seats. Are you sitting with anyone in particular? I mean, are you here as a plus one? You said you weren't up for an award.'

'I'm not here as a nominee,' I say. 'But –'

'Ben!' says an elderly man as he hurries past. 'I've been looking for you everywhere. Down there, please.'

He points to a row of seats on the opposite side of the room to where Isabella and Lily are sitting.

'Maybe I'll see you after the ceremony,' Ben tells me. He sees me watching the man. 'I'm not his plus one, if that's what you're wondering.'

I stifle a laugh. 'How do you know I'm not his plus one?'

'Because that's Ernest Pritchard, the organiser of this event. I met him and his terrifying wife earlier this evening.'

'Fair enough. I'll see you afterwards if I haven't died of boredom.'

'Put on your Oscars face,' he encourages me. 'This thing can't last longer than eight hours.'

I groan. 'I can look cheerful for two hours, maximum. After that, I'm faking an emergency and being carried out unconscious.'

'It can't involve the chocolate fountain,' he says. 'You've already tried that one, and I foiled it.'

'I have plenty more up my sleeve. Food poisoning is always a reliable excuse. I can say there was something wrong with the shrimp. Failing that, there's always the fire alarm.'

'Perhaps the presenter won't be too terrible,' he says.

'That shows how little you know. When you've attended a few more of these events, you'll realise how awful they are. I can't think where they find these people, but each one is worse than the last. This is a good face to pull if you feel you're about to scream with frustration.'

I open my eyes wide and curl my lips into a rictus grin, flapping my eyelashes at him. 'I can hold this one for almost ten minutes before I need to take a power nap.'

He smiles. 'I'll do my best to follow your advice.'

'Pinching your inner forearm works too,' I add. 'Or you can make up a game to play like Count the Toupees. If all else fails, imagine the presenter in their underwear. That always makes me laugh.'

'Thanks for the tip,' he says. 'Ernest is glaring at me, so I have to go.'

I slip into a seat behind Lily and Isabella as the music dies away.

Isabella turns around. 'I thought you'd deserted us,' she whispers.

'I was talking to someone,' I whisper back. I don't mention it was a very attractive someone with whom I hope to talk again as soon as possible.

'So I noticed,' she says. 'Why couldn't it have been me who fell into that chocolate fountain?'

'Almost fell in,' I correct her, and the woman sitting next to me glares at us to shush.

Ernest Pritchard strides onto the stage. 'Good evening, and welcome to our esteemed guests, local dignitaries, and award nominees. It is my distinct honour and privilege to be hosting tonight's fifteenth annual Local Spoon Awards, recognising excellence in cuisine across the entire New Forest area. I must add a special thanks to Pan-Tastic, suppliers of fine kitchen equipment, who are sponsoring tonight's event.'

He talks for a few more minutes, but I don't pay much attention. His speech is as boring as I predicted. But at least it's long …

'And finally,' says Ernest, 'I'd like to introduce our special guest, Ben Davies. It's a great honour to have him here today to hand out the awards, so please join me in welcoming him.'

I jolt upright. It can't be! Ben is a common enough name. But no sooner do I glimpse the tall figure striding towards the stage than I realise I'm wrong.

Ben climbs the steps, while I stare at my lap, not wanting to catch his eye. Fragments of our conversation float through my mind. Why didn't he tell me he was presenting the awards? It serves him right if he heard things he didn't want to hear about himself.

I realise how ridiculous I'm being. For all I know, Ben will be interesting and witty and hold the entire audience spellbound for the next couple of hours. I hope not. These seats aren't the most comfortable, and I'm already developing a cramp in my left calf.

'We have to thank Ben for coming this evening,' continues Ernest. 'As one of the food writers for *Whisk*, we all know what a hectic life he must lead. Which is why we're particularly obliged to him for taking time out of his busy schedule to be here with us tonight.'

My stomach flips. Did he say Ben was the food writer for *Whisk*? He can't have done. I must have misheard.

I lean forward and nudge Isabella. 'Where did he say Ben works?'

'*Whisk*. Haven't you seen his stuff? It's pretty good.'

I shake my head. 'I don't read that magazine.'

'You should,' she says. 'It's my favourite. I love their recipe ideas. Of course, all food columns are like catnip to me.'

I try to smile back, but it's a struggle. Of all the places this man could have chosen to work, why did it have to be *Whisk*? I have to get out of here as quickly as possible without him noticing.

'Are you ok?' Isabella asks, looking at me with concern.

'I'm fine. I have a touch of cramp. Maybe I'll just —'

I realise Ben has been speaking for a few minutes, and I haven't heard a word of it. He looks around the audience as he talks, as though searching for someone. I sink down in my chair as far as I can.

His gaze falls on me, and his lips twitch. 'I had a few more remarks planned, but I won't bore you with them. It's recently come to my attention that not everyone appreciates long speeches. So, without further ado, let me present the award for best new restaurant.'

He opens the envelope and pulls out a card. 'I'm absolutely certain this wasn't rigged,' he says with a smile, and I give a tiny gasp.

'I am, of course, joking,' he says without looking at me. 'The nominees are Beyond the Fork, The Old Mill, and Pam's Place. And the award goes to Beyond the Fork!'

There's a burst of applause as a young couple, both blushing madly, walk down to the stage to receive their award.

'What a disgrace!' the woman next to me hisses. 'That should have gone to The Old Mill, and they know it!'

'Not now, Sylvia!' says her companion, and she subsides.

The evening drags on as we sit through the categories of best locally sourced menu, craft brew, artisanal cocktail, family restaurant, vegan, charcuterie, wine list, interior design, most innovative menu, and even the best locally roasted coffee.

I don't dare glance at my watch in case it tells me we've gone past midnight and are now somewhere in the middle of next week.

'Our category is coming up next,' Lily whispers.

Isabella nods without speaking. I'm surprised to see how pale and tense her face is. She's always so full of jokes that it feels strange to see her taking something seriously. I cross the fingers on both my hands, then cross my legs too for good measure.

Ben opens the next envelope. 'I'm delighted to announce the award for best local bakery goes to The Sugarloaf Bakery in Honeywell.'

Lily gives a faint shriek, and Isabella lets out a whoop of delight.

'Come on!' she says, turning to me.

Lily stands dazedly, but I remain in my seat.

'I can't move. Cramp!' I illustrate this by giving a wince of pain.

'What a shame,' says Isabella. 'Come on, Lily!'

I watch them make their way onto the stage to accept their award from Ben. He smiles charmingly as he congratulates them. Lily still looks dazed, but Isabella is jubilant.

'Ladies and Gentlemen,' she says, leaning towards the microphone Ben is holding. 'It is a great honour and –'

'I'm afraid we don't have time for speeches,' says Ernest. 'We have several more categories to go.'

Isabella doesn't look convinced as Lily shepherds her off the stage. I join in the applause as loudly as I can. I'm delighted for them both. But I'm also desperate that Ben doesn't connect me with either of them. I'll slip out as soon as the awards end, text Isabella to say I was called away for an emergency, and hope for the best.

With any luck, Ben will be returning to London after the ceremony, and I can go into work tomorrow as though nothing has happened. Isabella and Lily will be so delighted with their award they won't even notice I'm not here tonight. As long as I don't set off the fire alarm as I leave, I should be fine.

Chapter Three

I'm the only member of staff to arrive at work on time the following morning. I'm not surprised. Lily and Isabella had a big night and I expect they've both overslept. I hope one of them turns up soon or I'll have to leave the kitchen and serve in the bakery, which means there won't be any fresh bread to sell.

I put the first batch of loaves into the oven and mix the pastry for the Bakewell tarts. I'm rolling it out when I hear the shop door open. I go to see who it is and find Isabella attempting to hang her old duffel coat on a peg.

'Shall I do that?' I ask, taking it from her.

She sinks into a chair and groans. 'We need to buy a new coat rack. None of the hooks seem to be in their usual places.'

I hang up her coat for her. 'How are you feeling today?'

'For some reason, I have a splitting headache and a horrible taste in my mouth. I can't think why. I must be going down with something. If it gets any worse, one of you will have to take me to the emergency room.'

'That will be me,' I say. 'Lily hasn't arrived yet.'

She raises her head from her arms with difficulty. 'That doesn't surprise me. She was drinking like a fish last night. I was quite shocked. Thank goodness I was on hand to get her home safely.'

'You didn't drive?' I ask, concerned.

She shakes her head, then groans again. 'That hurt. Of course I didn't drive. I think we took a taxi back home, but it's all a bit of a blur. As I say, I'm going down with something. I probably have a temperature.'

'It was a big win for you both,' I say. 'No wonder you feel rough. I'm sorry I didn't see you afterwards to congratulate you properly.'

'Didn't you? I could have sworn you did. I seem to remember dancing with you.'

'There wasn't any dancing,' I say, and she gives me a bleary look.

'I'm almost sure you're wrong. I have a distinct memory of dancing with someone. I think they were covered in chocolate. Or perhaps that was me.'

'You may be confusing it with me almost falling into the chocolate fountain. But that was earlier in the evening.'

'I don't remember that,' she says. 'But you were drinking an awful lot last night. Possibly you hallucinated it.'

I decide not to argue with her. For one thing, she's my boss. For another, I'm glad she doesn't realise I left as soon as the final award had been announced. Nor do I mention I only drank one glass of champagne. It seems unkind to let her know I'm not feeling as rough as she is. Best to allow her to imagine we're both fellow sufferers.

'Shall I make us both a coffee?' I ask.

She lifts her head for long enough to say, 'Make mine a triple,' before allowing it to crash back down again.

The bakery door opens, and Lily appears. Her face is a pale green colour and her usually tidy hair is dishevelled. She also appears to be walking on tiptoe.

Isabella squints at her. 'What are you doing?'

Lily collapses into a chair. 'It makes less noise when I walk like this.'

'Have you caught the same bug as Isabella?' I ask with barely concealed amusement.

Lily tries to focus on me, then gives up. 'Is Isabella off sick today? That's just like her. I made the effort to come into work even though it feels as though someone is running around inside my skull with a pneumatic drill. And now I find she's skulking at home in bed, telling you she's too sick to make it in. What did she say she had – the bubonic plague?'

'I'm sitting right next to you!' says Isabella in an injured tone.

Lily turns her head with difficulty. 'So you are. Then why did Meghan tell me you were home sick?'

'I'll make you a coffee too,' I say, deciding it's too much effort to clear up this misunderstanding.

'Thanks,' says Lily. 'Make mine a quadruple.'

Isabella mutters something about one-upmanship, and they both relapse into silence. It looks as though it's going to be a long day.

'Do you want to close the bakery this morning?' I ask as I measure out the coffee.

'No!' they say simultaneously, then wince in unison.

'We have to open today,' says Isabella. 'Everyone needs to hear about our award.'

'You could hang a sign on the door,' I suggest.

'I'm doing that the minute I can find someone to paint one large enough. But we have to tell our customers about our triumph in person. They're the ones who made it happen.'

Lily hiccups and claps her hand to her mouth. 'Excuse me!' She disappears into the back of the shop.

Isabella finishes her coffee and picks up Lily's. 'She won't be needing this. I'm feeling a little better now. Maybe it isn't the plague after all. It may be something a lot milder, like leprosy. I should be ok to work today. Can you tell Lily to go home to bed?'

'I'm not going to look for her,' I say. 'I don't know what I'll find. Besides, I have loaves to bake. If there's no bread, you won't have any customers to hear the glad tidings.'

Lily reappears, looking somewhat better. 'Sorry about that. False alarm. I'll be fine once I've finished my coffee.'

She looks around the tables. 'Where did it go?'

'I think Meghan drank it,' says Isabella. 'Maybe she can make you another.'

I point to the window. 'You have customers waiting. Shall I let them in?'

'I'll do that while you make Lily's coffee,' says Isabella. 'You drank hers, so it's only fair.'

When I've given Lily her coffee, I return to the kitchen to finish making the Bakewell tarts and start on a batch of eclairs. They're Isabella's favourites. If I have time, I'll make some macarons for Lily too. She loves those, but they're one of our best sellers, so she rarely gets her hands on them. I wonder whether either of them is regretting last night. I decide not. Winning the award for best local bakery was an enormous triumph. They deserved to enjoy their moment, no matter how awful they might feel today.

If I hadn't left early, this could have been me right now — slumped over a heap of bread dough, wondering whether the two halves of my brain would ever locate each other and join forces again. I feel a stab of resentment that I had to leave before all the fun started. It wasn't exactly Ben's fault, although he didn't have to accept the invitation to hand out the awards. He's just like the rest of them, unable to resist the idea of dressing up and listening to the sound of his own voice.

I put the final touches to the eclairs and return to the shop to check whether Lily and Isabella are still standing or whether they've collapsed groaning in a corner. To my surprise, Isabella looks almost her usual self.

'Do we have any more jam doughnuts?' she asks. 'Lily ate the last of them, and I want one with my lunch.'

'No, I didn't,' says Lily, who's cleaning the coffee machine in a lackadaisical manner. 'I haven't been able to face anything except coffee all morning.'

'Rookie mistake,' says Isabella. 'Whenever I go down with a dreadful virus like this, I eat more than usual. I think it confuses the germs.'

'I'll make some more this afternoon,' I promise. 'Is it all right if I take my lunch break now? I didn't get as far as the buffet last night, and I woke up too late to eat breakfast this morning.'

Isabella's eyes open wide. 'How have you not passed out? Get yourself something to eat at once. We can't afford to lose our pastry chef, not now we've won such a prestigious national award!'

'It was a local award,' says Lily, but Isabella ignores her.

'We have a couple of those steak pies left,' she tells me. 'Help yourself.'

Lily is peering out of the window. 'My vision is a little fuzzy, but isn't that the man we met last night – the one who gave us the award?'

Isabella cranes around her to look. 'That's right. Ben Davies. I thought he was driving up to London this morning. That's what he told me. I wonder why he didn't.'

I stand there frozen for a few seconds, clutching my steak pie. It can't be him. It just can't be. Lily said her vision was blurry, but I can't take any chances. I drop the pie back onto the tray and dive towards the kitchen.

'Don't tell him I'm here!' I hiss at Isabella.

'Why not?'

I wave my hands. 'There's no time to explain now, but it's desperately important. Please don't mention I work here as a pastry chef or that you and I have ever met each other.'

Her eyes light up. 'This sounds interesting. What's going on?'

With one last, desperate flap of my hands, I disappear into the kitchen. I don't know why Ben is here today, but it can't have anything to do with me. For all I know, he's heard about the quality of our steak pies and decided to sample them for himself before returning to London. In any case, he won't be visiting the kitchen.

I crouch behind the door and press my ear to the crack. The bell jangles, and I hear the sound of a man's voice. Isabella says something in reply. I strain to hear what it is, but I can only catch the odd word.

How long does it take to serve a customer a steak pie and wave them off the premises? I could have got rid of him in under a minute. Isabella still seems to be talking. I hear Ben's voice again, then footsteps. Thank goodness! I'll wait until he's left the shop, then make up some story to satisfy Lily and Isabella.

But the bell doesn't jangle again. The footsteps aren't going towards the shop door after all. Has Ben noticed a plate of millionaire's shortbread and decided to inspect it more closely? He really is an annoying man. I hope Isabella tips it over his head.

I hear her voice, much closer now. 'Don't worry, Lily, I'll show him. Can you mind the shop for a few minutes?'
She raises her voice to an artificially high volume. 'Alright, Ben, let's go and inspect the kitchen!'

Chapter Four

The door opens, and I duck behind a trolley laden with baking equipment. It isn't the best hiding place, but there's no time to think of a better one. What is Isabella thinking of bringing Ben in here? I told her not to betray any knowledge of my whereabouts, or even my existence. I know she loves to joke around, but she must have realised I was serious.

Maybe she thinks I've slipped out of the back door. If I had a shred of sense, that's exactly what I would have done. I glance over at the door, mentally calculating the distance between it and me. It's no good. Even if I could crawl over there without anyone seeing me, Ben would be bound to notice it opening and closing. I'll have to remain where I am for now and hope he doesn't stay for long.

Why is he here at all? He's a food writer, not a chef. There's no reason for him to be foraging around in our bakery kitchen. There's plenty of food in the shop if he's hungry. What would health and safety say if they knew people off the street were being offered unauthorised tours of our premises? It's a huge breach of the rules. Lily and Isabella would be stripped of their newly awarded title before they could say hazelnut meringue.

'It's larger than I expected,' says Ben's voice.

'That's because this bakery used to be a much bigger concern,' says Isabella. 'They baked everything on the premises. That all stopped under the previous owner, but Lily and I renovated the kitchen when we bought the place. It wasn't just that we wanted to add the cafe. We also plan to offer wider catering services now we've got the business off the ground.'

'You mentioned that last night,' says Ben.

Isabella told him about the bakery? That must have been after I left. What else did she mention?

My heart races, and I breathe deeply to calm myself. If Isabella told him about the business, it would have been Abby she talked about, not a temporary stand-in. Or would it? Isabella is a talker. She's one of the most gregarious people I know. Even more so when she's had a few drinks.

Did I tell Ben my surname? I rack my brains, trying to remember last night's sequence of events. I took a flying dive towards the chocolate fountain before he rugby tackled me and prevented complete disaster. He told me he was called Ben, and I told him my name was Meghan. So far, so good. As long as Isabella didn't become too confidential during their later conversation, I should be all right. There could have been hundreds of people called Meghan at last night's event.

I breathe a silent thanks to my parents for not saddling me with a name like Euphemia or Octavia. That might have caused Ben to ask questions. As it is, if he consumed as much alcohol as my bosses, I should be safe. He probably only has the haziest memory of what happened last night. I doubt he even remembers his rugby-tackling heroics.

Which leaves the question of why he's here today? It's unlikely he came across our bakery by chance on his drive home. Honeywell isn't on the route between Christchurch and London. Is he here to see Isabella? Most men seem to fall for her the moment they see her, which makes sense. She's beautiful, and she's intelligent and charming too. Some people have all the luck.

I hope Ben doesn't succumb to her charms. That would cause me immense complications. It was one thing to meet him at an awards ceremony when I could slip out unobserved. It would be quite another to be forced to avoid him until the end of my contract. I might even have to give up my job here. This seems unfair, but it may be the only solution. I can't spend the next few months hiding behind kitchen utensils or diving into the freezer whenever he appears. The bakery would go bust very quickly.

'Is there anything in particular you'd like to see?' Isabella asks him.

'Not really. I was just interested in your general set up. What do you have out the back – a staff garden?'

'I wish,' she says. 'That door leads to the car park.'

To my horror, she walks over to the door, and Ben follows her. I ease myself around the trolley, careful not to knock against any of the saucepans, and look for a better hiding place. I could make a dash for the shop, but there's too much open space. Ben and Isabella could turn around at any second, and he'd be bound to see me. If I'm to be discovered, it won't be crawling on all fours around the kitchen floor as though searching for scraps. I could claim to have lost a contact lens, but I somehow don't think that would be convincing.

'You see,' says Isabella, unlocking the door. 'A concrete path and a few cars. It isn't Narnia.'

'What a shame,' says Ben. 'If I worked here, I'd sneak into the kitchen at odd times and throw open the door in case I found a snow-covered forest with fauns running around. I loved those stories when I was young.'

I raise myself to a crouching position, ignoring the shooting pain in my thigh. I take one last hunted look around, then launch myself towards the industrial fridge. I'm tempted to climb inside it, but Isabella will probably offer to show Ben the chocolate torte she begged me to make yesterday. Instead, I wedge myself into the gap between the fridge and the wall, crouch down, and pull my apron over my head. At a cursory glance, I may look like a heap of tea towels.

'Would you like to see our new dough mixer?' asks Isabella. 'It's over there on that counter.'

I gasp in frustration, then clap my hand over my mouth. If it would be humiliating to be discovered crawling around the floor, it would be ten times worse to be found wedged down the side of the fridge.

I'm starting to feel claustrophobic. I can't stay here for the next half hour while Isabella demonstrates every single piece of kitchen equipment. And if Ben really is here to tell her he's fallen for her, I don't want to be an unwitting eavesdropper. She needs to remove him before I suffocate.

I reach into my pocket and pull out my phone. I can barely move my right arm, but I quickly type a text. Get him out of here!

Isabella's phone vibrates, and she looks at the screen. Her eyebrows shoot up. 'Sorry, Ben, I have to answer this.'

I panic as she taps the keys. Is my phone volume turned down? If not, the beep will give the game away.

My screen lights up, and I breathe a sigh of relief. I switched it to silent last night before the ceremony and must have forgotten to switch it back on this morning.

Where are you? says the text.

I grit my teeth as I type back. Never mind where I am. Just get him out of here!!!!

Isabella clears her throat. 'I'm awfully sorry, Ben, but there's somewhere I need to be rather urgently. Do you mind if we put this off until another time?'

'Of course,' he says. 'Please don't let me hold you up. I should get going too.'

My shoulders sag in relief. I won't feel easy until his car has cleared Honeywell airspace. Or roadspace. Not that we'll have any way of knowing the exact time this occurs unless Isabella can nip out and put a tag on his car without him realising. She's the type of person who's bound to have one in her bag for exactly this sort of emergency.

I decide this plan won't work. It would take far too many texts to explain to her what I wanted. Far better to let her remove him from the danger zone and trust to his wanting to get back to London in time for dinner. I'm so keyed up that I may well feel the disturbance in the force when he leaves the village anyway.

I slide my phone back into my pocket. As I do so, my elbow knocks against the side of the fridge with a dull thud.

Ben stops and looks around. 'What was that?'

'I didn't hear anything,' says Isabella, taking his arm and leading him towards the door. As she passes the fridge, she catches sight of me folded almost double in the tiny space. She makes a choking noise, which she turns into a cough.

'Are you ok?' asks Ben.

'Fine!' she says in an artificially high voice. 'I think I swallowed a crumb.'

He looks confused. 'When?'

'Earlier,' she says. 'Or maybe yesterday.'

I stifle a laugh, which is a mistake. Ben hears me. I hold my breath as he turns to look in my direction.

'Is there something inside your fridge?' he asks.

'An enormous chocolate torte,' says Isabella. 'Would you like a piece?'

'A chocolate torte wouldn't make a sound like that.'

'Oh, that,' she says. 'It happens sometimes. We think it's probably rats.'

Ben looks horrified. 'Rats?'

'I mean the pipes,' she amends. 'The plumber's coming tomorrow to have a look at them. You know what these old buildings are like. If it isn't one thing, it's another.'

She pushes him out of the door, and I hear their voices fade away. It still seems like hours before I hear the jangle of the shop bell.

'Goodbye, Ben! Safe travels!' Isabella calls loudly.

The kitchen door opens, and she comes back in, her shoulders shaking.

'It's safe to come out now,' she says, looking down at me.

'I can't,' I say. 'I'm stuck.'

I wish I could say she looks concerned. Most bosses, upon hearing their employees are in a difficult position, worry about possible lawsuits and spring into action. Not mine. Isabella only doubles up with fresh laughter.

'I mean it!' I insist. 'I can't move.'

She wipes her eyes and holds out her hand. I reluctantly take it and allow her to haul me out.

'It's like Pooh Bear getting stuck in Rabbit's doorway,' she says with a snort of mirth.

'It's nothing like that,' I say with dignity.

'Yes, it is. Have you been at the condensed milk again?'

'I haven't even had my lunch.'

'That's right! You were about to eat it when you saw Ben coming, then you disappeared. I'll heat that pie for you. But not,' she adds in a severe tone, 'until you've told me exactly what's going on.'

Chapter Five

I follow her back to the cafe and take a seat while she heats my pie.

'Thanks,' I say as she carries the plate over to my table. 'I really need this.'

She holds it out of my reach. 'Not so fast! Do you intend to explain what you're up to?'

I feign innocence. 'Eating my lunch, you mean?'

She moves the plate even further away. 'I mean nothing of the sort, and you know it. Out with it, young Meghan, or I'll be the one eating this pie while you wipe down the tables.'

'That's employee abuse. I'm sure it's written somewhere in my contract that I have the right to regular breaks and sustenance.'

'I wrote that contract,' she says. 'And I was careful not to include anything so ridiculous.'

I push back my chair. 'Fine, I'll go to the Red Lion for lunch before contacting my union for advice.'

'I'll call ahead and tell Shelley not to serve you,' she says. 'By the time I've finished making phone calls, there won't be a single establishment in this village willing to deal with you. You won't be able to buy so much as a stamp.'

'I never write letters.'

'Or a bar of chocolate,' she adds.

'I prefer toffees.'

'Come on, Meghan,' she says in a cajoling tone. 'Be reasonable. You can't expect to skulk around the kitchens, inserting yourself into spaces never designed for the human body, then refuse to tell your employers what you're up to.'

'I'm not up to anything!' I protest unconvincingly.

'Of course not. There must be a million good explanations for why you were lurking next to the fridge. The most obvious one is that you were testing out your new invisibility cloak. If so, I'm disappointed to inform you it was malfunctioning just now.'

'Nothing so exciting,' I say, wondering whether I can convince her I'm a secret health inspector sent down here to file a report on the state of her kitchen.

'Are you avoiding the paparazzi?' she asks, her face lighting up. 'You should have told me. I would have helped you. I could have laid a false trail to lure them away from Honeywell.'

'Considering that I begged you not to tell Ben where I was hiding, and the first thing you did was invite him into the kitchen for a five-hour tour, I don't have much faith in your luring abilities.'

She has the grace to look contrite. 'I thought you must have slipped out of the back door and gone to the pub. I never dreamed you'd still be in there. My head is still fuzzy from my unspecified viral malady, or I might have thought about it more clearly.'

'Why did you offer to take him into the kitchen at all? Is this some regular tour you plan to offer all our customers? If so, you'll be looking for a new pastry chef.'

'Ben was asking about our business last night,' she says. 'He seemed interested in what we do here. Lily and I invited him to stop by on his way to London and take a look.'

I stretch out my hand again. 'Are you going to give me that pie?'

Lily has been serving a customer during our argument. She closes the till and comes over to my table.

'Why are you waving that plate around?' she asks Isabella. 'Put it down before you drop it.'

'I'm using it as a bargaining tool,' says Isabella.

I make another futile attempt to snatch it from her. 'Blackmail tool, more like. Make her give it to me, Lily!'

Lily takes the plate from Isabella and hands it to me. 'I don't know what's happening, and I don't care. But please don't make so much noise.'

I take a bite of the pie before Isabella can stop me. 'Sorry about that. I'll be as quiet as a mouse for the rest of the day.'

Isabella plumps down in the chair opposite me. 'I won't! If you don't tell me what's going on right now, I'll scream.'

'Not if you want to keep me as a business partner,' says Lily. 'What are you arguing about?'

Isabella gives a frustrated sigh. 'Didn't you notice Meghan's disappearing act just now? As her boss, I'm asking for an explanation.'

Lily focuses on me with difficulty. 'That was strange. What were you doing?'

'Practising my ninja skills.'

'Right,' she says without much interest.

'No, it isn't right!' says Isabella. 'If you don't want me to call Ben right now, Meghan, you'd better come clean.'

'You wouldn't!'

'Wouldn't I?' She pulls out her phone and scrolls through her contacts.

'Fine!' I say. 'Put that down, and I'll tell you.'

She grins. 'I thought that would do it. All right, Meghan, I'm going to put my phone on the table here, nice and easy. That way, no one has to get hurt.'

'Thanks for that,' I say. 'In the interests of full disclosure, I have no weapons secreted about my person. And I haven't set the oven to self-destruct if I'm not back in the kitchen in the next three minutes.'

'We aren't doing this without coffee,' says Lily. 'At least, I'm not. Give me a minute and I'll make us all a drink.'

Isabella and I regard each other in wary silence until Lily returns. I consider making a grab for her phone but it's too far away.

'Here you go,' says Lily, handing us both a mug and sitting down. 'I have to say I'm quite intrigued.'

'You have no reason to be,' I warn her. 'Isabella's making a mountain out of a mole hill.'

I take a sip of my coffee, wondering how much to tell them.

'My name isn't really Meghan Randall,' I begin.

They both look startled, and I hurry on. 'I don't mean I'm an imposter, or a spy, or any of the thousand things Isabella is about to suggest. I mean that Meghan Randall is my work name.'

'What a great idea,' says Isabella. 'I wonder why I didn't think of that before I decided to set up business here as Isabella Campbell? I could have been Candy Shortbread or Cherry Slice.'

Lily is observing me carefully. 'Why do you use a different name for work?'

'I have every right to use it,' I say. 'It was my mother's surname before she married my father.'

'And what's his surname, if you don't mind me asking?'

'Blake-Taylor.'

Lily looks puzzled, but I see understanding dawning on Isabella's face.

'David Blake-Taylor?' she says. 'As in the guy who founded *Whisk* and went on to start a load of other magazines?'

'That's the one.'

'You're kidding!' she says.

'I'm afraid not.'

'It must be amazing to be able to say you're the daughter of David Blake-Taylor. I bet you had an incredible childhood.'

'A privileged one,' I say. 'It isn't always the same thing.'

'I suppose not. But why didn't you tell us?'

'Would you have treated me differently if I had?'

'Of course not!' She pauses. 'I mean, I hope not.'

I take another swig of coffee. 'Most people do. They want to know every detail about my family, or else they see me as someone who can do something for them.'

'We wouldn't have done that,' says Lily.

'I know that now, although I didn't when I applied for the job. But that isn't why I hid it. My father has never come to terms with me not wanting to go into the family business. My mother died when I was young. I was their only child, and Dad assumed I would take over and carry on when he retired. The problem is that I have no interest in becoming a media mogul.'

'Why not?' interrupts Isabella. 'It sounds fun. Private jets and yachts and five-star service wherever you go. Most people would jump at it.'

'Not me,' I say. 'I did a cookery course in Paris during my year off before university. When I got home, Dad was still keen for me to do my journalism degree. I did alright, but I didn't enjoy the course as much as he expected I would. My favourite part of it was my evening job. I worked in the kitchen of a local hotel, and I loved it. By the time I graduated, I knew I couldn't do what my father wanted, but I had no idea how to explain that to him. He thought I could mix my two sets of interests and become a food writer on his flagship magazine.'

'That must have been difficult,' says Lily. 'My parents are the exact opposite. They've always encouraged me to do what I wanted and follow my heart. I can never be sufficiently grateful to them for that. All they wanted was my happiness.'

'That's what my father wants too,' I say. 'The problem is, he can't understand how I could walk away from something that's been his whole life and given him so much satisfaction.'

'When did you break the news to him?' asks Isabella, who's looking more serious than usual.

'A couple of months ago. I finally told him I didn't want to work for him. He was surprisingly good about it. He agreed I should take a few months off and have some fun while I thought about my future. I suspect he's convinced I'll change my mind when I realise how hard real life is. He expects me to come running back to him with my tail between my legs, begging him for a job. He has a position lined up for me in the food writing department.'

Neither of them speaks. I half expect Isabella to make one of her usual jokes, but she doesn't.

'I planned to stay with a friend in Paris while I thought about my next steps,' I say. 'Then I saw your advertisement and thought I may as well apply, even though I didn't have as much experience as your regular chef. I was really excited when you offered me the job because it showed I didn't need my father's name to succeed.'

'We would have offered it to you either way,' says Isabella.

'Maybe, but I would never have been sure about that. As it is, you took me on because I had a bakery qualification, and you thought I would fit in. That meant a lot.'

'I can understand that,' says Lily. 'But I don't understand about Ben. Why did you hide in the kitchen today? Did you already know him? Is he an ex-boyfriend or something?'

Isabella is quicker. 'He works for your dad, doesn't he?'

'Yes. He's a food writer at *Whisk.*'

Her face flashes comprehension. 'Is that by any chance the job your father intended for you?'

'It is. Dad apparently cleared it with the editor and presented it to me as a fait accompli.'

Lily's eyes are wide with sympathy. 'Don't you and your father speak anymore?'

'It isn't as dramatic as that,' I say. 'We made up our quarrel and agreed I'd go to Paris for a few months while I considered my next steps. But we were both horribly stilted and polite around each other. We still are. It feels as though we're both shouting at each other from opposite trenches, and neither of us can hear each other. We can barely even see each other.'

'Where does Ben come into this?' asks Lily. 'Would he know your mother's maiden name?'

'Probably not, but I don't want him making the connection and mentioning it to people at work. My father has no idea I'm down here. He thinks I'm in Paris, and I'd like him to go on thinking that.'

I catch her surprised look and blush. 'I know how that sounds. I should be honest with him and let him deal with it. But I'm not yet ready for that. He's such a busy man that I doubt he has time to remember the details of what I'm up to. He just needs to know everything is fine, and then he won't give it another thought.'

Lily doesn't look convinced, but she doesn't argue further.

Isabella is looking thoughtful. 'Ben told us today he's writing an article on the Local Spoon Awards. He wants to come back here sometime and ask us some more questions.'

I groan. 'Of course he does. If you can't put him off, please give me adequate notice when he tells you he's coming here again.'

'We will,' she promises. 'And I'll make a list of possible hiding places for you.'

Lily isn't listening. She's peering out of the window. 'I see Bernie coming down the high street with his owners. Did you make a fresh batch of dog biscuits, Meghan? I think he's finished the previous lot.'

'They're in a tin in the kitchen,' I say. 'I'll get them now.'

'If you aren't back in two minutes, I'll come and search for you,' Isabella warns me. 'I realise you're used to living in swanky Parisian apartments rather than slumming it among the peasants of Honeywell. But that's what we're paying you to do, so you have no choice. And please – no hiding under the sink. We don't want to have to call a plumber when you inevitably get yourself stuck.'

Chapter Six

It could have been worse. I have to put up with Isabella's teasing for the next couple of days. She's particularly witty on the subject of possible hiding places in kitchens. But eventually she runs out of jokes, and things return to normal at the Sugarloaf. I would have preferred not to discuss my father and my reasons for taking this job without his knowledge. But what does it matter if I've had to be truthful with my workmates about my family background? Neither of them is likely to spread the news. Lily is far too discreet, and Isabella is big on female solidarity.

In the end, I'm forced to admit my private life isn't as important to those around me as it is to myself. I realise I've been blowing things out of proportion over the past few weeks. Even Dad, who presumably has a vested interest in what I do with my life, has shown almost no curiosity about what I'm currently up to.

He's sent me one brief email since I left on my supposed French adventure, and that was only to inform me of my Aunt Beatrice's hip operation. I haven't communicated with him either. My conscience pricks me occasionally, but it would feel worse to tell him a pack of lies. It was bad enough telling him I was going to Paris rather than Honeywell. Sending him a detailed string of fallacious French details would feel unnecessarily duplicitous.

I try to push him to the back of my mind, which is much easier than I expected because Isabella is full of plans for the coming month. She and Lily have decided that winning the award is a signal to expand their business.

'We have to strike while the iron's hot!' proclaims Isabella when she arrives one morning. 'We always intended to branch out the moment we could afford to. This publicity has come at the right time for us. We've had write-ups in three local newspapers, and Lily and I are being interviewed on the radio next week.'

'What do you have in mind?' I ask. 'Lily mentioned during my interview that you'd like to cater weddings one day.'

'We would,' she says. 'But we'd need a loan for that sort of thing. The bakery is doing well, but we don't want to take on more debt at the moment. We were wondering about offering cookery lessons.'

'Here at the bakery?'

'Or at Mayfield High School,' she says. 'They have a domestic science wing they hire out. They hosted a baking competition there a few years ago.'

'Which you won?' I ask, seeing the gleam in her eyes.

'It's complicated. Let's say it was a good day all around.'

'So, these cookery lessons,' I say to bring her back to the present. 'Who would be giving them?'

Her face is wary, and I groan. 'Let me guess!'

'Who else?' she says. 'Lily and I will help you, but we only know the basics. We need a trained professional if we want to attract plenty of customers.'

'What sort of lessons?' I ask. 'If you plan to hold them in a school kitchen, I don't suppose you're thinking of anything too extravagant.'

'That's up to you,' she says. 'What would you suggest?'

'Hiring someone especially for the occasion,' I say, but she shakes her head.

'We can't afford that. I realise it isn't in your contract, which was remiss of me. I should have added a clause saying you were obliged to cater to our every whim. I won't make that mistake again.'

I consider. I have little to do in the evenings. I've only been in Honeywell for a short time, and I've met no one except our customers and Eleanor. It could be fun, and it would be something to add to my resume.

'I'll give it a go,' I say. 'But does it have to be cookery lessons?'

She considers. 'What else do you have in mind – three-legged Zumba, or blindfold papier-mâché?'

'Nothing as exciting as that. I was wondering whether we could extend the theme of the Local Spoon Awards. I was surprised to see so many local businesses represented there.'

'I wasn't,' she says. 'Everyone thinks the New Forest is such a sleepy little area, but that couldn't be further from the truth. There's always something going on, and the food scene is thriving.'

'I'm starting to realise that. I can see the appeal of cookery lessons, but that's something you can think about at any time. My idea is to strike while the iron is hot and capitalise on the theme of local businesses.'

She pulls off her coat and sits at the table nearest to the door. 'I'm all ears.'

'I'm still thinking of something food related, but with more emphasis on the business side of it. Plenty of people were nominated for awards, but there are probably even more who weren't. I expect there are several of them in the immediate area. Why don't we get them together and run some classes on how best to produce and market their food-related ideas?'

Isabella looks at me in awe. 'That's perfect! It's exactly the sort of thing Lily and I needed when we first bought the bakery.

It was slightly different for us because The Sugarloaf Bakery was an established business – if you could call it that. But we were running on a wing and a prayer for the first couple of years. We could have done with someone who knew what they were doing and could guide us in the right direction.'

'I'm not sure I can do it full justice,' I warn her. 'I took a business course as part of my journalism degree, but it isn't my speciality.'

'I'm not thinking of your formal qualifications,' she says. 'I don't want to talk about it too much if you don't want to, but you obviously grew up around this stuff. You must have picked up lots of useful knowledge.'

'Some,' I admit. 'But I don't want to stand at the front telling everyone what they ought to be doing. I'd rather act as a facilitator and let everyone figure out what they need to do.'

She beams at me. 'I knew you wouldn't let us down.'

'I'll want a stellar reference when I leave,' I warn her.

'You can write your own, and I'll sign it,' she promises.

'You don't know what I plan to say about myself.'

'I don't much care. Thanks, Meghan. We've been wanting to get something like this off the ground for a while now, but something always gets in the way. Lily has been on maternity leave twice. She only came back from the second one a few weeks before Abby left. I didn't want to push things while we were looking for someone to replace Abby, and I wanted to give you time to settle in. Then we were nominated for the best bakery award and everything else went out of my head.'

I've done my utmost to pretend that ceremony never happened. As far as I'm concerned, none of us attended the awards evening or has ever met Ben. I'm particularly keen to forget the humiliating half hour I spent crawling around the kitchen on my hands and knees pretending not to exist.

'Let's have dinner tonight and talk about it,' says Isabella. 'My treat. We'll go to the Red Lion and sample some of Shelley's finest.'

'How can I say no? Will Lily be joining us?'

'I'll try to talk her into it,' she says. 'It's about time she had an evening away from the children. When she was on maternity leave, it was all I could do to persuade her to join me for a quick drink. Even then, she was checking her phone every two seconds to see what was happening at home. She was convinced the children would burn the house down if she was away for half an hour. Daisy is my goddaughter and the most perfectly behaved child anyone has ever met, so I knew she would never do that. I can't speak for Abby's godson. He hasn't had the benefit of my immense wisdom and finely honed child-rearing skills. But Daisy is an angel in human form and can be relied on to behave admirably and appropriately in any situation. She should have a column in The Lady. She could write about what the best babies are doing and wearing and finish each article with a few tips on baby etiquette.'

'She sounds amazing. I suppose she's rather young to join us at the Red Lion?'

Isabella sighs. 'Lily would say she's too young. I would say she isn't. It's an ongoing bone of contention between us. I believe you're never too young to learn how to eat pork scratchings. With your little finger crooked, in case you're wondering. But Lily can be very stubborn. I've often had to speak to her about it.'

The door opens, and Bernie the cavoodle bounds in. I check to see he's accompanied by an appropriate guardian. I've done this ever since he appeared out of nowhere during my first week working here. A customer was leaving the shop and held open the door for him, thinking Mrs Ogilvie or her sister Mabel was right behind. Bernie plopped himself down under the nearest table, and no one realised he was there for more than an hour, by which time his owners were frantic. Isabella finally noticed Bernie and called Mrs Ogilvie to let her know where he was, only to discover she'd contacted her vet, the police, and half the members of a group called the Silver Surfers. To Isabella's amusement, the group had already fanned out across the village green and was preparing to drag the pond.

It was a memorable afternoon, made even more so by the party we held in the bakery afterwards. Isabella dispensed free cake and tea to everyone who had helped in the hunt, and a woman called Mavis Sotherby gave a stirring speech somewhat reminiscent of Winston Churchill's 'We will fight them on the beaches'.

She finished by telling us anything was possible as long as people kept their heads and pulled together. And ensured their phones were switched on, she said with a meaningful look at Mrs Ogilvie, who was so busy hugging the errant Bernie she didn't hear. Fun as the party was, Lily told Isabella we couldn't afford to do it regularly, so we now check under the tables at intervals in case of canine intruders.

I cast a sharp glance at Bernie as he hurries in, his tongue lolling in a huge grin and his tail wagging. I relax when I see he's on his leash, and it's not just trailing behind him.

'Good afternoon, Mrs Ogilvie,' I say to the woman accompanying him.

'Wrong again!' she says with a grin. 'I'm Mabel. I don't think you've ever got it right, have you?'

'I'm sorry,' I apologise. 'I'm sure I will before I finish working here. I thought you must be Mrs Ogilvie because you didn't make a derogatory comment about Bernie when he made a beeline for the dog biscuits.'

She gives a shout of laughter. 'I didn't, did I? I must have run out of things to say about him. Don't tell Edie. She'll be insufferable.'

'I won't,' I promise. 'Your usual?'

She joins Bernie at the table next to the door. 'That's right. Earl Grey and a plum slice. Unless you have any lemon meringue tarts?'

'I'm sorry. I haven't got around to making any this week. I'll put them on my list for when I have a free moment.'

Isabella overhears and murmurs in my ear, 'You could have made a double batch in the time you wasted inspecting our fridge fittings.'

I ignore her and serve Mabel. Lily has already handed Bernie his usual dog biscuit, and he's now lying under Mabel's chair, chewing contentedly.

'Don't slobber all over my new shoes,' she tells him. 'I only bought them last week, and they have to last a good long time.'

She grins at me. 'I told Edie I got them in the sale. She'd have a fit if she saw the real price. But I don't care. If you add up what she spends on that mutt each year, she could buy herself a pair of shoes with diamond heels.'

'But she wouldn't get half as much pleasure from them,' says Lily. 'Diamond shoes don't rush over to greet you as though you're the most amazing person in the world.'

'Maybe not,' says Mabel. 'But nor do they chew up your bedspread when they get bored. Or eat your favourite socks. Or steal the last chicken breast.'

She pokes Bernie with her toe. 'You thought I didn't know about that, didn't you? Well, you're wrong. And if I hadn't hidden that marrow bone of yours in the laundry basket before Edie saw it, you'd never have seen it again. You know what Edie thinks about you eating bones, but you still did it right where she could see you. You weren't first in the queue when they were handing out brains, were you, young Bernie? It's lucky for you I'm around, or goodness knows where you'd end up.'

Chapter Seven

Isabella never lets the grass grow under her feet. Within a few days, she's organised and advertised the business classes. She tells me she's asked the first person who signed up to bring his ideas along to discuss during the first class.

Nine days later, I'm sitting in the village hall waiting for my pupils to turn up. According to the list Isabella handed me as I left work today, there should be five people here tonight. I'm glad I don't have to start my career as an educator by offering cookery classes. Business classes seem far less likely to result in fires or other accidents.

I hated our school cookery classes. Miss Eddison enjoyed the sound of her own voice so much that she spent the first two-thirds of each lessons either talking or demonstrating her superior cooking skills, leaving us almost no time to make our own dishes. I lost count of the number of failing grades I received because I only got as far as putting my dish in the oven before the bell rang.

Tonight's class is starting at seven o'clock, and the caretaker will come to check we're off the premises by nine o'clock. I hope at least some of them turn up. Most people will have to pass the pub on the way here, and it's started to rain. I don't want to sit here in lonely splendour for two hours wondering why no one wants the benefit of my immense wisdom.

My first pupil arrives at a quarter to seven. He's a man in his thirties with dark, curly hair and the brightest blue eyes I've ever seen. He gives me a cheerful smile and introduces himself as Greg Mitchell, the man who'll be presenting his idea tonight. He tells me he and his father are hoping to start a local gourmet popcorn business for some extra income, but they have no idea where to start.

'Do you enjoy cooking?' I ask him, and he grins.

'I can do a mean fry-up. Other than that, I'm a baked beans on toast sort of guy. Or else I have something delivered. But we should be able to manage popcorn if we can come up with a business plan.'

The other pupils drift in and introduce themselves. As well as Greg, I have Bethany, Charlie, Ellie, and Sue. I tick off the last name and turn to face the group. I'm surprised by how nervous I feel. This is a beginner's class, so it should be easy. But their expectant faces make me feel like a fraud. It feels arrogant to be passing myself off as some sort of business guru. What if they're looking for something from me I can't provide? They may expect to walk away after six weeks under my expert tutelage and become instant stars on The Apprentice.

I give them all a tentative smile. They smile back at me, and I relax. They don't expect anything of the kind. No one comes along to this sort of evening class expecting miracles. They want to have fun, and it's up to me to make sure they do.

'Welcome!' I say as confidently as I can. 'I'm delighted so many of you have signed up. I'll try to give you some useful pointers. I'd like to start by –'

I'm interrupted by the door behind me opening. I glance at my list. All present and correct. I turn around, expecting to see the caretaker. To my surprise, and no small degree of shock, I see Ben Davies standing in the doorway.

'What are you doing here?' I say before I can stop myself.

Why did I ask that? I should have pretended not to recognise him. As far as he's concerned, we met a while ago at an evening event, during which alcohol was flowing freely. No one remembers all their chance encounters under such circumstances. He doesn't know I also saw him the following day. And he never needs to.

He looks at me with startled recognition. 'Meghan?'

'That's right.' I pretend to search my memory. 'And you are … Ben?'

He takes a step into the room. 'You're the last person I expected to see here tonight.'

I give him a cool smile. 'I could say the same thing about you. What brings you here this evening?'

I cherish a faint hope he'll say his uncle is the caretaker of the village hall and he's stopped by for a quick chat before leaving the country on a ten-month holiday. No such luck.

'I've come to see one of these classes in operation,' he says. 'I noticed them advertised them on the bakery website. I didn't have anything planned for tonight, so I thought I'd come along and see them for myself. I hope that's alright with you?'

I plaster a welcoming smile onto my face. 'Of course. Why wouldn't it be? We were about to begin.'

'Great. Don't let me interrupt you,' he says, perching on the edge of a table.

I do my best to ignore him as I deliver my prepared speech of welcome. I finish by telling the class that Isabella has asked Greg to bring his product with him tonight.

'You'll all have a turn,' I promise them. 'But we had to begin somewhere. Ben, of course, won't be participating. He's just here to observe. He may not even want to stay for the full class.'

Greg pulls out several bags of popcorn and hands them around.

'My Dad and I have always wanted to start a business together,' he says. 'This seemed like a good idea. We plan to offer a variety of flavours and market locally to start with. But we need some tips about running a small business on a small budget.'

Everyone tastes the popcorn and offers suggestions about packaging and distribution while Greg nods and takes notes. To my surprise, I don't have to say much. The members of the group are full of ideas about local events and social media marketing. I chip in occasionally to remind them of things they may have overlooked and to talk about brand awareness and how best to advertise on a small budget.

Before we know it, it's nine o'clock, and the caretaker has arrived. He clears his throat loudly and gives me a meaningful look.

'Well done, everyone,' I say. 'I think we've all learned something tonight. Sue, you're up next week. If you're bringing ice cream samples, I've been told it's fine for you to arrive early and put them in the freezer in the kitchen. There will be a Jazzercise class going on, so you may need to dodge the flailing limbs.'

Everyone says goodbye and disappears off to the pub. I stay behind to make sure we've left the hall as tidy as we found it. I'm mildly annoyed when Ben elects to stay too.

'That was great,' he says with enthusiasm, helping me stack the chairs. 'You handled the questions really well, and you got everyone involved. I learned a lot tonight.'

'Aren't you a food writer?' I ask.

'I am.'

'Then you must already know quite a lot about food-related businesses.'

'A bit,' he says. 'It would be great if you offered cookery classes too. I'd definitely sign up for those. I don't cook very well, but you don't need to be a chef to be a food writer. Anyway, my current job is only for six months. Who knows what subjects I'll need to write about next?'

'Six months?' I ask.

'That's right. I thought when I started that I must be covering someone's parental leave, but it doesn't appear to be that. If I do well, I'm hoping they decide to make my position permanent.'

'Right,' I say.

'So, how long have you been doing this?' he asks.

'These lessons?'

'I meant working at the Sugarloaf. You didn't mention it when we met the other night.'

'You didn't tell me where you worked either,' I say in a light tone.

He looks amused. 'Would you have been less scathing about award presenters if I had?'

'Probably not. Did you enjoy the evening?'

'I enjoyed the earlier part of it,' he says. 'And I was looking forward to the after-party, mainly because I wanted to talk to you. I looked for you everywhere, but you'd disappeared like a modern-day Cinderella. Did the mice bring your carriage for you?'

'Nothing so romantic. I wasn't feeling well, and I left as soon as it finished.'

'That's a shame,' he says. 'It couldn't have been the buffet because you told me you hadn't made it that far. Was it the chocolate fountain?'

I laugh despite myself. 'Of course not. You saved me from an ignominious dipping.'

'I did, but I'm wondering now whether that was a mistake. I could have presented you as one of the trophies – a life-sized chocolate Oscar.'

'Isabella would love the idea of chocolate trophies,' I say. 'I'll suggest it to her. She's bound to want to share some ideas with the organisers about next year's event. Anyway, there's no need for you to wait. I'm sure you're dying to join the others at the pub. I'm afraid I can't make it. I have an early start tomorrow.'

He picks up his bag. 'It's a shame you can't join us, but I understand. I'll see you next week, if not before.'

I frown. 'Are you planning to come back again?'

'I most certainly am if there's room. I've enjoyed myself very much, and who knows when I'll have need of some business knowledge? I'd be foolish not to take advantage of your expertise while it's on offer.'

'It's up to you,' I say, trying to keep my lack of enthusiasm out of my voice. 'You'll have to speak to Isabella about it. She may not want extra people joining us.'

It's obvious Ben can tell I don't want him attending my classes. But for some reason he refuses to take the hint.

'I'll do that next time I see her,' he says. 'In the meantime, just in case she suddenly disappears under mysterious circumstances, perhaps you should give me your phone number so I know where to find at least one of you.'

He must see the wary look in my eyes because he laughs. 'I'm not going to steal your identity.'

I give an involuntary gasp, and he looks surprised. 'You don't have to give it to me. How about if I give you mine instead?'

'What for?' I ask, and he grins.

'To show I have no nefarious intentions. Seriously, Meghan, I thought it would be nice to have your number so I could ask you out for a drink sometime.'

I flush and scribble my number on a napkin. 'I'm pretty busy.'

'Me too,' he says, pocketing it. 'But I can always make time for a drink.'

'Most journalists can.'

He raises an eyebrow. 'Have you known many journalists?'

I remember he only knew me from The Sugarloaf Bakery. 'None. But they're always drinking like fish on TV shows.'

'I don't have time to watch much television,' he says.

I'm glad to hear that. If he's so busy, he probably doesn't have the time to dig into other people's genealogies either. With any luck, I should be able to fly completely under his radar.

Chapter Eight

'How did it go?' asks Isabella when I arrive at work the next day. 'I'm sorry neither of us could be there last night. I can come along to help next week if you need me.'

I pull off my jacket and reach for my overall. 'It went alright, I think. Everyone turned up, and no one stormed out halfway through.'

'That's the definition of a good evening class. Will they all come back next week?'

'I hope so. No one demanded a refund as they left or threatened to make an official complaint.'

'Better and better,' she says. 'I knew you'd be a success.'

I switch on the coffee machine. 'I didn't. I was nervous at the start, but it went better than I expected.'

I measure out the coffee, not looking at her. 'I had an extra pupil last night.'

'Oh, yes? I hope you remembered to charge them.'

'I wasn't sure what you wanted me to do about that.' I hesitate. 'It was Ben.'

She looks surprised. 'Really?'

'Yes, he said he'd seen the classes advertised on the website. What I don't understand is why he was in this area at all. I thought he worked in London, but he seems to spend most of his time hanging around Honeywell. Is he thinking of buying a second home here?'

'No idea,' she says. 'You'd have to ask him that.'

I have no intention of asking Ben anything of the sort. Maybe my original theory is correct, and he's after Isabella. Did he only ask for my number last night so he could talk me into putting in a good word for him with my boss?

Usually, I'd be happy to oblige, but not this time. The last thing I want is Ben Davies spending more time in Honeywell. He should go back to London and stay there. If he's looking for a new girlfriend, he'd be better off searching for one who lives in the same postcode as him. For one thing, it would be better for the environment. For another, a new girlfriend might stop him coming down here so often.

For all I know, he has a wife and several adorable children tucked away in a dinky little town house in Chelsea. In which case, he should be spending his time with them, not lurking around random bakeries and turning up unexpectedly at local church halls demanding to learn how to run a small business.

'I'm afraid we'll all be seeing a lot more of him,' says Isabella. 'But it isn't my fault. Haven't I told you his latest plan?'

I sigh. 'It's safe to say you haven't told me anything. You never do. You either announce things after the fact, or you leave me to discover what you're up to when it's almost too late for me to find a place to hide.'

Her face lights up. 'Did you do that last night too? I wish I'd been there.'

'I wish you'd been there too, but not for that reason. No, I didn't hide.'

'Why not?' she asks. 'There are plenty of places to choose from in the church hall. I've hidden in several of them myself.'

'I'd just started the lesson when he walked in. I turned around, and there he was.'

'If it had been me, I'd have clapped my hands over my face and pretended I was about to be sick,' she says. 'Then I'd have made a run for it.'

'We can't all be as quick thinking as you. And what do you mean, we'll be seeing a lot more of him?'

'He's writing a piece on how local businesses are responding to the recession. It seems his editor really liked the article he wrote about the awards and suggested Ben should dig deeper. Ben told her about some of the small businesses that were nominated. Between the two of them, they came up with the idea for this in-depth magazine piece.'

I make myself a latte and carry it to a table by the window where I can see if anyone approaches. I'm not up for more surprises this morning. If any more nosy journalists plan to walk down our high street, I intend to be prepared.

Isabella picks up a plate of croissants and joins me. 'Did Ben recognise you?'

'Unfortunately, yes.'

'Did he realise who you really were?'

I pick up a croissant and take a bite. 'I don't think so. He didn't appear to put two and two together. It isn't surprising. He has no reason to connect me with his employer.'

'Maybe you aren't as important as you think you are,' she says.

'I don't think I'm important. I just don't want my father finding out I'm not in Paris.'

'And none of us will tell him,' she says. 'But Ben will obviously be in the area for a few weeks, and it will make it difficult if our chef keeps squeezing herself behind our kitchen appliances. It isn't how the best kitchens operate.'

I survey her over the top of my croissant but don't answer.

She disposes of her croissant in two enormous bites. 'I know you aren't keen to see him again, but it's great for us. We can capitalise on all this publicity. Your business lessons are just the beginning.'

'What else do you have in mind?' I ask suspiciously. 'Remember I belong to a union.'

She waves a dismissive hand. 'Don't be so negative. Lily and I will do most of it ourselves. But you won't mind lending the occasional hand?'

'I'd rather not commit to anything until I've seen it in writing. I'm not sure I have enough spare hands, occasional or otherwise.'

She pushes the plate towards me. 'Have another croissant before I eat them all.'

'I'm fine, thanks. I'm not saying you shouldn't explore new avenues, but expansion means more than offering random services and hoping for the best.'

'I know that,' she says. 'Lily and I had thousands of ideas while we were building up the bakery from nothing. And now we're in an excellent position to do something about them. We've got some publicity, we have a loyal customer base, and we're a part of the community. People will support us as much as they can. I know they will.'

'I'm sure you're right, but it isn't you I'm worried about. It's me. I'm newly qualified, I don't have a lot of experience, and I'm only here for six months. Wouldn't it be better to leave things until Abby returns? From what I've heard of her, she's experienced and capable. She'd be far better positioned to carry out your plans than I am.'

Isabella finishes the last croissant and brushes the crumbs off her skirt. 'Abby's great, but so are you. Lily and I have every confidence in you. And these classes seem a great place to start.'

'Fine,' I say. 'But only as long as Ben doesn't figure out who I really am. The minute you let that slip, I'm out of here. Do you understand?'

She gives me a mock salute. 'Yes, ma'am. I won't breathe a word.'

I'm not convinced. But it's useless to dwell on it. I've made my point. All I can do is hope she remembers.

'I'd better start work,' I say. 'I need to get on with the Danish pastries, and you never get much done until you're convinced they're well underway.'

She frowns. 'My powers of concentration are legendary. Once I apply myself to a task, there's no distracting me until it's completed. The shop could go up in flames, and I would continue with my book-keeping, completely unaware of it all.'

Lily, who's just arrived, gives a derisive snort.

Isabella gives her a pained look. 'I sometimes wonder why I'm partnering with someone who's determined to wilfully misunderstand me.'

'No one else would have you,' says Lily. 'Go and check the accounts aren't overdue.'

Isabella catches my arm as I walk over to the kitchen. 'If you're making puff pastry Danishes, the pastry takes seventeen minutes to make, six minutes to roll out, and fifteen minutes in the oven. You need a further three minutes to apply the icing and allow the pastries to cool enough to eat without taking the skin off your tongue. Right now, it's 8:43. I'll see you in my office at 9:24 exactly.'

'I thought you didn't micro-manage,' I say.

'I don't, but I'm a perfectionist. It's one of the many qualities I bring to my role. It plays a vital role in ensuring the success of this business.'

She looks at her watch again. 'It's now 8:44. I'm a patient employer, but I have my limits.'

'Go!' Lily tells me. 'If you value your job.'

I grin at Isabella and walk as slowly as I dare towards the kitchen, hearing her heavy sigh as I go.

Chapter Nine

Ben texts me a couple of days later. I can't think what possessed me to give him my number. Or if I do have an idea, I'm not admitting it to myself.

I thought I might hear from him the day after the class, but it wasn't a disappointment when he didn't call. Why would it have been? I'm trying to avoid him, not spend unnecessary evenings with him. When two days passed without hearing from him, I resolved to put him out of my mind.

I look at my phone screen when his text arrives, angling it away from view. I needn't have worried. There are only three people in the cafe. They're sitting at the far end of the room, talking and laughing as they consume cream teas at breakneck speed.

I suppress an urge to tell them it took me half an hour to make those scones so the least they could do is savour them and read my message.

Hi, Meghan. Great class on Tuesday. Would you like to meet for a drink at The Red Lion this weekend? I'm free tomorrow evening. Ben

I close my phone, thinking hard. The safest option would be to refuse. He hasn't realised who I am, and I'd prefer it to stay that way. But I don't want to alienate him entirely. He's writing an article about our business, so we need to keep him on board.

'What are you looking at?' asks Isabella, coming into the shop with an armful of folders.

'Nothing,' I say.

'You were staring out of the window, entranced,' she says. 'I thought at very least some famous film star had arrived in Honeywell and was hot footing it down the high street to taste our famous Danish pastries.'

I slip my phone into my pocket. 'I was daydreaming. Are you ready to take over in here while I get back to the kitchen?'

Her eyes rest on my pocket. 'Don't let me interrupt whatever you were doing.'

'I wasn't doing anything,' I say rather more sharply than I intended.

'No problem,' she says.

'I'm sorry, Isabella. I didn't mean to snap at you. I was thinking about a text I've just received from Ben.'

'Ben the journalist?'

'How many other Bens do you know?'

She draws a deep breath and ticks them off on her fingers. 'There's Ben Hibbert, who works on my Uncle's Farm. Ben Walker, who delivers the post in Little Compton. Ben Wilson, who –'

I stop her before she can move on to the wider New Forest area. 'Fine, you win. I'm talking about Ben from the awards evening.'

'And the following day,' she says, her lips twitching.

'And the evening class,' I add.

'What a busy social life you two lead. And now he's texting you. Do I scent a romance?'

'You do not. He took my number because I work here and because he was thinking about signing up for the full course.'

'Of course,' she agrees. 'I should have known it was strictly professional. I apologise. And he's texted you today to ask about something business related?'

'Not exactly,' I admit. 'He's asked me out for a drink at The Red Lion.'

'A business drink?'

'He didn't say. How does one distinguish a business drink from any other kind?'

She considers. 'You could wear a suit.'

'I haven't brought one with me.'

'Or carry a briefcase,' she says. 'Or clutch a copy of the Financial Times.'

'I don't think the corner shop sells that.'

She doesn't appear to hear me. 'And you could say things like synergy and core competencies.'

'I have no idea what they mean. No one does.'

'You aren't making this easy for me,' she says. 'When is this drink taking place?'

'At the weekend.'

'Then it isn't a business drink. It's some other type of drink.'

'How many types are there?' I ask, intrigued.

'Hundreds! People go out for celebratory drinks, networking drinks, impromptu drinks, casual drinks –'

I break in before she gets too carried away. 'Not that first one. We have nothing to celebrate.'

'Except our award,' she reminds me.

'True, but you've already drunk your bodyweight in alcohol to celebrate that.'

'Several people's bodyweights,' she agrees with a reminiscent smile.

'And it isn't networking,' I say. 'We aren't in the same line of business. At least, we are in a way, but he doesn't know that.'

'So, it's an impromptu drink?' she asks.

'Not really. Impromptu implies spur of the moment, and he's asked me for tomorrow night.'

'You're so fussy,' she complains. 'Fine, then we've narrowed it down to casual drinks, unless you have any further objections.'

'Casual works for me. My issue is that I'm not sure whether to accept.'

'Why not? Don't you like him?'

'He's all right, I suppose. But you know why I don't want him to discover who I am.'

She gives a delighted smile. 'I knew I'd left something off my list. Spy drinks!'

'What?' I ask.

'You know what I mean. The sort of occasion when spies meet – oh, so casually – in a pub miles from anywhere. They pretend not to know each other, but they really do. One of them orders a drink, then the other spy wanders over and orders the same drink. A few minutes later, the first spy goes to the bathroom, and the second person switches their drinks.'

I'm struggling to keep up. 'Why would they do that?'

'You'd have to ask them. Maybe the second person has dropped the secret plans into the first person's drink.'

I try to envisage this. 'Wouldn't they get soggy?'

She gives an exasperated sigh. 'They use waterproof microfilm.'

'Wouldn't someone notice if there was a foreign object in their drink?'

'How should I know? Not if the microfilm was transparent and the drink wasn't. I expect spies order Guinness to be on the safe side. You could drop a very long message into a pint of that without anyone noticing it.'

I drag the conversation back to reality. 'I'm sure you could, but Ben hasn't invited me for a spy drink.'

'You can't be sure of that,' she insists. 'No self-respecting spy would text and say Hi, Meghan, I have some stolen plans I need to hand over. Why not meet me for a piece of pie and a dead-letter drop?'

'Who said anything about pie?' I ask, even more confused.

A dreamy look comes over her face. 'I did.'

'He said a drink.'

'Did he state there would under no circumstances be pie?' she asks.

'I don't think he did.'

'There you go. Pie is clearly implied. So, are you planning to accept?'

'I'm not sure. It might be wiser to refuse. But I mustn't annoy him before he writes this article about the bakery.'

'Don't even go there,' she says. 'This isn't the eighteenth century where you have to do what your employer wants or risk losing your job.'

'Why the eighteenth century in particular?'

She ignores me. 'If Ben gives us a bad write-up because one of our staff refuses to go out with him, that's his issue. To do him justice, I don't believe the thought would cross his mind. He seems like a nice guy. Either way, you don't get to use me and Lily as an excuse. Own your decisions. Go if you want to. Don't go if you don't want to. It's up to you.'

'You're right,' I say. 'That wasn't the reason. I'm worried about giving myself away. It's easy to say very little in a work situation. It's more difficult when you're meeting someone for a casual drink.'

'Or a spy drink,' she reminds me.

'Casual,' I insist, and she laughs.

'You don't need to drink much. Concentrate on the pie instead.'

'Why don't you go in my place?' I suggest. 'You're the one who's so keen to see this happen, and you aren't trying to conceal your identity.'

She shakes her head. 'Are you forgetting he invited you? He has my number, and Lily's too. Yet he texted you. What does that tell you?'

'That he likes to do things in reverse alphabetical order?'

'That he wants to meet you,' she says. 'I don't understand what your problem is. If he was going to work out who you are, he'd have done it by now. But he hasn't, which doesn't surprise me. Men are simple creatures.'

I lift my hands in a gesture of surrender. 'I give in. I have nothing planned for this weekend. I'll text back and tell him I'll meet him for a drink. But if something goes wrong, I'm blaming you.'

'Nothing will go wrong,' she says. 'Now we've sorted that out, can you please make a start on the sausage rolls? I haven't had a bite to eat since my after-lunch snack, and I need something to keep me going until closing time.'

Chapter Ten

I arrange to meet Ben at the Red Lion on Saturday evening. I almost change my mind as I walk along the high street. I could go back home and see whether my landlady would like to share a takeaway and watch an old James Bond film – or preferably something less spy-related. But that would be cowardly. No one is half as important in other people's lives as they think they are. I'm not the centre of Ben's world, and he doesn't spend his time thinking about me, let alone speculating about what my mother's maiden name may have been.

As far as he's concerned, I'm someone he met at an awards ceremony and bumped into unexpectedly a few days later. He's in the area, and he thought it would be nice to meet up for a drink. That's all. Unless Isabella is right and he's planning to drop the secret plans for the latest government submarine into my plate of chips when I'm not looking.

Ben is waiting outside when I arrive. 'Hi, Meghan. You found it ok?'

'It would have been more noteworthy if I hadn't. There's only one pub in the village, and I can see it from the bakery.

Besides, I've been here before. Even I couldn't go to the wrong one.'

'You make a good point. Shall we go in? I think it's about to rain.'

He follows me inside, and we wait at the bar to be served.

'What can I get you?' he asks.

'I've had strict instructions to try their Pimm's.'

'Instructions from your boss?'

'How did you guess?'

He grins. 'She's given me a long list of all the places I should visit and what I should order. She was most definite about it.'

'That sounds like Isabella. I'll find us somewhere to sit.'

I manage to grab a table next to the window at the back of the pub. I didn't realise they had such a large garden outside. All the tables are occupied. Several dogs are running around chasing each other. Others are waiting hopefully next to their owners in case someone needs help with finishing their meal. Beyond the fence, I catch glimpses of a large field leading down to a line of trees.

Ben sets down two glasses on the table and drops a couple of bags of crisps next to them. 'Which flavour do you prefer?'

'Salt and vinegar. They're my favourite.'

'I somehow thought a chef would be more adventurous,' he says, opening his bag of prawn cocktail.

'I'm adventurous. But why mess with perfection? There's a reason why other flavours come and go, but salt and vinegar crisps remain a top seller.'

'I'll remember that for the future,' he says. 'In the meantime, it would be a shame to waste these others.'

I take a sip of my drink. 'Isabella is right. This is delicious. She said I should try their Pimm's in the summer and their mulled wine in the winter.'

'It will be autumn in a couple of months,' he says. 'Does that mean we can try both?'

'I don't think they start serving mulled wine until closer to Christmas.'

'I'll reluctantly wait until then,' he says.

'Won't you have finished your article long before that?'

'I would hope so. It should only take a couple of weeks.'

'So, why will you be here at Christmas?' I ask.

He looks surprised. 'Why wouldn't I be? I live here.'

'You live in London!'

'No, I don't. I live in Christchurch.'

'Are you sure?'

He looks amused. 'Perfectly. I've lived there for the past ten years. Why should you doubt it?'

'But you work for *Whisk*. That's in London.'

'True,' he says. 'But only the permanent senior staff members are based there. The more junior staff can live where they like. As long as I can get to the office when I'm needed, no one minds where I sleep.'

This hadn't occurred to me until now. Dad lives in Hampstead Heath, and so does Uncle Matt. If I'd taken the job as food writer, I would have stayed in my London flat. But it makes sense that not all the staff live locally, especially someone like Ben, who's only working there for a few months.

I take a gulp of my Pimm's. 'Is that why they asked you to present those awards? Because you live locally.'

He smiles. 'I'd like to think they invited me because tales of my work ethic and extraordinary literary talent have reached the provinces. But I suspect the answer is yes. They were looking for someone to hand out the awards, and one of the committee mentioned I was local, which would save on travelling expenses.'

'I thought it was because you worked for *Whisk*,' I say, finishing my drink and making a start on my crisps.

'Let's say it was a lucky coincidence. It's a good magazine, but it isn't so big that people are fighting to get hold of their staff.'

I'm not sure I like him speaking like that about *Whisk*. It may not be as big as *Cosmopolitan* or *House and Garden*, but it has a healthy circulation, and it attracts plenty of advertising. I can't mention this to Ben. It's unlikely that a pastry chef in a small countryside bakery would happen to have the circulation numbers of a London based magazine at her fingertips, let alone their exact advertising revenue and forward projections for the coming year.

'Did you say you're only there on a six-month contract?' I ask to change the subject.

'That's right. I was working at a small magazine called What to Eat and Drink before that, but they laid me off.'

'That magazine went bust, didn't it?'

He looks surprised. 'You've heard of it?'

I can't tell him I've not only heard of it, but I also know the exact circumstances under which it went under. I doubt there's a magazine in the country with a circulation of more than a thousand I haven't heard of. Dad has always insisted on giving me a thorough grounding in the business. He's made me study profits and projections ever since I was old enough to read a financial report.

'I think I read something about it,' I improvise. 'How long did it take you to find this job?'

'About two months. I was luckier than some of my colleagues. I wasn't exclusively writing about food, but it was close enough for me to be able to apply for this job when it came up. It was a relief when I was offered the position, even if it is only for six months.'

'Do you have something lined up for when this finishes?'

'Not really. I'm keeping a look out for anything that comes up. If I do a really good job, I'm hoping they'll decide to keep me on at *Whisk*. I'm not sure why the contract is short-term, but maybe that's how they do these things, taking someone on spec for a few months without the legal hassle of having to offer them something permanent.'

'No, it isn't,' I say. 'That's not how *Whisk* operates.'

He gives me an odd look. 'How do you know?'

I knew it was a mistake to have a drink with him. Why didn't I tell him I was a lifelong teetotaller and allergic to all forms of bar snacks?

'I don't know for sure,' I say. 'What I mean is I can't imagine a business operating like that. It wouldn't be ethical for one thing. And it wouldn't be cost-effective. Even if they hire qualified people, there's a learning curve in any new job. Every business operates differently and has its own culture. Taking people on purely for the short term makes no sense. It's a bad business strategy.'

'You could be right,' he says. 'Is that how it works in the bakery business – all the owners investing in their employee's futures?'

Is he laughing at me? I tilt up my chin and stare back at him defiantly. 'As a matter of fact, my bakery really cares about their staff.'

'How long have you been working there?'

'A couple of months.'

'So, you're still on a learning curve?' he asks.

'I am. Obviously, I know how to make everything I need to, but I'm still getting used to the way the business operates. The evening classes, for example. I didn't expect to have to do those when I arrived.'

'They weren't in your contract?'

'Not specifically. I took a business course at university, which meant Isabella decided I was the perfect person to run this course. If we hadn't won the award, I don't think she'd have started offering the classes until their regular pastry chef returned. Abby is in Scotland until the end of the summer. Her partner is helping to set up a restaurant there, and she's apparently taking the opportunity to write a cookbook.'

'So, you aren't their regular pastry chef,' he asks.

'As it happens, I'm on a six-month contract like you,' I say reluctantly. 'That's all I was looking for.'

'You didn't want something more permanent?'

'Not at the moment. I haven't quite decided what my next steps will be.'

'It seems like a good place to work,' he says.

'It's the best. My bosses are both lovely, and I'm learning a lot.'

He finishes his drink. 'I imagine you are. You did a great job with the class the other evening.'

'I'm not sure about that.'

'You did,' he insists. 'I've signed up for the rest of the course. Isabella was delighted to have another pupil.'

I'll bet she was. Why should she care that each time I meet Ben I end up in more of a tangle than the last time? To be fair to her, she's after publicity, and Ben is the person who can give it to her.

'I'll do my best to make sure you enjoy it,' I say politely, wondering whether there's any way I can get out of teaching the rest of the classes. Could I fake severe food poisoning? I could put it down to having foraged for mushrooms which I then misidentified and cooked. I could use it as a teaching moment about the dangers of eating too much local food. I'll have to give it some serious thought.

I pick up our empty glasses. 'Why don't I get us some more drinks?'

'I won't say no to that,' says Ben. 'While you're there, could you take a look at their other crisps? They seem to have some interesting-looking varieties. I can't be certain, but I thought I saw a box of hedgehog-and-tomato flavour.'

'Are you sure they weren't beef and tomato?'

He grins. 'That would make more sense. What a shame. I was looking forward to trying them. It would have made a great article. You can't think how much our readers enjoy reading about bizarrely flavoured snacks. People in London live quite sheltered lives, and it gives them something to get excited about.'

Chapter Eleven

'How did it go?' asks Isabella when she arrives at work on Monday.

I glance up from the till where I'm trying to work out whether we have enough cash to get through the morning without taking a quick trip to the bank. 'How did what go?'

'Your date! I thought you might have messaged me yesterday. When I didn't hear anything, I assumed you were sleeping it off.'

'I went for a walk in the forest yesterday,' I say. 'The weather was lovely, so I made the most of my day off.'

'Some of us had to work,' she says with a martyred expression. 'But don't let that make you feel bad.'

I look at my watch. 'It's almost ten o'clock. I've been here since six thirty. Doesn't that make you feel bad?'

She picks up a vanilla eclair and takes a thoughtful bite. 'You would think so, but no. And don't change the subject. The fact remains that you had all day yesterday to contact me and tell me how it went, and you didn't. I hope you have a decent excuse.'

'Am I obligated to keep my employers up to date with every detail of my personal life? I didn't notice that in the contract.'

She finishes the eclair and takes another. 'It's becoming obvious that our current contracts are sadly lacking. I blame Lily's lack of foresight. I'll have to overhaul them before we employ anyone else. In the meantime, let's agree it's an unwritten part of your job description. More of a verbal agreement.'

'One I don't remember making,' I say. 'If you eat any more of those eclairs, there will be none left for the customers.'

She crams the final piece into her mouth. 'It's better this way because no one will know they were even an option. Whereas if two people come in and realise there's only one eclair on offer, it could lead to some unpleasant scenes. That's the last thing we want in a respectable bakery. We have a reputation to maintain.'

'So, you're doing the bakery a favour? I should have guessed. I'll make another batch this afternoon.'

'Thank you,' she says. 'But don't imagine you can distract me with promises of cake. Unlike the White Queen, I can't be fobbed off with the idea of cakes yesterday and cakes tomorrow.'

'That was jam,' I say. 'What do you want to know?'

She measures coffee beans into the machine, steams the milk, and hands me a mug. 'I want to hear how your date went. Every single detail. I have plenty of time.'

I peer out of the window. 'Is that Lily's mother coming up the street?'

She sighs. 'Aren't customers the worst? I sometimes wonder why we bother. It would be much easier to run our business without them. And there would be far less competition for the eclairs.'

The door opens, and Angela Carson walks in. She beams at us. 'Good morning. Isn't it a beautiful day? I'm here for a Cobb loaf if you have one. Lily and the children are coming over for lunch.'

'I made some Cobb loaves this morning,' I tell her. 'And pizza rolls too if you're interested. I know Lily likes those.'

'So does Isabella,' says my boss plaintively.

'Which is why I made a double batch,' I reassure her.

I hand Mrs Carson her loaf. 'Is there anything else I can get you? A cup of coffee, perhaps?'

She looks at her watch. 'I don't have time, I'm afraid. They'll be here in half an hour.'

'Meghan is trying to distract me from the subject she and I were discussing,' says Isabella. 'She won't succeed.'

Mrs Carson pulls out her purse. 'What was that, dear?'

Isabella beams. 'Meghan had a date with a very hot prospect on Saturday evening.' She dodges the kick I aim at her ankle.

'It wasn't a date,' I say yet again.

'Was that with the food writer?' asks Mrs Carson.

'How did you know that?' I ask before I can stop myself. I should have said I could neither confirm nor deny the rumour, but I'm terrible at thinking on my feet.

'My husband Martin was chatting with Jack's father after their golf game yesterday,' she says. 'Jack is Lily's partner, Meghan. Have you met him yet?'

'Only in passing. He usually has the children in tow, so we haven't had much chance to talk.'

'Jack's father mentioned to Martin that he'd seen you at the Red Lion,' she goes on. 'He described the man you were with, and Lily said it must have been him. Ben, I think his name was. She told us he's very good looking.'

'I hope Jack wasn't there when she said that,' says Isabella. 'We all know what a fragile ego men have.'

Mrs Carson smiles. 'Jack didn't seem too bothered.'

Isabella sighs. 'That's because he also has a massive amount of unearned self-confidence.'

'Don't you like him?' I ask, and they both laugh.

'I adore him,' says Isabella. 'If Lily hadn't got to him first, I'd have snapped him up. But, as Lily's friend, it's my job to keep his head from swelling too much. She's far too easy-going to keep him in check.'

'Jack doesn't need keeping in check,' says Mrs Carson. 'He's a lovely lad. He and Lily make a wonderful couple.'

'They do,' says Isabella. 'But I may have a partner of my own one of these days, and I need the practise.'

'I hope you do,' says Mrs Carson. 'I can't think why you're still single. It can't be from want of opportunity. You're the prettiest girl in the village.'

Isabella grins. 'I'll tell Lily you said so.'

'I meant single girl,' says Mrs Carson. 'As you well know.'

She catches my eyes and blushes. 'I meant local single girls. Weren't you about to tell us about your date, Meghan?'

I look up the high street, hoping to see a wave of customers heading our way. It's annoyingly empty.

'Meghan is extremely shy and retiring,' says Isabella. 'I may have more luck getting the details out of her when we don't have an audience.'

Mrs Carson picks up her loaf. 'Of course. And it's none of my business. I'm sorry, Meghan. It's the downside of living in a small community. You can't do anything without half the village knowing about it.'

'I'm beginning to realise that,' I say. 'As usual, Isabella is making a storm in a teacup. I don't know what she wants me to tell her. I met Ben for a drink. We had that drink, and I went home.'

Isabella looks disappointed. 'That's it? You didn't get on so well that drinks turned into dinner, followed by him spontaneously flying you to Paris in the company's private jet?'

'Not that I remember. As far as I know, his employer doesn't have a private jet. I can't speak for the bakery. I wouldn't be surprised to discover you have a helicopter pad hidden somewhere behind the building.'

'Not yet,' she says regretfully. 'But it's on my wish list for when business picks up. I could pop over to Milan for a genuine Minestrone Milanese and be back in time to supervise Lily closing up for the evening.'

'I have to go,' says Angela Carson. 'I'm glad you're settling into the village, Meghan. We'll be sorry to see you leave when Abby gets back.'

'We have her for a few more months,' says Isabella, opening the door for her. 'And we intend to wring every last ounce of value out of her before she leaves.'

We watch Mrs Carson trot briskly down the high street with her bags.

'That woman has more energy than most people half her age,' says Isabella. 'She looks after Daisy three days a week, and she takes Ethan as well when Lily needs her to. She's a member of half the clubs in the village, and she still finds time to check on all the elderly people in her street and make sure they get to their appointments and eat properly.'

'And keep a watchful eye on your staff's personal lives,' I add.

'That was never going to remain a secret,' she says. 'Martin is always out and about, and he knows everyone who lives in the village. He and Angela work as a team to keep the place in order.'

'I like that,' I say. 'Not the part where I get my privacy invaded, but the rest of it. London can be rather impersonal, depending on where you live.'

'Where does your father live?' she asks.

'Hampstead Heath. He and Mum bought the house when they got married, and he's never left it. I'm glad he didn't. She died when I was ten. It feels like my only connection to her.'

She looks thoughtful. 'Isn't your father a bigger connection to her than a house?'

I consider this. 'I suppose he should be. But he and I are so … disconnected at the moment. I don't know whether that will ever change. If it doesn't, I like to think of him living in the house they bought together and made into a home.'

She gives my shoulder a sympathetic squeeze. 'You and he will work it out. See if you don't. Families are funny things. My family drives me to distraction, but I wouldn't be without them. Even Georgia, but never tell her I said that.'

'I promise I won't. Does she ever come in here?'

'Thankfully not. I'd have to be polite to her if she did, which would go against the grain.'

'You could refuse to serve her,' I suggest.

'I'd be delighted, but Lily would never hear of it. She's a stickler for being courteous to all our customers. I don't understand it, but it's easier to do as I'm told than to argue. If Georgia came in here, she'd be bound to find something to complain about and demand a refund. She and Wendy Protheroe have a lot in common. You haven't met Wendy yet, but I'm sure you will before you leave. She's worth watching when she's in action. She returns at least half of everything she buys here, and her excuses get more bizarre each time. Of the two of them, I think I'd rather have Georgia, which is saying a lot. Perhaps there's something in the concept of family after all.'

'Speaking of family,' I say, 'it's my father's birthday soon. I'll have to send him an e-card.'

'Why not a real one?' she asks.

'Because I'm supposed to be in Paris. I can't send him a card with a Honeywell postmark and a British stamp. I'll have to find an appropriate e-card.

Isabella's eyes light up. 'I have a better idea.'

'If you're about to suggest I hand-deliver it, don't bother,' I warn her. 'I'm not making up some complicated story about having taken the Eurostar back home just for his birthday. He'd be bound to ask me a load of questions I couldn't answer. Either I'd get the mythical train times wrong or I wouldn't have heard about something major that's happening in Paris.'

'I wasn't going to suggest that,' she says. 'It would mean giving you time off work, and I'm always reluctant to allow my staff to get ideas above their station and learn about workers' rights and benefits. I have a far simpler solution. When's his birthday?'

'Two weeks on Friday.'

'That gives us plenty of time,' she says. 'Pop along to the post office at lunchtime and buy him a card. We'll send it by express post to that friend you were meant to be staying with and get her to mail it to your father from Paris.'

I gaze at her in awe. 'That's a great idea.'

She purses up her mouth. 'Why do people always say that as though it's a surprise? All my ideas are great ideas. Some are more brilliant than others, but all of them are better than ninety percent of anything other people come up with.'

'And you claim it's Jack who needs his ego keeping in check?' I murmur.

She ignores me. 'It's almost lunchtime. I can hold the fort in here. Go and choose a card now, and we'll send it off this afternoon.'

'If they have an appropriate selection,' I say, pulling off my apron. 'Won't Dad expect something French?'

'I don't think the post office runs to those,' she says. 'It's very remiss of them. At any moment, a Honeywell resident might need a Congratulations on Your Divorce card written in Esperanto. I'll have a word with them about laying in an international selection. But it's too late to do anything about that right now. You'll have to do your best with what they have. As long as it isn't a sympathy card or one left over from Easter, you should be all right. Happy Birthday Dad will be fine. It isn't a special birthday, is it?'

'He'll be sixty-three.'

'Soixante-trois,' she says knowledgeably.

'Do you speak French?' I ask.

'Mais oui!' She catches my eye and bursts out laughing. 'Only what I can remember from my school days. Slip along now and get that card before the hordes of ravenous lunch customers descend on us. I'll check Google Translate for appropriate festive phrases while I wait for you to return.'

Chapter Twelve

I start preparing for our third evening class in my very few spare moments. Last week went pretty well. Sue brought along more ice cream than any group of seven people could reasonably eat, although we made a creditable attempt. I think she has every chance of turning her product into a successful business, as long as she masters portion control when she actually comes to sell it.

Ben was there again last week. I suppose I should be flattered a food writer is interested enough in what I have to say to commit to attending all the lessons. But I'm aware it's really part of his research on local businesses and not because he thinks my lessons are intrinsically valuable.

This week, it's Ellie's turn. She wants to set up a local jam-making business.

'All set?' asks Isabella as I help her close up the shop for the evening.

'Almost literally,' I say. 'We're talking about jam tonight.'

'Fantastic!' she exclaims. 'Jam is my absolute favourite!'

'What kind of jam?'

She looks confused. 'All kinds.'

'Of course. I'm not sure why I asked. I'll bring you a pot tomorrow if there's any left over.'

She looks delighted. 'I'll skip breakfast in preparation.'

'I wouldn't take the risk,' I warn her. 'There may not be enough left for me to take any home.'

'You're right,' she says. 'But I'll skip my after-breakfast snack just in case. Don't be late!'

'I'm never late,' I say. 'Unlike my employer.'

She gives me a dignified look. 'I'm not late. I'm differently timed. You'll notice I'm always here when it counts.'

'I'll take your word for it. See you tomorrow.'

Eleanor isn't there when I get home. I make myself a cup of tea and a toasted sandwich, then leave for the class. I don't want Isabella hearing that I arrived late. She would never let me live it down.

I arrive at the church hall to find it already unlocked. It isn't raining this week, so hopefully everyone will turn up. I've just put out the chairs and opened my folder of notes when the door opens. I turn to see Ben grinning at me.

'How's it going?' he asks.

'Great, thanks. I wasn't sure you'd come every single week.'

'Why not? I've paid for the full course.'

'You might have changed your mind or decided it would be simpler just to ask me for my notes.'

'That would be cheating,' he says self-righteously. 'I'm surprised to hear you suggest such a thing. Is that what you did at school – copied someone else's notes?'

'I was an excellent student,' I say. 'I would never have dreamed of taking short cuts.'

'And yet you assume I would?'

'That's different. You're only here because of that article you're writing about local businesses. No one would blame you if you cut a few corners.'

He smiles. 'It almost sounds as though you don't want me here.'

'That's ridiculous. The more people who attend, the better. Isabella is anxious to make a profit from this course.'

'In any case, that isn't why I'm here,' he says. 'You're right to say I could get the details in other ways. But it wouldn't be half as much fun without the full Meghan Randall experience.'

I shoot him a quick look, but he doesn't seem to notice. There's no reason he should. I remind myself yet again it's only my guilty conscience that makes me react to my name like this. It's a common enough surname.

The rest of my pupils drift in clutching folders. Ellie arrives carrying a large cardboard box. With any luck, she's brought enough of her product for Isabella to enjoy with a stack of scones tomorrow morning.

I wave to her. 'The floor is all yours. What did you bring, and how can we help you?'

Ellie opens the box and pulls out several jars. 'I've always made my own jam. My grandmother taught me how to do it when I was young, and I still love making it. It makes me feel very close to her.'

'You could put her picture on the label,' interrupts Greg. 'You could call your product Grandma's something or other.'

I hold up my hand. 'Why don't we let Ellie finish before we make suggestions? She may already have a name in mind.'

Ellie looks embarrassed. 'Not really. I don't have many ideas at all. Perhaps this wasn't a good idea. I should come back when I've thought things through a bit more.'

'Not at all,' says Ben. 'That's what these classes are for. All you need is one idea. The rest will come later.'

She gives him a grateful smile. 'I hope so. Well, that's it really. I'd like to sell jam locally, but I have no idea how to go about setting up a business. I don't even know whether there's a market for it.'

'There's a market for most things,' I say. 'You need to find your niche. Jam is a great product because it's not a one-off purchase. People buy it over and over again. But you have to come up with a selling point for your particular brand. You can't compete with supermarket prices, but that doesn't matter. Plenty of businesses sell the same products as the supermarkets. So, what's different about your jams?'

Ellie looks confused. 'There isn't anything different.'

'That isn't true,' says Greg. 'Your jam is homemade.'

'Which means it tastes better,' agrees Charlie. 'Or your customers think it does, which comes to the same thing.'

'It definitely tastes better,' says Sue. 'You gave me a jar of your Christmas marmalade last year, Ellie. It was amazing. I barely got any because my son found it and polished it off in a couple of days.'

Ellie looks pleased. 'I didn't know you liked it so much. I'll make you some more this year.'

'So, we've identified one unique selling point,' I say. 'Can we come up with others?'

Everyone is leaning forward in their chairs, thoroughly engaged. I listen as they discuss Ellie's jams and the local market for them. By the time we've finished, Ellie has drafted a basic marketing plan and has a list of things to research before next week.

'Do you have a name for your new business?' I ask.

She shakes her head. 'I like the idea of mentioning my grandmother in the publicity material, but I don't want to base the whole product around her. It feels as though I'd be trying to market it to older people, whereas I'm trying to appeal to anyone who wants to buy locally sourced and produced food. That may include the older demographic, but I don't want to limit myself.'

'And you said you had no idea where to start,' I say. 'Listen to you! You're bursting with ideas.'

Her face turns pink. 'It's because I'm doing it with a group. It doesn't feel half so daunting when the whole class is involved.'

I make a mental note to pass this along to Isabella, although she may already have realised it. I wasn't sure this sort of class would appeal to anyone, but it seems I was wrong. Not for the first time, I realise that Isabella, for all her joking around, is more astute than most people give her credit for. She loves people, and she seems to possess an instinctive understanding of what makes them tick. It's an understanding that comes less naturally to me. Looking around at everyone's excited faces as they inspect the jars and taste the jam, I'm glad she talked me into doing this.

'We should brainstorm a name,' I say. 'It's the most important part of a product. If you get that wrong, nothing else will be right. You might have the best product in the world, but if you call it something boring or irrelevant, your business will fail before you start.'

'Rural Roots?' suggests Charlie.

'What are the roots?' asks Ellie.

'It tells your customers the business is local,' he says.

Ellie considers this. 'To me, it suggests there are roots in the product.'

'You could use beetroot in some of them,' says Greg. 'Or ginger root.'

She doesn't look convinced. 'It sounds rather forced.'

'Ellie's right,' I say. 'If you have to change your product to accommodate its name, you have the wrong name.'

'How about Hometown Harvest?' asks Bethany.

'Too old-fashioned,' says Greg.

'But jam *is* old-fashioned,' says Sue. 'That's part of its charm. Everyone remembers eating jam in their childhood. It's nostalgic, and nostalgia sells.'

'Maybe,' says Ellie. 'It still doesn't feel quite right.'

'Backyard Bounty?' suggests Charlie. 'I assume you'll be using locally grown fruits wherever possible?'

Ben raises a tentative hand, which makes me smile.

'You aren't in school,' I tell him. 'You're allowed to speak up at any time.'

He grins back at me. 'I didn't know whether that applied to me too. Apparently, I'm only here on sufferance.'

'I never said that!'

'Something like it, he says. 'You told me I'm not really a local entrepreneur.'

'What did you want to say?' I ask before he can say anything more about my less than welcoming attitude.

'I wanted to suggest a name,' he says, turning to Ellie. 'How about Ellie's Jellies?'

There's a shout of laughter from the rest of the group.

Ellie looks delighted. 'What a great idea! I love it.'

Ben nods. 'I'm glad. I'll lease it to you for five hundred pounds and ten percent of your gross profits.'

Her face falls, and he laughs. 'Or you can have it for free. Your choice.'

'I'll buy you a drink later,' she promises. 'Thanks, Ben. I don't know why that didn't occur to me at once.'

'Sometimes you can be too close to something to see it clearly,' he says.

Did he glance at me when he said that? I can't think why he should.

I look at the clock next to the stage. 'That about wraps it up for this week. You have got a lot of work to do before our next meeting, Ellie. And we didn't get very far with your logo. Maybe that will be easier now you have a name for the business. We can cover the concept of logo design another time if any of you are interested.'

There's a chorus of agreement, and everyone starts packing up to go. Ben helps me stack the chairs at the side of the hall.

'Will you be joining us at the Red Lion this week?' he asks.

'I wish I could, but I have a 6 a.m. start tomorrow.'

'That's a shame. Is that when you start every day?'

'Not on Saturdays. But most days, yes. It's the worst part about my job. We can't all lie in bed half the morning scribbling a few words on our laptops.'

'Typing,' he says. 'You scribble on paper and type on a computer. It's one of the first things they teach in journalism courses.'

'I'm sure you're right. Anyway, I don't dare join you for a drink or Isabella may discover me face down in the mixer, fast asleep, when she comes in tomorrow morning. She'd tell me it was a waste of good brioche dough.'

'Fair enough,' he says. 'Would you like to have dinner with me on Saturday night instead? If you don't have an early start on Sunday, it won't matter if you fall asleep in the middle of the restaurant.'

I almost refuse, but there's no reason not to accept if I want to. Ben doesn't know who I am, and he never will. The chances of us having more than one dinner together are small. With my track history, one date is about the limit of my romantic adventures. We'll probably discover we've run out of things to talk about during our last few meetings and don't want to see each other again. We can enjoy a pleasant meal together on Saturday and leave it at that.

He gives me a quizzical look. 'I didn't think it was a complicated question.'

I smile back at him. 'It isn't. Dinner sounds great. Let me know where, and when, and I'll be there. Are you thinking of the Red Lion?'

'I'm not that unoriginal,' he says in a reproachful tone. 'We went there for our first date, and I never repeat my effects.'

So, he thinks our evening at the Red Lion was a date? I decide not to mention that to Isabella. Better to let her keep believing it was a spy-related encounter. That way, I can avoid too many questions from her until I've made up my mind how I feel about Ben.

'I don't want to hurry you,' he says. 'But the caretaker has been hanging around for the past five minutes with the look of someone who's eager to lock up and go home.'

I emerge from my reverie to see the caretaker hovering in the doorway.

'Sorry, Mr Bright,' I apologise. 'We've finished here. See you next week.'

I walk to the high street with Ben and say goodbye to him outside the Red Lion.

'Sure you can't manage a small lemonade?' he asks.

'I'd better not. I need some sleep before tomorrow.'

'All right. I'll find somewhere that serves lemonade on Saturday.'

'There's a burger place on the bypass,' I say.

He shakes his head in disgust. 'I'm not sure I like your opinion of me. I'll have to pull out all the stops to erase whatever unfortunate impression I may have made.'

He bends and quickly kisses my cheek. 'See you on Saturday.'

He waves and disappears into the pub before I have the chance to respond.

I arrive home at half past nine, exhausted. I should ask Isabella for a raise. My contract definitely didn't include all these extras.

Eleanor is in the kitchen when I arrive home. 'How did it go?' she asks.

'People seemed to enjoy it.'

'I think you're brave to do these classes,' she says, pouring me a cup of tea. 'Everyone enjoyed the ice cream lesson last week. I bumped into Sue in the post office, and she told me all about it.'

'Really?' I say, feeling more cheerful. 'I'm happy to hear that. Isabella is hoping to expand the business and offer more of this sort of thing. These classes are a trial to see how they go. With me as the guinea pig.'

'You're doing fine,' she says. 'Although you look tired.'

'I am. And I have an early start in the morning, so I should go to bed soon. Thanks for the tea and the pep talk.'

I take a quick shower and open my phone to check my alarm is set. There's a message notification on the screen. I'm too tired to look at it right now. It will be Isabella reminding me for the fourth time to bring the jam with me tomorrow. Or she may be offering to pop over and collect it from me tonight to be on the safe side.

My phone pings again. She must be getting desperate. I swipe the text, and my heart jumps when I see it's from Dad. He hardly ever contacts me. We used to speak almost every day, but things have been very cool between us for months, and I've hardly heard from him. I don't contact him either. I wouldn't know what to say to him. My decision about the magazine hangs heavily between us, and I'm conscious of being a disappointment to him. It's easier to keep him at a distance than to open up the huge can of worms that is our relationship and my career decisions.

But I won't sleep now if I don't read it. I'll lie awake imagining all sorts. It's best to rip off the sticking plaster and find out the worst. I let my eyes travel down the screen.

Hi Meghan! I was very touched to receive your lovely birthday card. Thank you for sending it all the way from France. It reminded me of how much I miss you. Now for the good news. I need to come over to Paris soon. It would be lovely to catch up with you. So, would you like to meet for dinner on the 18th? I can book a table at La Cave. I'd love to see you and hear how you're getting on over there. Let me know if you can make it. Thanks again for the card. Love Dad x

Chapter Thirteen

I knew I shouldn't have read that message. I'm exhausted, but I can't sleep for hours. Why did I have to send Dad a birthday card? I could have pretended to forget his birthday altogether. That wouldn't have been kind, but it wouldn't have made him quite so keen to see me.

I have a few options, none of them appealing. I could pretend I haven't received his text. But then he's bound to send another one. Even worse, he may call. I could text him to say I'm travelling around France for a month and can't meet him. But that runs the risk of him deciding to join me for some much-needed R and R.

Maybe I could say I'm hiking in the Himalayas. Dad has never been known to walk anywhere if he can take a taxi. Better still, a limousine. He might hire sherpas to carry him up the mountain, but it isn't likely. I remember I won't actually be in the Himalayas. If I'm starting to confuse my fictional life with reality, I'll never be able to convince anyone else.

I'm not comfortable lying to anyone, particularly Dad. I wish he didn't keep putting me in situations where I feel as though it's my only option. I hate not telling him why I'm not in Paris. I meant to go. I really did. But then this job came up, and I happened to see it. I didn't expect Lily and Isabella to offer me the position, but when they did, I couldn't turn it down.

And why does it matter to Dad where I am? He agreed to me taking a break so I could clear my head and decide what I want for the future. I can do that just as well here in Honeywell as in Suzanna's apartment.

I could still call him and tell him what I'm really doing. It's the simplest and least risky course to take. But I don't want to. I'm enjoying my freedom and independence too much.

I'm still undecided what to do by the time I arrive at work. Lily and Isabella won't be here for another couple of hours. I'll be all alone in the kitchen, and I do my best thinking when I'm kneading dough.

I need to make sourdough rolls and focaccia. And Isabella has eaten the last of the plum slices. I could punish her by refusing to make more until I'm less busy, but I don't have the heart. I love watching her dispose of my products. There aren't many moments of pure pleasure in life, but that's definitely one of them.

I set up the mixer and measure out the ingredients. I switch it on and turn on the industrial oven. Isabella told me when I first arrived that it was larger than the one into which Hansel and Gretel pushed the witch, and she wasn't exaggerating.

As I mix the dough for the focaccia, I try to decide what to do about Dad, but it's no good. I keep finding myself at an impasse. I circle between telling him the truth and informing him I'm on submarine training. Several times, I remind myself I should behave like an adult, but I can't convince myself.

The shop door opens at half past eight. I put my head around the door to check that burglars aren't taking advantage of the shop's apparent emptiness to steal our last doughnuts, but it's only Lily, looking paler than usual.

'Are you ok?' I ask her, and she smiles.

'I'm fine. Just one of those nights. My offspring have decided to work in tandem. I swear they make out a timetable together and agree when each of them should wake up. Never at the same time, of course. That would be far too convenient. They're like the figures on those German weather clocks. As soon as one disappears, out comes the other one.'

The door flies open, and Isabella appears.

'You're both here on time!' she says, looking surprised.

'I've been here for two hours,' I say.

'And I arrived before you,' Lily points out.

'I would have been here half an hour ago if I'd woken up,' says Isabella. 'I think there's something wrong with my phone. I set it very carefully each night, but it never goes off.'

'I don't believe you,' says Lily, holding out her hand. 'Give it to me.'

Isabella pulls out her phone. 'The code is 1234.'

'That isn't secure,' says Lily. 'We'll have to change it.'

Isabella tries to take the phone from her. 'Don't you dare! It's the only number I can remember.'

'You're an accountant,' says Lily. 'That can't be true.'

'Yes, it is. Financial accounts are quite different. They're written down. No one expects you to memorise all the columns in a spreadsheet.'

'Change it,' advises Lily. 'And don't write the new code on a post it note and leave it lying around for customers to find.'

She presses a few more buttons. 'Give me a minute.'

Isabella sighs. 'I was doing fine without you.'

'No, you weren't,' says Lily. 'Don't you use this phone for internet banking too?'

'Yes, but there's never any money in my account.'

'Lily's right,' I say. 'You shouldn't use easily guessed codes for your phone or bank card.'

Isabella shoots me a guilty look, and I raise an eyebrow. 'Please don't tell me you use the same code for both?'

'All right, I won't,' she says. 'Can I have my phone back, please?'

Lily holds it away from her. 'In a second.'

The phone buzzes and emits a ring tone that sounds like a cockerel crowing. Isabella looks innocent. 'I haven't heard that noise before.'

'I have,' says Lily. 'I hear it whenever a new batch of cakes is ready. I assume it's the ring tone you use for alarms you consider important.'

Isabella snatches her phone. 'What can I say? I'm a creature of habit.'

'One who's all out of excuses,' says Lily. 'Your alarm works perfectly.'

'It did that time,' says Isabella. 'But who's to say Georgia doesn't tiptoe in each morning and switch it off to get me into trouble at work?'

'Why would she do that?' I ask.

'You've still not met her. She's pure evil. It's exactly the sort of thing she would do. Although I guess she's free from suspicion in this case because she never gets up before me. It's a puzzle. Perhaps it has something to do with the electricity supply in Compton.'

Lily rolls her eyes. 'Your uncle runs an awful lot of machinery on his farm without being affected by any mysterious power cuts.'

'You know nothing about farming,' Isabella tells her. 'We still use Verey lights and parachute flares when we get lost in the fields.'

Lily switches on the coffee machine. 'I don't have time for this. Someone has to open the shop and check yesterday's takings against the stock.'

'If they don't quite match, I'm sure there will be a simple explanation,' says Isabella.

'I'll make the coffee,' I say. 'Can you two give me some advice while I do?'

Isabella plumps herself down in a chair and rests her chin on her hands. 'There's nothing I like better than giving advice. Especially on subjects about which I know absolutely nothing.'

'There's nothing at all you like better?' says Lily sardonically.

Isabella isn't fazed. 'Except cake. But that goes without saying. Speaking of which, are there any macarons left? They go beautifully with handing out advice. Someone should write a book about pairing various cakes with various types of problems.'

'We only have a few macarons left,' says Lily. 'And we need those for the customers. Don't forget it's poker club today.'

'Do they use them as poker chips?' I ask, confused.

'Not as far as I know,' says Isabella. 'But it's a great idea. I'll suggest it to Vera when they arrive. It would be great for our bottom line. There's nothing like fragile, crumbly poker chips to keep small businesses in profit. I may mention it in my next TED talk.'

'You can't have a macaron,' says Lily. 'But those coconut slices need to be eaten by this evening.'

'Pass them over,' says Isabella. 'And I'll do my poor best with them.'

She settles herself comfortably with the plate of cakes, accepts the mug I hand her, and looks expectantly at me. I wish I hadn't started this. She's clearly anticipating something juicy, and my problem isn't an interesting one.

'It's nothing really,' I say. 'Just something to do with my father.'

'Shoot!' she says, her mouth full of coconut slice.

'You remember we had the bright idea of sending him a birthday card from Paris?'

'I had the bright idea,' she corrects me. 'I remember it distinctly.'

'You had it,' I agree. 'But it's backfired.'

She swallows her last mouthful and picks up a second slice. 'That doesn't sound likely. My brilliant ideas never backfire. They're all well thought through and highly organised.'

She ignores Lily's snort of derision. 'Maybe it was your part of the scheme that backfired, Meghan. What happened?'

'He was so pleased to hear from me that he's decided to visit me in Paris,' I say in despair.

Isabella gives a shout of laughter. 'You should have seen that one coming.'

'You didn't,' I say.

'Part of becoming an adult is learning to take responsibility for your actions. I'm surprised no one has ever told you that.'

'Never mind whose plan it was,' I say. 'The point is, I have no idea what to do.'

Lily looks sympathetic. 'Could you call your father and let him know where you really are?'

'Not a hope!' says Isabella. 'Where would be the fun in that?'

'I'm not looking for fun,' I say. 'I'm looking for a solution.'

'You're looking for both,' she says. 'There's no rule saying solutions have to be boring.'

She sinks her teeth into her cake and chews thoughtfully. Finally, her eyes light up. 'I knew coconut slices would do the trick. Of course! I have the obvious solution.'

'I very much doubt it,' says Lily.

Isabella picks up a third slice. 'Do you realise how difficult it is when everyone around you shows so little confidence in your abilities? When I say I have the obvious solution, I have the obvious solution.'

She turns to me. 'You're sure you don't want to visit your father in London?'

I shake my head. 'Definitely not.'

'And you don't want him visiting you here in Honeywell,' she goes on. 'Which means there's only one thing for it. You'll have to get on a train and meet him in Paris!'

Chapter Fourteen

I meet Ben for dinner on Saturday evening. He's suggested we try a new place that's just opened in Christchurch. He offers to come over to Honeywell to pick me up, but I refuse. I'd prefer to have my own vehicle on hand in case a quick getaway is required. I'd also like to have a look at the town before I meet him. Most of the shops will be closed, but I want to visit the Priory and see the old Keep.

I arrive at the restaurant at seven o'clock to find Ben waiting outside.

'I'm not late, am I?' I ask him, and he smiles.

'Not unless you're on Austrian time. I've only just arrived. Did you find somewhere to park?'

'A little car park down Anvil Street. I wanted to look around the town before I met you, and it seemed a convenient place.'

'You should have knocked on my door,' he says. 'I live in the next street.'

'How was I supposed to know that? This is the first time I've visited Christchurch, and I didn't know your address.'

He holds open the restaurant door. 'You only had to ask.'

A server shows us to a table near the back of the restaurant. 'This should be nice and quiet for you.'

'Thanks,' says Ben.

'Why would we want a quiet table?' I ask as I sit down.

'Maybe the server thinks you look as though you're hard of hearing. Or he considers us elderly and wants to warn us they have a children's entertainment hour starting at seven.'

'In which case, I'll take my food to go,' I say.

'You don't like children?'

'Children are fine in their place, but not en masse at the end of a busy week. And definitely not when their entertainments include clowns.'

'I love clowns,' he says. 'Show me a circus, and I'm there.'

'I've never been to a circus.'

'You've been missing out,' he says. 'What do you do for fun?'

'Other things. But not that. It isn't my type of thing.'

'How can you be sure if you've never been to one?'

I pick up my menu and scan it. 'You don't need to try every single thing to know whether you'll like it. For instance, I'm not too keen on seafood, which means I won't be ordering the calamari al forno. I've never had it, but I have a pretty good idea I wouldn't enjoy it. The same goes for circuses. I don't like crowds and noise, and people in masks creep me out.'

'That shows how little you know,' he says. 'No self-respecting clown would wear a mask. They paint their faces. It's an art form.'

'It still doesn't mean I want to spend my hard earned money watching them.'

'I don't have the luxury of turning up my nose at anything,' he says. 'I'm a journalist. I have to go where I'm sent and pretend to enjoy it, or my boss will know the reason why.'

I search around for a new subject before I give myself away. 'Do you like to travel?'

'I love it,' he says. 'I have a wish list as long as my arm, but it's an expensive hobby.'

'Not if you hitchhike and stay in hostels.'

'I've done a bit of that. But it would be fun to go on an all-expenses-paid holiday to Mauritius and lounge around on the beach with people bringing you cocktails every ten minutes.'

'I've been there,' I say. 'Not with all my expenses paid, but it was great fun.'

'Lucky you. Where else have you been?'

We discuss the various places we've visited until our food arrives. I'm delighted to see they serve generous portions here. I worked right through lunch, and I'm hungry.

'It must be nice to eat something that someone else has prepared,' says Ben.

'What do you mean?'

'You're a chef. You make food for other people.'

'I'm a pastry chef. I don't get too many requests for linguine or risotto. We serve soup and toasted sandwiches at lunchtime, but nothing too complicated.'

'But you must have trained as an all-round chef first?'

'I've only done a year of formal training. I didn't expect to be offered a job based on that, but Lily and Isabella were happy to take a chance on me. And this job is only for six months. Hopefully, I can't do too much damage before Abby returns.'

'There's no chance they'll keep you on when she gets back?' he asks.

'I'd love that, but no. They only need one pastry chef, and that's Abby. But I intend to learn as much as I can while I'm here.'

He regards me thoughtfully. 'Do you see yourself doing this forever?'

'Forever is a long time.'

'Agreed. Let me rephrase that. Do you see yourself doing this for the next ten years?'

I take a bite of my linguine to buy myself some time. I've asked myself this question a million times, and I'm no nearer to arriving at an answer.

'It's complicated,' I say at last, and he laughs.

'It always is. What's the problem? Are you trying to coordinate your life with someone else's?'

I know what he means, but he's closer to the truth than he imagines. That's exactly what Dad wants me to do – what he's always wanted me to do. He loves the life he's built for himself, and he expects me to be a part of it.

'Not exactly,' I say. 'But in a way.'

'Are you seeing someone else?' he asks.

'Of course not. I wouldn't be here tonight if I were.'

'I was hoping not,' he says. 'I never date more than one person at a time. I'm glad you feel the same way.'

I remember Isabella's list of drink possibilities.

'Not all meals have to be dates,' I tell him. 'There are celebratory meals, impromptu meals, networking meals, impromptu meals …' I almost add spy meals but stop myself in time.

Ben rescues me before I can become even more entangled.

'I very much hope this is an actual date. I've wanted to ask you out ever since you took that flying leap towards the chocolate fountain.'

'That's the hero complex coming out in you,' I say, and he laughs.

'Perhaps. No one gets the chance to play the hero very often these days, not since the last dragons were banished from England.'

'Banished?' I say. 'Weren't they wiped out by all the sword-wielding heroes? That's what we learned at school.'

'I was giving you the sanitised version. I didn't want you to have nightmares tonight.'

'I never have nightmares,' I tell him. 'At least, not dragon-related. I might have some if I ate the calamari, which is one of the reasons I didn't order it.'

'Very wise. But we're getting away from the subject of my chocolate-based heroics. I'd hate for us to stray too far from that. As a modest person, I couldn't very well allude to it myself. But now that you have, it would be a shame to change the subject too quickly.'

I sigh. 'And I thought you were different to other men.'

He surveys me thoughtfully. 'I'm not sure how to take that. It could bode extremely well for me or extremely badly.'

I meet his questioning glance with an enigmatic smile. 'That's the price you pay for fishing for compliments.'

'I asked for that,' he says. 'Let's agree that what I did for you was nothing special – just a lucky combination of lightning-fast reflexes and incredible muscular strength.'

He catches my eye and grins. 'Not that there was much strength required. You were as light as a feather in my arms.'

'That's better,' I say. 'You were treading on thin ice there for a moment.'

'I would have asked you out on a date whether or not you'd dived into that fountain,' he says. 'I noticed you the minute you came into the room that evening, and I was looking for an opportunity to introduce myself. If I'd had any sense, I would have loosened that piece of carpet myself.'

'A missed opportunity,' I say. 'But you wouldn't have had the chance to ask me out. The ceremony was about to begin when we met, and I left straight afterwards. It was a lucky coincidence that you happened to walk into my place of work the following morning.'

'Don't you believe in the mystical workings of fate?' he asks.

'Not in the slightest. I'm not superstitious, and I don't believe in fate, destiny, karma, or any of those things people use as an excuse not to take responsibility for their own lives.'

'You're so unromantic,' he complains.

'Not at all. I'm a realist. Life is what you make of it.'

He reaches over and takes my hand. 'In which case, I'm glad I decided to pursue you when I had the chance and ask you out to dinner.'

'Another coincidence. You didn't know I was taking those classes when you turned up to take a look.'

'Maybe not,' he says. 'But I didn't have to come back the following week. I could have taken a few notes for my article and left it at that.'

'I thought you were interested in the subject of small businesses. That's what you told me at the time.'

He grins. 'I was more interested in the person giving the classes than in the small businesses themselves. Not that I haven't learned a lot of useful information,' he adds hastily.

I can't help laughing. 'I'll make sure there's a quiz during our final class, and we'll see how true that statement is. Shall we get going? We're the last ones here, and that server looks as though he'd like to go home.'

We wander back along the high street towards the place where I parked my car. Ben takes my hand as we walk, and I don't object. We've already established this was a date rather than a networking or any other type of meal. Besides, I like this man more than anyone I've met for a long time. He's easy to talk to, and we share the same sense of humour. It's been too long since I've allowed myself to get close to anyone, and there's no reason not to have some fun.

It won't go further than that, if only because I still haven't told him who I am. It isn't necessary to spill the entire details of your life on the first date with someone. But neither is it normal not to mention such a huge point of connection. I don't plan to do that, not least because I can't think how to do so at this stage without opening a massive can of worms and taking the risk of putting Ben off me altogether.

So, for now, this will have to remain a casual thing. We'll both have some fun before moving on to whatever the next part of our lives may hold. We'll be the epitome of a summer romance, and I'm fine with that. I'm sure he is too. Someone as good looking as Ben won't be short of offers. By September, he probably won't even remember me.

We've reached my car without me noticing. He gives me a quizzical look as I stand there, waiting for him to open the door. 'Have you forgotten your car key?'

I return to reality with a start and rummage in my bag. 'I'm sorry. I was a long way away.'

'Clearly. I got the sense I'd lost you somewhere around Clerkwell Street.'

'I was thinking of something else,' I apologise again.

'Always what people like to hear at the end of what they thought was a very successful date.'

I laugh. 'I had a lovely time, thank you. My mind tends to wander when I'm tired. It was nothing to do with you.'

I'm about to open my car door when I catch his gaze fixed on me. There's something in his eyes that makes my heart beat faster. It's a mixture of amusement and something else. I can't tear my eyes away from his face. Very slowly, he leans towards me, and I feel the world slow down around us as though time is holding its breath.

It's a warm evening, but his closeness sends a shiver down my spine. The warmth of his breath brushes against my face, and I feel a rush of anticipation. His gaze locked on mine, he closes the distance between us and lifts his hand to my cheek. His thumb traces a line along my jaw as he lowers his head to kiss me. Without conscious thought, I slip my arms around his neck, aware only of the pounding of my heart as he deepens the kiss.

He draws back at last and surveys me with the hint of a smile. 'I hope your mind wasn't wandering too much just then?'

'Just when?' I ask with assumed indifference.

He opens my car door for me. 'I'll tell you some other time when you're not so tired.'

He kisses me again lightly. 'Thank you for a wonderful evening. I'll call you tomorrow, and maybe we can arrange something for later in the week?'

I climb in and start the engine before smiling up at him. 'It's a very definite date!'

Chapter Fifteen

I wake the following morning and look at my phone. There are five missed calls from Ben. Why is he calling me at this time of the morning? And why has he called five times? I check my messages to see whether he's told me what he wants, but there's nothing there.

I sit bolt upright, my thoughts racing wildly. I only said goodbye him last night. What could have happened in the meantime that was so important he had to call me five times? I'd like to think he's missed me so much that he can't wait to speak to me again. But surely if that was the case he would have sent me a message with a string of whatever emojis he thought appropriate to the occasion. He hasn't sent me any messages like that so far because until last night we weren't officially dating.

It will be interesting to see what sort of a text messager he is when he's actually seeing someone. Will he end each one with a flurry of hearts and bunches of flowers? I hope not. That really isn't my style. Or will he be one of those strong, silent men who confines himself to communicating whatever he has to say in as few words as possible, caveman style? I imagine the way to win

Isabella's heart would be to preface each message with a string of cupcakes and sign off with a row of eclairs.

My heart plummets when I realise Ben hasn't texted at all. Instead, he's called. Repeatedly. That can't be good. Maybe he got carried away by all our talk of dates last night and didn't really intend to kiss me. When he got home, he may have realised what he'd done and called me immediately to let me know the whole thing was a terrible mistake, and I shouldn't read anything into it.

I should have gone with my initial instinct and never agreed to date him in the first place. It's all Isabella's fault with her talk of business drinks and spy drinks and whatever other nonsense categories she came up with. She talked me into having a perfectly innocent drink with Ben, which ended by giving him ideas and asking me to dinner. And, like the idiot I am, I gave in, bamboozled by his handsome face and sense of humour and irresistible charm.

I won't make that mistake again. The next time a tall, handsome, near stranger with kind eyes asks me to have dinner with him, I'll turn on my heel and run away to eat at the nearest fast food outlet all by myself.

My phone vibrates in my hand, making me jump. It's still on silent, so I can pretend I'm asleep if I want to. I almost drop the phone back onto the bedside table and pull the quilt over my head. I could make snoring sounds for extra effect. I remember Ben won't be able to see or hear any of this. I also remember I'm an adult and should be past playing silly games. I'm quite capable of answering my phone, listening to him explain he's made a huge mistake and doesn't want to see me again, then telling him I feel exactly the same way and hanging up with my dignity intact.

I cautiously jab at the button and lift the phone to my ear, taking a deep, steadying breath before I speak.

'Hello?' To my annoyance, my voice comes out in a hoarse croak.

There's a pause before I hear Ben's voice. 'Are you ok?'

I clear my throat. 'I'm fine, thank you. How can I help you?'

There's an even longer pause before he speaks again. 'Are you sure?'

'I'm fine,' I repeat crossly. 'Why are you calling?'

His voice sounds distinctly amused. 'Because I want to talk to you.'

This is the perfect opportunity to get in first and tell him this isn't working out for me. That should take the wind out of his sails. I'm trying to formulate an exquisitely polite yet mildly cutting phrase, but he gets in first.

'I've been trying to call you for the past hour.'

'I know you have. But I was asleep.'

'I didn't wake you, did I?'

I toy with the idea of informing him that he did. And as a result, I no longer wish to see him. Thoughtlessness so early in a relationship never bodes well.

'Only you mentioned that you switch off notifications at night,' he goes on. 'So I thought I'd be quite safe.'

'I do,' I admit. 'I only woke up a few minutes ago and saw you'd been trying to call me. I was about to call you back.'

He sounds relieved. 'That's good. I'm sorry to be calling on a Sunday morning, but I wanted to see whether you were free today.'

This isn't at all what I was expecting. If he wanted to break up with me, he surely wouldn't feel the need to do it face to face after only one date. He could just tell me now.

'To do what?' I ask cautiously.

'I have to go out to lunch at short notice. My editor called and asked me to review a pub called The Crooked Branch in the New Forest. Someone else was going to do it, but they've dropped out at the last minute, and we've promised to give this place a write up. What do you think?'

'About the write up?'

He laughs. 'I'll take care of that. I meant about lunch. Would you care to accompany me as my mystery plus one?'

I frown at the phone, not sure what he means. 'How can I be a mystery plus one if you know who I am?'

'You're not a mystery to me,' he says patiently. 'I'm the one who's a mystery. My editor usually asks me to go incognito to this sort of place so I don't get any special treatment.'

'Got it!' I say, relieved. 'So, if I go with you, I also have to go incognito?'

'That's the general idea. Although in your case it doesn't matter so much. I mean, all customers are incognito unless they happen to be personal friends of the management. I'm the one who has to hide my identity.'

I'm starting to feel more cheerful. It doesn't sound as though he's intending to break up with me in the near future. It wouldn't do much for his incognito-ness if he staged a big public break up and risked drawing attention to himself by causing a row at his table.

'I'd love to go,' I say. 'What sort of food is it?'

'I'm not entirely sure. Their website was down this morning. But it's some sort of pub, so it ought to be the usual thing – steak and kidney pie, fish and chips, jam roly-poly, or whatever.'

'Most pubs seem to be more adventurous than that these days,' I say. 'But I get the general idea. I hope they have somewhere we can eat outside. It's a lovely day.'

'I'll pick you up at twelve thirty, if that's ok. We have a reservation at one o'clock under the name of Higham. Presumably the magazine used an alias for me.'

'Should I wear a disguise?' I ask, warming to the idea.

'I think you absolutely should,' he says without missing a beat. 'The more bizarre, the better. Do you have a false moustache and eye patch?'

'I'm afraid not,' I say regretfully. 'And I don't have time to pop out and buy them now. We'll have to do the best we can with what we have. Is it too late for you to grow a beard?'

'I'm afraid I shaved this morning,' he says apologetically. 'So, even a trace of designer stubble is out of the question.'

I sigh. 'I don't think you take your job nearly as seriously as you should. We'll have to go as we are and trust to our excellent acting skills to pull the wool over their eyes.'

I take a quick shower and inspect my wardrobe, wondering what to wear. We'll be eating at a pub, so I won't need anything too formal. But I'd like to look nice for our official second date. The fact that it's combined with work is immaterial. Ben didn't have to invite me to go with him. He could have eaten in lonely splendour and put it on his expenses. He must do that all the time.

The fact that he's asked me to go along must mean he's keen to see me again, and he thinks he'll have a better time if I'm there. I sort through my wardrobe, wishing I'd brought more with me from London. I didn't expect to have much of a social life when I came to Honeywell, so I packed the minimum. I'm regretting that now. Maybe I can find the time to go shopping sometime this week. If Ben and I are now dating, I'll want more than my usual jeans and T shirts.

On the other hand, I don't want to get too far ahead of myself. We've had one official date. And one possible round of spy drinks a couple of weeks before that. It would be tempting fate to invest in a whole new wardrobe when I have no idea where this is going. I pull out one of my two summer dresses – the one with the tiny floral print and puffed sleeves, then wander downstairs to make myself a coffee. Ben isn't arriving for another couple of hours, and my caffeine levels are dangerously depleted.

Eleanor is sitting at the kitchen table with a newspaper open in front of her.

'Anything going on in the world that I should know about?' I ask, switching on the kettle.

She waves a pen at me. 'I have no idea. I'm in the middle of doing the crossword.'

I lean over to look. 'The short one or the long one?'

'The long one.'

I sit down opposite her. 'You're on your own. I'm not great at puzzles at the best of times, and I'm not fully awake yet.'

She points to the kitchen clock. 'It's past ten o'clock.'

'I know, but I didn't sleep too well. And when I did fall asleep, I had some weird dreams.'

'Maybe you ate too much cheese at the restaurant last night,' she suggests. 'People say that can cause bad dreams.'

'I'd have needed to eat several kilos of the stuff to give me the sort of dreams I was having.'

She squints at the paper, then quickly scribbles something. 'Octopus! I thought it must be. What sort of dreams were they?'

'I think one of them had something to do with the bakery. Isabella was conducting a funeral service for a chocolate cake, and everyone was crying. I can't remember why. I remember her telling me I'd cremated it by putting the oven on too high, then giving me a formal warning.'

'It sounds as though you had a bad night,' she says sympathetically. 'Was Ben there at this funeral service?'

I feel my cheeks heat. 'I'm not sure why you would think that.'

She grins and fills in a few more squares. 'I apologise if I've jumped to any wrong conclusions. Do I take it he's still just a friend?'

I stare out of the kitchen window so I don't have to meet her mocking gaze. 'If you must know, things have progressed slightly between us.'

'I'm delighted to hear it,' she says. 'I've never known anyone take so long to admit what's staring them right in the face.'

'I'm a naturally cautious person,' I say. I'm not sure whether this is true, but it's better than mentioning I've been keeping my distance from Ben because I'm keeping so many secrets from him.

'What are you up to today?' she asks. 'Would you like to come over to Harry's for lunch? He'd cooking a Sunday roast, and he always makes far too much.'

'That would have been lovely. But I have plans.'

Her quick smile makes me flush even more deeply. 'With Ben?'

'As it happens.'

'I'm glad to see the pair of you are making up for lost time. Life is short, and there's no point in wasting any of it. I'd better go and get ready. I don't have time to think about this final clue. I'll have to wait until I see Harry. He'll have finished it in five minutes flat.'

I look at the crossword she's left lying on the table. I don't enjoy puzzles as a rule, but I like to finish what I've started. Eleanor doesn't seem to have any such scruples. I stare at the clue for a second, thinking hard. *Beat it or quickly clear away.*

I pick up the pen she's left on the table, lean forward, and fill in the missing letters – *Whisk*. I only hope it isn't some kind of omen for our date today.

Chapter Sixteen

Ben knocks at the front door exactly on time. I'm glad Eleanor is upstairs. I'm not sure how to greet him. He solves my dilemma for me, pulling me into his arms and kissing me as though he doesn't care whether anyone else is in the house.

He releases me at last. 'You look lovely.'

'You've smudged my mascara,' I complain.

He peers at my eyes. 'It looks fine to me.'

'That's because I'm not wearing any. But if I had been, you would have smudged it.'

He takes my hand and walks me towards his car. 'I'll try to bear that in mind when I kiss you in the future.'

So, he plans future kisses? That's good to know. Just for the record, of course.

We drive through the New Forest to Midford, which is about six miles from Honeywell. The final half mile is down a gravel path that twists and turns and dips into a grassy area, where we see several parked cars. Ben pulls into the last space, and we climb out.

'Hungry?' he asks.

'Surprisingly so after the enormous meal we ate last night.'

'That was ages ago. I've had eggs and bacon since then, and I'm ready for my lunch. Let's hope the food here is good.'

We walk towards the main entrance. The pub is noisy even at this distance. Music is blaring out of the open windows, and there's an odd thumping noise.

'Are you sure you've got the right place?' I ask Ben.

'Unless someone has bought the pub between yesterday and this morning. It's a bit loud, isn't it?'

'Maybe it's someone's birthday,' I suggest. 'The staff may be playing their favourite song.'

We push open the door, and the volume increases. I take a step inside, wondering whether my ear drums will survive the next couple of hours.

A young woman greets us. She's wearing jeans and a checked shirt, and her hair is hidden under an enormous cowboy hat. It's hard to tell what she's saying over the noise of the music, but I can just make out the words welcome and booking.

'Reservation for Higham!' yells Ben.

She nods. 'Y'all wait there, and I'll be right back!'

She disappears, leaving Ben and me standing looking at each other.

'Y'all?' I mouth, and he grins.

The woman returns carrying a couple of menus. 'Come right this way, folks! Would you prefer the gold rush or the stagecoach table?'

'The what?' I ask.

She gestures towards the far end of the room. 'You're lucky they're both still free. We had a cancellation earlier.'

She appears to recollect herself and adds, 'Probably a shootin' over Bentley way.'

'A shooting?' I say, alarmed. Maybe I should have read Eleanor's paper in more detail before venturing out.

'Sure thing, hon,' she says cheerfully. 'Happens just 'bout every day around these parts. So, which is it to be?'

I dart a look at Ben, who doesn't seem disturbed by the idea of having brought me to such a violent area.

He smiles back at me. 'Which table would you like?'

'Erm, the gold rush?' I say at random. I'm not sure what's going on here, but I don't want to say so.

'Good choice!' The server pulls out a chair and gestures for me to sit. 'It's my favourite table too.'

She glances around, lowers her voice, and whispers. 'You can see the entire room from here. If Dead-Eye Derek comes in lookin' for trouble, you'll have a clear line of sight, and you can escape through the kitchen.'

She drops the menus on the table. 'I'll give you a minute to look at these.'

Ben sits down and picks up a menu. 'Let's have a look.'

I snatch it off him. 'What's going on? What was all that about a shooting?'

He looks amused. 'I wouldn't take it too seriously.'

'I can see you wouldn't. But what sort of place is this? I thought you said this was an English country pub.'

He removes his menu from my grasp. 'So I was led to believe. But I'm a great believer in going with the flow. I vote we sit back and enjoy the show, whatever it is.'

I narrow my eyes at him. 'I don't mind giving it a chance, but only until the bullets start flying. Then I'm out of here. You heard what she said – there's an exit through the kitchen.'

He squeezes my hand. 'I promise not to let anything terrible happen to you.'

'That isn't a promise you can make. They're expecting Dead-Eye Derek any moment, and he never misses his man.'

Ben doesn't look too worried. 'You've forgotten you're here with Eagle-Eye Ben. He's known far and wide throughout the territories as a crack shot. Last year, he shot a row of drinks off a shelf at the Red Lion with one eye closed.'

I open my menu. 'I don't think so. Honeywell is a small place. Something like that would be all round the village before you'd finished your game pie.'

'Trust me,' he says. 'I've saved you from a sticky fate once. If need be, I promise I'll do it again.'

I scan the menu, but there's no sign of the English classics Ben promised me when he invited me to join him for lunch. Instead, the dishes appear to be appropriate for a saloon bar in 19th century Gulch Creek.

'What are Wagon Wheel Wings?' I ask, looking at the starters.

'Some sort of chicken, I think. I like the look of the Cowpoke Cornbread.'

'Depending on what a cowpoke turns out to be,' I say. 'Is it the same as a cowpat?'

'Goodness, I hope not! Perhaps I'll have the Gold Rush Buffalo Nuggets instead. They should be safe enough. Unless they're made with real buffalo.'

'I wouldn't take the risk,' I say. 'Are these genuine gold nuggets scattered across the tablecloth?'

Ben picks up his fork, which is in the shape of a miniature mining pick, and mimes swinging it at the lumps of metal. 'I'm afraid not. These are what are commonly known as fool's gold. But those gold coins look real.'

I pick one up and peel back the foil. 'They're chocolate. What a let-down.'

'Would you have preferred to sit at the Stagecoach table?' he asks. 'It's not too late to move.'

'I'll stick with the chocolate coins. Seriously, Ben, what is all this? You told me we were coming here to sample Olde English Country Fare, and we rock up to find ourselves in the middle of a Wild West saloon. Have we travelled back in time, or have I banged my head and ended up unconscious in a hospital ward?'

'I can't vouch for the time travel thing,' he says. 'From everything I've read, those portals open up without warning in the most unexpected places. But I think I'd have noticed if you'd banged your head between the time I picked you up and our arrival here.'

The server arrives back at our table and flashes us a huge smile. 'Hi, I'm Caitlin, and I'll be lookin' after you today. Well, folks, how y'all doing with your menus? Are you ready to order?'

She looks so enthusiastic that I don't like to burst her bubble.

'I'd like to try the Wagon Wheel wings,' I say. 'Followed by the Trailblazer Tacos.'

She jots it down. 'And to drink?'

'A glass of white wine.'

She gives me a pitying smile. 'That there's a big city drink, hon. We don't serve none of those fancy beverages hereabouts.'

She points to the drinks section. 'You take a look at that while I take your husband's order.'

'He's not my –' I begin.

Ben is quicker. He lays a hand on mine. 'Shh, honey. Let your man talk.'

He ignores my glare and continues smoothly. 'I'm thinkin' about samplin' your tasty lookin' nuggets.'

She scribbles on her pad. 'Great choice. Ma Maverick made them fresh this morning. And to follow?'

'I can't decide between the Outlaw's BBQ ribs and the Rattlesnake Rolls,' he says. 'Do they use fresh rattlesnake?'

She gives him a pitying look. 'That's not real rattlesnake, darlin'. You'd have to pay quite a premium for that. They're pulled pork with a salsa dip.'

'Sounds great,' he says. 'I'll have those and a Whiskey Barrel Root Beer.'

'And your wife?'

I point to the menu. 'I'd like a Desert Oasis Punch, please.'

'Comin' right up.'

She gathers up our menus, flashes us another dazzling smile, and disappears in the direction of the kitchen.

I survey Ben, who's grinning at me. 'Was that supposed to be an American accent?'

'Surest thing you know, hon,' he says. 'What else accent would an old cow poke like me be usin'?'

'It sounded more like an Irish accent to me. With touches of Welsh.'

He looks hurt. 'If I'd a' known you'd be so poison mean, I would never ha' married you.'

'And that's another thing. Why did you let her think I was your wife?'

He leans over and speaks in a half whisper. 'These are old-fashioned times. Why else would you and I be lunching together unchaperoned? I didn't want to shock the poor woman.'

I raise an eyebrow. 'I'm sure unmarried people could eat together in public even in the Wild West.'

He lowers his voice further. 'But only in a respectable establishment, not a place like this.'

I open my eyes wide and fan myself with my menu. 'What are you suggesting?'

'I'm not sure. But I don't like the sound of Ma Maverick. Who knows what kind of operation she's running? We should keep our heads down if we want to get out of here in one piece.'

I pull out my phone and jab at the keys.

'Put that thing away!' he hisses. 'Do you want them to take you for a witch?'

I look up from my screen. 'It's not a time slip. And neither have I banged my head. Apparently, this pub does a themed lunch once a month. Did no one mention that to you?'

He reaches for a chocolate coin. 'I go where I'm sent. It's more than my life's worth to ask questions. You can't imagine what it's like working at *Whisk*.'

I can imagine it very well, but this is neither the time nor the place to say so.

'I wish we'd known ahead of time,' I say. 'We could have dressed appropriately. Everyone else here is wearing checked shirts and jeans and cowboy boots. We're the only ones who don't look as though we've made an effort.'

'You could tie your shirt at the waist,' he suggests.

'I'm wearing a dress.'

'That makes it more difficult,' he agrees.

His eyes light up when he sees our red and white checked napkins. 'We should be able to do something with these.'

He ties his napkin around his neck and opens the top buttons of his shirt. He rolls up his sleeves and grins at me. 'How do I look?'

He looks surprisingly good, but I'm not about to say so.

'Stay away from any card sharps,' I advise. 'They'll see you as a perfect mark.'

'How about you?' he counters.

I pick up my napkin and twist it into a bandana. I fish in my pocket for a hair tie and pull my hair back into a ponytail, then wrap the bandana around it. 'That's the best I can do.'

'I like it,' he says. 'That look suits you. All you need is a gun belt, and you'd make an excellent cowgirl.'

Caitlin returns with our starters.

'Do you have any cowboy stuff the customers can borrow?' asks Ben.

'Sure thing!' she says. 'I'm glad to see y'all getting into the spirit of the thing. I'll bring them over.'

She returns a minute later carrying a ten gallon hat filled with accessories. 'Take your pick.'

Ben delves into the hat and emerges with a sheriff's badge and a lasso. He pins the badge onto his shirt and whirls the lasso around his head.

'Careful,' warns Caitlin. 'You break it, you buy it! And it won't come cheap. Everything in Ma Maverick's establishment is of the finest quality.'

I select what looks like a water pistol. Caitlin assures me it will shoot the pips out of a playing card at a hundred paces.

'Don't point that thing at me,' says Ben. 'I'm law enforcement.'

I twirl the gun around my finger and promptly drop it into the jug of water. 'Sorry, these things take practise.'

I reach into the hat again and pull out a twisted leather bracelet and a pair of clip on cactus earrings. 'That will do for now. In the future, I'd like you to address me as Calamity Meg.'

'Only if you call me Wild Ben Hickok,' says Ben.

'Y'all look great,' says Caitlin. 'I'll let you get on with your meals. You must be hungry.'

Ben spears one of his nuggets. 'Just what I need after a hard morning randomly shootin' strangers and diggin' up gold.'

He chews thoughtfully. 'I've never eaten macaroni cheese nuggets, but they work.'

'These wings are lovely,' I say. 'Really spicy. People seem to have eaten well in the Wild West.'

Ben picks up his cocktail barrel and takes a sip. 'I'm not so sure about this. What on earth is root beer?'

'No idea,' I say, taking a slug of my own drink. It's my first Desert Oasis Punch, but with any luck, it won't be my last. It's delicious – fruity and refreshing, with a kick of vodka.

Ben looks at my glass regretfully, but I don't relent. 'Order one of your own if you don't like what you have.'

'I can't think why I married you,' he grumbles.

Caitlin brings our main courses, which are also excellent. My tacos are hot and fresh, and Ben's pulled pork rolls look appetising.

He sees me looking at them. 'Not a hope. You didn't share your drink with me.'

I shrug. 'I'm not too keen on rattlesnake. It burns my tongue.'

We finish with Cactus Blossom Cheesecake and Prairie Pecan Pie. Ben splits each dessert in half and hands me a bowl.

'We should have done this all along,' he says. 'I can write a much better article if we each compare two different things.'

'And if we're still not full, that Pioneer Peach Cobbler looks good,' I say, plunging my spoon into the pecan pie.

Chapter Seventeen

I push back my plate at last. 'I can't eat another bite, even to help you write this article. You're on your own.'

'You've eaten an impressive amount,' he says. 'As have I. And what we didn't sample, I can just make up.'

'Do you really do that?' I ask. 'Your articles seem so authentic.'

He looks surprised. 'You read my stuff?'

'Occasionally.' I catch his eye and grin. 'Perhaps a bit more than that. Isabella was saying how well you write, so I thought I'd check out some of your articles.'

'And you find them authentic? I'm delighted to hear it. I wish you could put in a good word for me with my boss.'

I could, of course, but I'd prefer not to mention that.

'You don't need anyone else to tell your bosses how well you're doing,' I say. 'But if you ever want a reference, ask Isabella. She's a big fan of your work.'

'I'll remember that when I come to the end of my contract,' he says. 'It may tip the balance for me.'

'Your own performance will do that. If you want to work for *Whisk* permanently, you should say so. They'd be fools to let you go.'

I'm amused to see a faint colour steal into his cheeks. Ben always seems so self-possessed, but he probably needs encouragement like anyone else.

'What are you going to say about this place?' I ask. 'You were expecting to write about the usual country pub with its authentic traditional cuisine. Your editor will get a surprise when she reads about your gun-toting, lasso-twirling afternoon in the middle of the British countryside. She may think you're playing an elaborate practical joke on her.'

He grins. 'Or that I was extremely drunk and got confused about where I was. I'll write the truth, of course. I enjoyed a wonderful meal in the Wild West with my … lunch companion and only just made it out alive.'

'We should be alright,' I say. 'Derek Whatshisname hasn't turned up. If you hurry and get the bill, we can make a run for the car before any brawls break out.'

He shakes his head. 'We can't leave yet. We haven't found out what's going on in the other room. The music in there has, if anything, got louder while we've been eating. As a fearless investigative journalist, I have to check it out.'

'You're a food writer,' I say. 'Leave the investigating to someone else. *Whisk* must have a crime reporter who could come and do that for you.'

'We're a respectable magazine,' he says. 'We write about food and home décor, not criminal gangs.'

He waves to Caitlin. 'Could we have our bill, please?'

'Comin' right up!'

'Do we have to go into the other room?' I ask Ben. 'I'm not a fan of loud music, and it sounds as though the ceiling is about to fall down at any moment.'

'You can wait in the car if you like. But I'm duty bound to investigate whatever I come across in the food related arena.'

'Those awards were bad enough,' I say. 'Come on, then. Let's get it over with.'

We push through the door into the side room. A wave of sound hits us, and I take an involuntary step backwards.

'Don't be shy,' says Ben. 'No one will dare to mess with Calamity Meg.'

'I wouldn't be so sure,' I mutter, but I allow him to propel me into the room.

A man is standing on a makeshift stage at the far end, shouting instructions through a megaphone.

Ben's face lights up. 'Line dancing! I've always wanted to try it.'

'I haven't,' I say, trying to pull my hand free.

His grip tightens. 'Of course, you have. You can't leave me to do this all by myself. I need someone to watch my back.'

'I returned my pistol to Caitlin,' I say. 'You'll have to find yourself another bodyguard.'

'Join the line, folks!' shouts the man with the megaphone. 'We're about to start a new one.'

Ben pulls me into the line of dancers, and we stamp and twirl as instructed. I try not to step on anyone's toes, but I'm not sure I succeed. It's surprisingly energetic. By the time the dance ends, I'm hot and gasping for breath.

'You should have warned me before I ate all that dessert,' I tell Ben.

'Another hour of this, and we'll have room to sample all the others,' he encourages me.

I shake my head. 'I've danced enough. I'll sit over there and watch you.'

The man on the stage gestures for silence. 'We'll start the dancing again in half an hour. In the meantime, we have a challenge for those of you who are up to it. I'd like you all to say a big hello to our old friend Bert!'

I look around for someone answering to that name, wondering what they expect us to do next. The double doors at the end crash open, and four men appear, pushing what appears to be –

'Is that what I think it is?' asks Ben.

The crowd cheers as the men heave a large bull into the centre of the room. Someone produces an extension cord and plugs it in.

I stare at it in horror. 'Bert's a mechanical bull?'

'Looks like it,' says Ben. 'Will you be having a go?'

'I'm not dressed for it,' I say, thankful I'm wearing a summer dress. It gives me the perfect excuse not to go anywhere near the bovine monstrosity.

'Who would like to go first?' shouts the man with the megaphone, and there's a ripple of laughter among the crowd.

'Is it safe?' asks a voice.

The man gives a derisive snort. 'This is the Wild West. Of course, it isn't safe!'

'I'll give it a go!' says a man who looks as though he's consumed rather too many Snakebite Sarsaparillas. He strides forward and swings his leg over the saddle.

'I'll put you on the lowest setting to begin with,' says the operator.

'Don't patronise me!' says the man. 'I can cope with any setting you throw at me.'

The operator ghosts a wink at the audience. 'Them's fighting words, pardner! Off you go.'

He flicks a switch, and the bull jerks forward. Its rider attempts to stay upright, but either the motion of the bull or the number of drinks he's consumed are too much for him. He slides sideways, landing on the floor with a crash, to the accompaniment of jeers and laughter from his friends.

'You couldn't have done any better!' he shouts at them. 'They put it on the highest setting.'

'Actually, that was the lowest setting,' the operator informs him. 'Would you care to have another go? There's a prize for the person who stays on the longest.'

'Nah, it's stupid. I'm out of here.' The rider gathers the last shreds of his dignity around him and stalks off towards the bar.

Several other people try their luck, with varying results.

'It's harder than it looks,' gasps one man after he's been thrown off for the third time.

'How about you?' I ask Ben. 'I know how keen you are to report on all the details of our lunch. I'll hold your jacket for you.'

He groans. 'Do I have to?'

'In the interests of the magazine, I would say you do. You wouldn't like it to get around that Wild Ben Hickok is a fraud.'

'Would you like to try it first?' he suggests with a hopeful smile.

'My bakery hasn't insured me for dangerous sports. Up you get!'

He hands me his jacket and walks over to the bull.

'The trick is to sit well forward and grip with your thighs,' advises the operator.

'I'll be happy as long as I don't throw up in front of my date,' says Ben. 'Go on, then. Do your worst.'

The man switches on the machine, and the bull lurches forward. For a moment, I think Ben is going to fly straight over its head, but he manages to grab the reins and regain his balance. The bull starts rocking from side to side with deceptive gentleness, and I find myself willing Ben not to let down his guard. The bull gives another sudden jerk and starts bucking wildly in random directions. Ben's legs flail in an attempt to find stability. His expression veers from determination, through pure panic, to a resigned acceptance, and I choke back a laugh.

I expect him to come flying off into the crowd at any moment, but he hangs on for several minutes, his face scarlet and his teeth set. Finally, the bull bucks backwards, spinning as it goes, and Ben comes off, only remembering to let go of the reins at the last minute. It seems as though he's about to hit the nearest bystanders, but his trajectory slows, and he crashes to the ground next to me in a tangled heap of limbs.

I help him to his feet. 'Are you ok?'

He rubs his elbow. 'A couple of broken legs, a dislocated shoulder, and a possible concussion. Nothing to complain about.'

I pat his hand. 'That's my brave little soldier. Have you had enough, or would you like another go?'

Before he can answer, there's a sudden commotion at the other side of the room.

'Stick 'em up, folks!'

I turn to see a man holding what looks like a potato gun. He's brandishing it wildly as he glares at the crowd.

'I've heard tell of a wagon load of gold passin' through these here parts!' he shouts. 'Tell me where it is, and ain't no one gonna get hurt!'

Ben slips his arm around me protectively. 'Let me guess – the famous Dead-Eye Derek?'

'Or his twin brother,' I say. 'Do you want to get out of here while we still can?'

Ben surveys the man, who's waving his plastic gun even more wildly. 'Not a hope. I'm just about sick of these gunslingers throwing their weight around. The Crooked Branch isn't big enough to hold the two of us.'

'If we left now, there would be plenty of room for him,' I point out.

He gives me a withering look. 'I've been waiting for a long time for this chance. I'm not backing out now. Either Derek or I won't leave this place alive.'

'That's a bit drastic,' I say.

He ignores this. 'You stay here while I tackle him.'

I clasp my hands. 'With two broken legs and a concussion? My hero!'

He pulls him towards him and kisses me. 'That's to remember me by until I come back!'

'If you come back. Derek looks as though he means business.'

Ben glances at Derek, who appears to have taken Caitlin hostage. She's swooning dramatically in his arms and trying not to giggle. 'No time to waste.'

He grabs a fake horseshoe from a nearby table and strolls towards the gunslinger. 'Hey, Derek!'

The man swivels around, keeping Caitlin between him and Ben. 'Don't take one more step if you want her to live!'

Ben keeps walking. 'This is between you and me. Let her go, and we'll fight this out man to man.'

Derek shakes his head. 'Tell me where the gold is, and I'll let her go.'

'I can't do that,' says Ben. 'That gold belongs to the town, not to some two-bit, hornswoggling, no-good lowlife like you.'

Derek raises his gun. 'In which case, none of you is leavin' this place alive!'

I edge around the outside of the crowd and come up behind Derek.

'Hey, loser!' I shout.

He spins around to see who it is, and Ben lifts his arm and throws the horseshoe with surprising accuracy. It sails through the air in a dramatic arc, collides with Derek's gun with a loud clang, and sends it spinning across the floor.

The crowd erupts into cheers and laughter as Derek releases his hostage and raises his hands in surrender.

Several bystanders leap towards him and pin his arms behind his back.

Ben picks up the gun, tucks it into his belt, and walks over to me. 'I told you I'd come back for you.'

'You'd have been in real trouble if it hadn't been for me,' I say.

'I was getting the job done,' he insists. 'But you were great. Have you done this kind of thing before?'

'A couple of times. Some of our customers can be quite tricky, and we have to resort to desperate measures. But don't put that in your article! Isabella would never forgive me.'

Derek walks past us in the custody of two of the servers.

He stops next to Ben. 'Sheriff tells me I'm lookin' at twenty years. I'll come lookin' for you when I'm out.'

Ben stares him down. 'I'll be sure to leave the porch light on for you.'

Derek gives us one last sneer and disappears through the swing doors with his captors.

'Have you finished here?' I ask Ben. 'Or are there any more desperate criminals you'd like to tackle?'

'My work here is done,' he says, linking his arm through mine. 'Would you like to buy me a drink to celebrate my extreme heroism?'

'No need,' says Caitlin. 'The drinks are on the house. Not only have you saved us from the worst criminal ever to infest the law-abidin' streets of Rustler's Ridge, but you stayed on the mechanical bull for the longest time.'

She pulls her hat from her head and hands it to Ben. 'This is for you to remember us by.'

She grins at us and disappears towards the bar.

Ben drops the hat on my head and surveys me. 'I've seen another side of you today, Calamity Meg, and it suits you.'

'You too,' I say. 'And there I was, thinking of you as Clark Kent, the mild-mannered journalist.'

'We didn't need Superman to deal with today's situation. You and I together were more than a match for Dead-eyed Derek.'

'We made a good team,' I agree. 'And now all that's left is for you to write up an account of our quiet lunchtime date. I can't wait to read your article when it comes out.'

Chapter Eighteen

I'm pleased with how well the evening classes are going. They seem to be running themselves. Everyone is so full of ideas and so eager to help everyone else that I'm more of a light-touch moderator.

'Have you enjoyed trying something new?' Eleanor asks one morning at breakfast.

'I have,' I say. 'I'm planning an afternoon event at the bakery when we've finished. Isabella insists on calling it a Show and Tell. I think she's been spending too much time with Daisy. But everyone seems to be looking forward to it. It will give everyone the opportunity to present their ideas to an audience and see what sort of reception they get.'

'How many people have been coming along?' she asks.

'Five.' I hesitate. 'Six if you count Ben.'

She helps herself to a second slice of toast. 'I'm glad he's finding them helpful, even though he's a journalist with absolutely no plans to start a local food business.'

She catches my eye and laughs. 'I'm honestly not trying to spy on you, Meghan. You must be aware of my comings and goings too.'

'I notice you don't come home until late most evenings,' I say. 'But I don't ask questions. It isn't delicate.'

The corners of her mouth lift slightly. 'I have nothing to hide. I've already told you about me and Harry.'

'He's been into the bakery a couple of times,' I say. 'He usually has a little girl with him.'

'That's his daughter, Emily. She's a sweetheart.'

'How long have you been seeing each other?'

'About a year,' she says. 'But we knew each other for a while before that.'

'Whereas I've only known Ben for a short time.'

She smiles. 'I'm afraid my lodgers have to police themselves. We're all adults, and I have enough on my plate without worrying about someone else's business.'

'I'm glad to hear it. Thanks for the toast. I have to run or I'll be late.'

No one else is there when I arrive at the bakery. I let myself in and switch on the coffee machine. I need a double espresso to counteract the stress of my dash up here and my worry about being late. Isabella always insists caffeine is a well-known calming agent, guaranteed to soothe and relax.

I hear her arrive twenty minutes later, arguing with Lily about something or other. I can't catch what it is, and I don't have time to find out. I go into the shop at eleven to ask whether they need anything prepared for the lunch rush and find them still engaged in a heated discussion.

'What's up?' I ask, placing a tray of cinnamon rolls on the nearest table.

Isabella's eyes light up, and she makes a dart for them.

Lily jumps in front of the table, blocking it from Isabella's view. 'Not until we've sorted this out.'

Isabella almost stamps her foot. 'You can't stop me from having a light snack in the middle of the morning. It's a human right.'

'No one is stopping you,' says Lily. 'I'm only saying you can't have one until we've made a decision.'

I pick up a calzone and sit at a nearby table to eat it. 'What are you both arguing about, or is it a secret?'

Isabella makes a feint, then dodges around Lily to secure a cinnamon roll.

'Ha!' she says, lifting it out of Lily's reach. 'It's a good thing you're only half my height.'

She takes a bite before Lily can stop here. 'Ouch! That's hot.'

'Serves you right,' says Lily.

'I've only just taken them out of the oven,' I say.

'You could have warned me,' grumbles Isabella. 'How was I to know?'

I tear my calzone in half. 'You've owned this bakery for … how many years? And it's only just occurred to you that some of our products are hot?'

'I'm aware,' she says. 'But you've walked all the way from the kitchen to the shop with them. That should have given them plenty of time to cool down.'

I ignore her and concentrate on my calzone. It feels like an age since I had my breakfast, although it's only a few hours. But I've been kneading and mixing, not to mention running to work this morning. My stomach is screaming for something to eat. Is this how Isabella feels all the time? In which case, I should feel more sympathy for her.

'So, what are you arguing about?' I ask.

'We're trying to decide on a logo,' says Lily.

'It's for branding purposes,' explains Isabella, taking a more cautious bite of her roll.

'What are you trying to brand?' I ask.

'The bakery, of course!'

'I thought so, but I wasn't sure. You might have been trying to brand yourselves. Like social media influencers do.'

Isabella looks interested. 'I never thought of that. What an excellent idea! Why didn't that occur to me before?'

'Don't set her off,' Lily begs me. 'It's difficult enough to get her to concentrate on anything as it is without sending her off down rabbit holes.'

'Sorry,' I say apologetically. 'So, you want to brand the bakery?'

Lily nods. 'I was reading an article about running a business in the age of social media. It said the first thing you have to do is get yourself a logo.'

'It's a good idea,' I say. 'What I don't understand is why you're fighting about it.'

'We aren't fighting about it,' says Lily. 'At least, not really.'

She catches Isabella's eye and grins. 'Thank goodness we don't have any customers in at the moment.'

'I'd love to help you when I have time,' I say. 'Maybe after work this evening?'

'At the pub?' asks Isabella hopefully.

'If you like.'

'Sounds good,' says Lily. 'I'll check that Jack will be home in time to look after the children. I could do with an evening out.'

She wanders off to the back of the shop, and Isabella gives me an approving smile. 'I'm glad you suggested that. Lily doesn't get out enough in my opinion. If I ever have children, I won't give up Shelley's cooking for anything.'

'I'll remind you of that if you ever have children,' I say.

We all meet at the Red Lion at seven o'clock. It's as busy as ever. I recognise several of the locals, which gives me a cosy feeling. I haven't been in Honeywell for long, and already I'm starting to feel at home here. Some places are like that, and this is one of them.

We order our food and find ourselves a table while we wait for it to arrive.

'So, you want to brand the business?' I say. 'It's a great idea, especially if you're hoping to expand.'

'We're never going to agree,' says Isabella gloomily. 'Lily doesn't have a creative bone in her body.'

'I have plenty of creative bones!' says Lily indignantly. 'But all your ideas are ridiculous.'

'I don't think so,' says Isabella. 'All my ideas have been wonderful. You just need to open your mind a little.'

'She wants to design a superhero flying across Honeywell carrying a plate of cakes,' Lily tells me in a despairing tone.

'It doesn't have to be a superhero,' says Isabella. 'But I think it should be. Bringing joy and sustenance to the starving population of Honeywell.'

'She means herself,' says Lily.

'What other ideas have you had?' I ask before they can start bickering again.

'Isabella suggested a loaf of bread wearing sunglasses and playing a guitar,' says Lily. 'I mean, why?'

'Because our bakery is incredibly cool,' says Isabella. 'I was thinking of making the loaf look like Elvis. In his earlier incarnation, of course. We don't want people thinking our products make you unhealthy.'

'We're not having an Elvis logo,' says Lily.

'What would you like?' I ask her.

'Something simple. Maybe using the intertwined letters *SB* and a small and tasteful loaf of bread.'

Isabella gives an ostentatious yawn. 'How very twentieth century.'

Lily freezes her with a look. 'It may not be as avant-garde as your idea for a flying teapot fighting off alien invaders, but it tells people what our business is about.'

'I'm not wedded to the flying teapot,' says Isabella. 'I also like the idea of a unicorn juggling doughnuts and cream buns. In fact, I'm leaning towards that one more and more.'

Our food arrives before Lily can tell her exactly what she thinks of this idea. Isabella appears to lose interest in the discussion as she digs into her game pie.

'Isn't this the best smell in the entire world?' she asks. 'I wish I could bottle it and sell it as an expensive designer scent.'

'Why bother?' asks Lily. 'You smell like that most of the time anyway.'

Isabella looks up from her plate. 'I'm fairly sure you mean that as an insult, but I'll take it as a compliment.'

Lily takes a bite of her pie and sighs. 'I'm sorry. I don't mean to be snappy. I haven't been sleeping well this week.'

'I can imagine,' I say sympathetically. 'It must be difficult to juggle two small children with running your own business.'

Isabella finishes her pie and casts a hopeful look at mine. I pull my plate towards me and start to eat before she suggests we share it.

'Why aren't you sleeping well?' she asks Lily. 'It can't be because of Daisy, the angel child. Is Abby's godson causing trouble? Would you like me to pop around and have a word with him? I'd like to hear what he has to say for himself.'

Lily gives her a tired smile. 'He's only a year old. He isn't talking yet.'

'Are you sure?' asks Isabella doubtfully. 'I seem to remember Daisy speaking in whole sentences by that age. Perhaps she had a better role model as a godparent. I would also point out that her godmother has stayed in this area for her entire life, providing guidance and stability and calm good sense whenever needed. You can't put a price on that.'

'Abby will be back in a couple of months,' says Lily. 'Ethan won't have noticed her absence. All he cares about is eating and refusing to sleep and laughing at Jack and Daisy when they do a puppet show for him.'

'You're the expert,' says Isabella. 'Seriously, I'm sorry you're exhausted. Why don't you take a few days off? Meghan and I are more than capable of looking after the bakery.'

'That's true,' I agree. 'Although I was hoping you'd give me some time off to go to Paris soon.'

Isabella's eyebrows shoot up. 'You're taking my advice and travelling over for the day?'

'If need be. But if you can spare me for an extra day, I'd like to stay for the weekend.'

'I didn't really think you'd go,' says Lily.

'I don't see what else I can do. If I tell my father I can't meet him that day, he's bound to go over to Paris another time and expect to meet me then. I'm committed to this now. I may as well get it over with. I'll take the train over and have dinner with him. Then, depending on whether you can spare me, I'll stay for the weekend and spend some time with my friend Suzanna. I'll be back in time for work on Monday morning.'

'Is Ben going too?' asks Lily.

'Why would Ben be going?'

Isabella rolls her eyes. 'Because you and he are dating. You aren't really planning to go to Paris all by yourself when you have a perfectly good boyfriend to go with?'

'I hadn't thought about it,' I say.

'You should invite him to go with you,' says Lily. 'You'd have a lovely time.'

'I'm not sure.'

'Of course you are,' says Isabella. 'When are you next seeing him? Ask him then. I bet he says yes.'

Lily nods. 'She's right. You could ask Ben to accompany you to a remote island with no electricity and running water, and he'd say yes. He really likes you.'

'You can't know that,' I say.

'Don't argue with an exhausted woman,' Isabella advises me. 'Especially not when she's right. You and Ben are clearly made for each other. If I hear you've snuck off to Paris alone because you were too chicken to invite him, I'll be most annoyed. It may even affect your performance review.'

'I've already told you I'm in a union,' I remind her.

'Your union rep would agree with me. They'd tell you not to be so ridiculous and to call and invite your boyfriend on a trip to the most romantic city on earth.'

'I'm not sure what kind of a union you think I've joined,' I say. 'But it doesn't matter. I'll invite him. He'll probably be busy, though.'

'Ten portions of crème brûlée says he isn't,' says Isabella, handing me the dessert menu. 'Now let's not argue anymore about this stupid logo while Lily's tired. You and I can discuss it this week and come up with a compromise.'

'Remember I have to sign off on it too,' Lily warns her.

'I'll keep an eye on her,' I promise. 'No unicorns, no alien invaders, and no superheros.'

'You think you've put a spoke in my wheel,' says Isabella, waving to the server. 'But I have hundreds more excellent ideas. One way or another, we'll get ourselves a logo so amazing it's taught in business courses for decades to come.'

I arrive home around ten o'clock and finally pluck up the courage to book my ticket on the Eurostar. I open the website, then close it again, not sure I want to do this. But what choice do I have?

I check the train times and, before I can talk myself out of it, book my ticket. Even if Ben can't make it, it will be lovely to see Suzanna. I'll meet Dad somewhere for dinner and keep the conversation light and breezy and well away from the topic of bakeries and future careers.

Then I can return home relaxed and refreshed and ready to face the rigours of the bakery once more. Why haven't I thought about doing this before? I'm surprised Lily and Isabella don't offer it as an option for their staff as an annual bonus. If this trip goes well, maybe I'll suggest it to them.

Chapter Nineteen

Ben picks me up at six thirty on Friday evening. He's taking me to The Wild Horse for dinner. He mentioned the place in passing last week and was surprised to hear I'd never been there.

'We'll have to do something about that,' he said.

I thought he would forget about it, but he didn't. I like the fact he pays attention to other people and never forgets conversations or tiny details. When I mentioned how much I missed Caffeine Joe's, my favourite coffee shop back home, he dropped in the next time he was in London and bought me a bag of their beans. The cafe roasts them on the premises, and they make the best coffee I've ever tasted.

I'm using them as slowly as possible, partly because I want them to last but mainly because it was such a thoughtful gesture on his part. Attention to detail is part of any journalist's training, but Ben goes the extra mile. It isn't only his excellent memory. It's the interest he takes in people's lives and the way he gets them to talk about themselves.

I don't have that gift. I'm a competent journalist who writes clearly and works hard. But I don't love it as Ben does. You don't have to enjoy your job more than anything else in the world to be good at it, but it certainly helps. From talking to Ben, it's obvious he loves what he does, which makes me realise I wouldn't be going into journalism for the right reasons.

More importantly, it doesn't seem fair on people who actually want to do the job. I've never been comfortable with the idea of working for my father. Everyone should start on a level playing field, and it feels wrong for people to be given an unearned advantage. But I also understand Dad doesn't want to leave his family business to someone outside the family.

Not for the first time, I feel a flash of resentment that he and Mum waited so long to have me. If they'd started their family earlier, they could have had a string of children willing and eager to take over from them when they retired, and I could have gone off to do whatever I wanted with a clean conscience. Instead of which, they had me when Mum was nearly forty, and she died five years later, leaving Dad to figure out how to raise a child by himself. And leaving me to grow up knowing I was all he had left, and that he wanted to give me everything he possibly could.

'All ready?' asks Ben, opening the car door for me.

'I skipped lunch especially.'

'You didn't?' he says in a shocked tone.

I laugh. 'You looked exactly like Isabella when you said that. I miss meals all the time. Things get hectic at work, then I suddenly realise it's time to close up and I haven't stopped for my lunch break.'

'I couldn't concentrate on my work if I hadn't eaten anything since breakfast,' he says.

'That's because you're a man.'

He snorts. 'Not even close. I've never met a female journalist who wasn't packing an emergency Mars bar or a bag of trail mix.'

I almost mention he's met me, but I think better of it. I'm planning to tell him the truth about myself at some point, but not now. If he reacts badly, it will spoil our meal, and I've been looking forward to eating at The Wild Horse all week. Isabella raves about the place. Then again, she raves about any establishment selling food or food-adjacent products.

Ben asks me about my week, and I tell him how Bernie got his lead tangled in a chair and brought a tableful of cream teas crashing to the floor. Mrs Ogilvie was most indignant with whoever had left the chair right in Bernie's path.

'How about you?' I ask. 'Did you go up to London this week?'

'Only for one day. I went up for the Monday morning staff meeting. It isn't essential for me to be there, but I like to show my face so my employers don't forget me entirely. Six months may not be enough time to make a lasting impression, but I do my best.'

'I can't imagine they won't jump at the chance to have you,' I say.

'That shows what you know about journalism,' he says. 'It's a cut-throat business. It isn't like the sort of work you do, where you're offered a job, sign a contract, and that's it.'

'I may not know much about it,' I say. 'But no ethical business rides rough-shod over its staff. I doubt *Whisk* is an exception.'

'Maybe,' he says. 'But the fact remains that they've only given me a short-term contract. Either they have someone else lined up or they're testing the waters.'

'Didn't you ask them when they offered you the job?'

'I did, but they weren't too forthcoming, and I didn't want to rock the boat. I was just happy to get in the door. The guy who started the magazine is a legend in the industry. He and his wife had to start it from his garage with a loan from his wife's father.'

I don't mention that I've grown up with this story. I know every detail of it. Dad used to describe the magazine's beginnings to me – how Grandpa insisted on giving them his life savings because he believed implicitly in what his daughter and son-in-law were trying to do. It's a touching story, but it adds yet another layer of pressure to my future decisions.

'It sounds great,' I say. 'I read *Whisk* occasionally, although not as avidly as my boss does. As you know, Isabella is a long-term subscriber.'

'She's mentioned it several times,' he says. 'She's passionate about the idea of food, isn't she? I wonder whether she's thought about going into the writing business. She could pitch a few ideas to Julianne. She's always open to fresh talent.'

'I think Isabella is keener on the practical side of the food business,' I say. 'By which I mean the tasting side. And she and Lily are so busy with the bakery that I'm surprised they have the energy to consider expanding at all. I fall asleep about nine o'clock myself these days. I can't remember being this tired.'

'I expect you're right,' he says. 'And I don't need the competition from such a renowned food lover as Isabella.'

'You should talk to your employers,' I say. 'Tell them what you've told me. You love working for them, and you're hoping they'll make it a permanent position. What's the worst that could happen?'

'They could tell me it's never happening,' he says. 'They may be counting down the days until my six months are up and they can get rid of me.'

'I doubt it. They liked the original article you did about the food awards enough to commission you to do this series on small businesses. If I were you, I'd strike while the iron's hot.'

'Maybe,' he says, although he doesn't look convinced.

It's strange to think someone like Ben could be insecure. He's good at what he does. In addition, he's personable and intelligent, not to mention attractive. Not that I imagine Uncle Matt put that last quality on his wish list for the new food writer. But Ben's picture probably looks good on the website. What am I saying? I know it looks good on the website. I check it almost every day. I'm not sure why. It isn't to collect information about Ben. I can see him in person whenever I like.

Is it because I want to feel connected to Dad, even if only cyber-connected? If so, it isn't helping. Short of one of us joining the next Mars mission, he and I are as disconnected as any two people could be. I still can't believe what's happened between us. We used to be so close. I couldn't wait to rush home from school and tell him about my grades or the fact I'd been chosen to be the third camel's hind legs in my class nativity play. He would drop whatever he was doing and listen carefully before catching me up in his arms and telling me I was his favourite person in the whole wide world.

When did that change? Was it during university? I certainly never played a camel there, either as the back or the front legs. But I had achievements to celebrate – consistently good grades and the odd prize. I told Dad about them all during my first year, and he was as delighted as ever. But I stopped doing that by the time I entered my final year. Either he was no longer interested in my life or I was less keen to share it with him. I can't remember which it was. All I remember was that a coolness developed between us, and I could never put my finger on exactly why.

Did I feel taken for granted as graduation approached – as though Dad was less concerned with what I was achieving as a person and more interested in how I would fit into the world he'd created for me? All I know is that I began to pull away, and he let me. By the time I graduated, and he expected me to start working at *Whisk*, I didn't feel he was able to see the real me anymore.

In his turn, he retreated from me, avoiding all the conversations I started. It was as though he was reluctant to give me the opportunity to say something both of us might regret. By the time I plucked up the courage to tell him I didn't want what he had planned for me, there was already a gulf between us, and it was one neither of us knew how to bridge.

At least Dad has had the grace to accept my decision and not keep pestering me to change my mind. I offered him the olive branch of taking a few months to think about what I really wanted, and he accepted it. It felt easier to do it in stages, to ease back from past expectations long enough for him to forget he'd ever wanted me to join his company and eventually take over from him.

So, why are we still estranged? We both know the score, and we've both accepted we want different things for my life. I thought that would be enough to let us move past it and carry on with our relationship as before. But it hasn't worked out that way, and I have no idea what to do about it.

If things were less tense between us, I might have been tempted to tell him the truth about Paris. I really meant to go there, but I got sidetracked by this job. And every day I spend at The Sugarloaf Bakery confirms my decision to pursue a career in baking. I should tell him the truth. It would be the mature, respectful thing to do.

And I know I won't do it. I've tried to convince myself I could tell Dad the truth when we meet in Paris. If our dinner together goes well, I could take a deep breath and make a clean breast of the whole thing. I'm sure he wouldn't be nearly as hurt as I've imagined. He might even laugh about how ridiculous it was for me to travel all the way to Paris just to explain that I don't live there.

'Are you ok?' asks Ben.

I return to reality with a bump. 'Sorry, I was miles away. About three hundred miles away, in fact. I was thinking about Paris.'

'That's a coincidence,' he says. 'So was I.'

'Really? Or are you going to claim to have ESP to impress me?'

'If you aren't impressed with me by now, I suspect you'll never be,' he says with a grin. 'I was thinking about an article I've been writing on the history of croissants.'

'I'm travelling to Paris next Thursday,' I say. 'I have to meet … someone … on Friday evening. I'm afraid I can't say more about that just now. It's a … business thing. I was originally planning to do the whole trip in a day, but I've changed my mind. I have a friend who lives there, and I've decided to spend a few nights at her place over the weekend. I was wondering whether you'd like to come too?'

His face lights up. 'I'd love to! I have to be in London for a Thursday afternoon meeting, but I could fly out after that. What time is your flight?'

'Isabella kindly gave me a few days off, so I'm taking the Eurostar on Thursday morning. It's an easy trip.'

'I can travel out on Friday morning if that works?' he says. 'I'm sure I can find myself a suitable hotel out there. It would be wonderful to do some sightseeing with you. There's safety in numbers. Do you speak French?'

'As a matter of fact, I do. Enough to get by at any rate. How about you?'

'*La plume de ma tante* sort of thing,' he says. 'Otherwise, I rely on raising my voice and speaking very slowly with random gestures.'

'The French always appreciate that. That's why our two countries have such a close relationship.'

'I knew there was a reason,' he says. 'But if you're willing to translate for me, I won't need to annoy anyone with my waving hands and blank looks.'

He takes my hand and smiles at me. 'Thanks for inviting me.'

'I hope you love it as much as I do. It's a special city.'

I imagine us wandering along the banks of the Seine, hand in hand, dodging a stream of men in striped jerseys playing the accordion.

'I can't think of anyone I'd rather take my first trip to Paris with,' he says.

'You've never been?'

'I've always meant to, but I've never managed it.'

'You'll love it,' I say with confidence.

He leans over to kiss me. 'I'd love anywhere if it was with you.'

'Death Valley?' I say. 'Siberia?'

He laughs. 'I'd give them a try. But we aren't going there. We're going to Paris, the city of –'

He catches my eye and breaks off. 'Pandas,' he finishes.

'I've never heard that one.'

'For someone who's so well-travelled, you're remarkably ignorant. It's lucky you'll have me there to educate you.' He throws out his hands. 'To know Paris is to know a great deal!'

'Who said that?'

'I have no idea, but someone did. Also "Secrets travel fast in Paris." I think that one was Napoleon Bonaparte.'

'It's nice to know your education wasn't wasted,' I say. 'The only one I remember is Audrey Hepburn saying that Paris is always a good idea.'

He waves to the server for the bill. 'That was a movie. Movies don't count. It has to be something that was said by a real person.'

'Audrey Hepburn *was* a real person.'

'It still doesn't count. I'm off home now to look up quotes about Paris. You've done me the honour of inviting me to accompany you. The least I can do is educate and entertain you while we're there.'

'You're extremely close to having that invitation rescinded,' I warn him, and he laughs again.

'Fine, I'll keep my quotes to myself. Even the most famous Humphrey Bogart one.'

I push back my chair and reach for my coat. 'Here's looking at you, kid?'

'Not quite. I'll save his quote for when we get back home. If you haven't got fed up with me before then and ditched me in the back streets of Paris.'

'Keep bombarding me with quotes, and I won't rule it out.'

He smiles down at me. 'Seriously, Meghan, thanks for inviting me. I'm really looking forward to it.'

I slip my arm through his. 'Me too. It should be a weekend to remember.'

Chapter Twenty

I've booked myself a seat on the ten-thirty Eurostar on Thursday. I would have liked to have taken an earlier one, but that would have meant spending the previous night in London, which would cost too much. If I still had a relationship with Dad, I could have stayed with him. As it is, I'm on my own. I take the earliest possible train up to London and arrive at St Pancras with half an hour to spare. I buy myself a magazine and wait on the platform.

I'm almost regretting taking the train over instead of flying. I could have travelled with Ben, which would have been fun. This is our first trip away, and it happens to be to one of the most romantic cities on earth. It would have been nice to do the whole thing together. I know he's only going because of me, while I'm going for less than creditable reasons of my own, but it still feels romantic. I've spent a lot of time in Paris over the years, but never with anyone special. And Ben, although I've only known him for a short time, is definitely special. I don't want to get ahead of myself, but things are going well, and I'm happy about that.

I wish for the hundredth time I'd told him the truth from the start instead of keeping secrets. Why should he care whose daughter I am or what I studied at university? It has nothing to do with who I am as a person. I should have told him my real name straightaway and simply let the chips fall where they may. It might have resulted in a few uncomfortable moments, but Ben's a reasonable guy. He wouldn't have held it against me.

By waiting this long, I've created an awkwardness I have no idea how to address. More than an awkwardness. I've lied to him. Maybe not in so many words, but I've fudged and obfuscated to the point where I may as well have said I was the Queen of Sheba.

I'll have to explain myself at some point, but I don't know when or how. Certainly not during this weekend. I'm looking forward to it, and I want it to be perfect. I want to wander around the familiar sights with the man I … like very much … and soak up the romance of the city so I can take it back with me when we leave and keep it tucked away among my memories for the rest of my life.

With any luck, Ben will find the whole thing amusing when I finally come clean. He's amused by so many things. It's one of the many things I like about him.

The trip passes quickly. I alternately gaze out of the window and doze. I'm used to early starts, but waking up to catch a train feels different from getting up early to go to the bakery.

Almost before I know it, the train is slowing down, and we're arriving in Paris. I pick up my bag and emerge into the warm summer day. I take a taxi to Suzanna's apartment, where I find a note telling me she'll be home by six o'clock.

I spend the afternoon wandering around the local park, taking a trip down memory lane. It hasn't changed at all since I was last here. The flowers and fountains are exactly the same. I lived here for a whole year, but all my memories are of warm sunny days and long, sultry evenings. There must have been plenty of cold, rainy days too, but somehow those haven't stuck in my memory.

Suzanna arrives home a few minutes after six, and we spend the evening at our favourite restaurant, eating chicken chasseur and catching up on what's been happening to each of us since we last met. She travels quite a bit, and I'm interested to hear all about her recent trip to Monaco. I tell her all about my time in Honeywell and the fun I've had working at The Sugarloaf Bakery. She shrieks with laughter as I describe some of Isabella's plans for logos.

'It sounds as though you're having fun,' she says. 'Do you ever regret not coming to stay with me here?'

'Now that I'm here, I do. But not really. I've had a wonderful few months, and I've learned a lot. It's confirmed me in my decision to become a pastry chef.'

I don't mention Ben. I'm not sure why. Suzanna and I have always discussed our relationships, given each other advice, and supported one another through breakups. It would be the most natural thing in the world to tell her about him. But I don't know how to discuss him without bringing up the subject of Dad, which I would prefer not to do. I mustn't bring all my problems with me and spoil what I'm expecting to be a halcyon few days. There will be plenty of time to think about them when I get home.

I should have known it would be no good. I've never been able to keep anything from her.

She quirks an eyebrow at me. 'You've told me all about your job and your landlady and the history of this Honeypot place –'

'Honeywell,' I say.

'Whatever. The fact is that you've talked about them all at some length without once mentioning you've met someone.'

'What makes you think I've met someone?'

She rolls her eyes. 'Call it female intuition.'

'I don't believe in that.'

'Neither do I. Come on, Meghan. We've known each other half our lives. Plenty long enough to know when you're hiding something from me. You'd be terrible at poker.'

'That's where you're wrong!' I say triumphantly. 'I played poker with a group of elderly women the other day and won two Eccles cakes and a pot of Earl Grey.'

'It sounds fascinating,' she says. 'I expect they have many quaint customs in such an isolated place. They must need something to get them through the long winter nights. You'll have to tell me more about them sometime. Right now, I'd like to hear about Mr Tall, Dark and Handsome.'

'Setting aside the fact I haven't admitted his existence, what makes you think he's any of those things?'

'Fine,' she says. 'Mr Short, Blond and Ugly, if you prefer. I don't care what he looks like, but I do want to hear all about him.'

There's no point in trying to deceive her. I have enough deception and half-truths in my life without adding to them. There's no reason I shouldn't tell her about Ben.

She reads my expression correctly. 'Quite right. You know you're dying to talk about him. Shall I get us another brandy?'

I put my hand over my glass. 'I'll fall asleep if I have any more. And I'll have a headache tomorrow.'

'Sleep it off,' she advises. 'I won't wake you.'

'I can't. I'm meeting –'

I catch her eye, and she bursts out laughing. 'I knew you'd mention him at some point. Is Mr Wonderful coming to Paris too? Is he already here? You should have brought him with you this evening. I'd like to meet him.'

'He doesn't arrive until tomorrow morning. He couldn't travel out with me because he had a meeting. So, he's booked himself a flight tomorrow morning. We've decided to make a weekend of it.'

'Will he be staying at our apartment?' she asks.

I'm annoyed to feel myself flush. 'He's booked himself a hotel in the city.'

'So, you're staying there with him?'

'I'm not sure. We haven't discussed that yet. I thought we could just see how it all goes.'

'Fair enough,' she says. 'Leave the key to the apartment in the usual place if you won't be staying there over the weekend. What sort of meeting did he have to stay for? What does he do?'

I almost make something up, but I'm not quick enough.

She catches my pause and raises an eyebrow. 'Now you have to tell me. Is it top secret? Are you not allowed to discuss it? Is he here to negotiate a nuclear non-proliferation treaty on behalf of the government?'

'Not that he's told me. If I say I'd rather not discuss his job, would you drop the subject?'

'Not remotely. If you aren't prepared to tell me what he does, tell me his name and I'll search for him online. Unless his employers have erased all traces of him in the cyberworld.'

'He hasn't mentioned that. As a matter of fact, he's a food writer.'

She looks surprised. 'Now, there's a coincidence.'

'Isn't it?'

'It must give you a lot to talk about,' she adds.

'We don't talk much about work.'

She grins. 'I imagine not. But it's good to start off with something in common.'

I almost leave it there, but the urge to discuss this with someone is too strong. 'I haven't told him I studied journalism.'

'Why not?'

'It hasn't come up,' I say weakly.

She pounces on this. 'How can it not have come up? I can understand you don't want to spend all your time discussing work. But you must have exchanged basic details when you met.'

'Of course, we did. I told him my name.'

Actually, I didn't tell him my full name. But I told him a part of it, which should be good enough for anyone.

'But why all the secrecy?' she asks. 'Why not tell him you had journalism in common?'

'Because of where he works.'

I see dawning comprehension in her face and nod. 'That's right. Ben is a food writer for *Whisk*.'

She looks puzzled. 'Is that how you met? At the magazine?'

'No, we met at a food award thing. I would never have talked to him if I'd realised who he was.'

'You aren't making any sense,' she complains. 'Why wouldn't you have talked to him?'

'It's a long story, and I don't have the energy to tell you all about it tonight. The short version is that when I first met Ben, I had no idea who he was, and he didn't know who I was. When I realised he was doing the job I'd turned down, I wanted to keep it that way.'

'The job your father offered you?' she asks, and I nod.

'That would have been awkward,' she says slowly. 'I can see why you didn't bring it up when you first met. It isn't the most tactful of ice breakers. But surely, when you got to know him better, the subject must have come up.'

I finish my coffee. 'It never seemed to. I've thought about telling him the truth several times, but I've never found a good opportunity.'

She gives a snort of laughter. 'And when will that be? While you're exchanging wedding vows? "I, Meghan … and, by the way, I almost took that job before you had a chance to apply for it … in sickness and in health …" Honestly, Meghan, what were you thinking? It will be a far bigger deal now than if you'd mentioned it at once.'

I don't argue with her. I've been thinking the same thing for a while. As hard as I try to persuade myself that Ben won't see it as a big deal, I'm not convinced.

'I can't do anything about that now,' I say. 'I'll deal with the situation when it arises.'

She nods. 'Does your father know you're dating one of his employees?'

'Absolutely not! And he isn't going to.'

'Not even when you and this Ben guy have been married for twenty years?'

'We've only been seeing each other for a short time,' I say. 'It's all very casual.'

'Your expression each time you say his name says otherwise.'

'He is lovely,' I admit. 'I've never dated someone who's so easy to talk to. He's smart too, and he has a great sense of humour.'

She clasps her hands and tips her head on one side. 'He sounds dreamy!'

I grin. 'Fine, but you're the one who insisted on discussing him.'

She stops smiling. 'Seriously, Meghan, what about your dad? Won't he be hurt if he finds out you're secretly dating one of his employees?'

I bite my lip. 'That isn't the biggest secret I'm keeping from him. Not by a long shot. You know he thinks I'm living in Paris with you.'

There's a long pause before she answers. 'Are you never going to tell him you're living in Honeybun?'

'Honeywell,' I correct her. 'And I'm not sure. I didn't mean things to happen like this. It all got out of control. You'd been inviting me to stay for ages. Then I saw the ad for my current job and decided to give it a go. I didn't think I'd get it. When I did, I wasn't sure what to do. Dad and I were barely speaking by that point. I decided that if he thought I was safely in Paris, he would stop worrying about me and calm down. This job is only for six months. My plan was to go and see him when it finished and then tell him I'd decided to become a chef and he'd just have to deal with it. I hoped after he'd had some space, he would realise how ridiculous he was being.'

'It's one plan,' she says. 'I'm not sure it would have been mine.'

'It's too late to re-think it now,' I say. 'He's been happy thinking I'm here in Paris. And I'm taking the chance to think about my future without all the pressure he's been putting on me. The only problem is …'

She's grinning at me, and it's obvious she has a strong inkling of what the problem is. 'Tell me.'

'He was so pleased to receive his birthday card that he told me he was coming to Paris for some meetings, and he'd love to have dinner with me.'

She's laughing so hard the tears are streaming down her face. 'Is that the real reason you're here?'

I answer with as much dignity as possible. 'It seemed like the best idea.'

She wipes her eyes. 'I'm glad we had dinner together tonight. I haven't laughed this much in a long time. Well, if you're set on keeping this whole thing a secret, despite everything, all I can do is wish you luck. You're going to need it!'

Chapter Twenty-One

Suzanna has left by the time I wake up the following morning. I was more tired than I realised. I had a long day yesterday, and our late night didn't help. I potter through to the kitchen and make myself some breakfast. It's surreal being back in this apartment after such a long time. Half of me feels like a stranger who doesn't belong here, and the other half feels as though I never left.

I wonder what my life would have been like had I actually come to stay here instead of only pretending to. I'm sure I would have had fun, but I would never have worked at the Sugarloaf and met Lily and Isabella. More importantly, I would never have met Ben. It's strange how things work out. I didn't even want to go along to that awards evening. If it hadn't been so important to my employers, I would have made my excuses and stayed safely at home.

Maybe Isabella would have been the one to nearly fall into the chocolate fountain and be rescued by Ben. And everything would have gone differently. I remind myself that Ben isn't obligated to start dating every woman he saves from a chocolatey disaster. But it feels so much like a rom-com trope that I can't quite bring myself to believe it. I can almost hear the voiceover. *He was presenting an award. She was hot footing it to the buffet table.*

If we hadn't met in the way we did, would Ben and I have been fated to meet some other way? I know some people believe in fate, but I'm not sure I do. There are so many events that never happen because all the necessary circumstances haven't fallen into the place. And plenty of other things that happen because they do.

I shake myself free of these thoughts. This isn't a productive path to go down. I did it a million times after my mother died, and I've come to realise there's no point. Worse than that, it's damaging and destructive. My mother died, and no one could have prevented it. The only thing we can do, as with so many things in life, is to live with it and deal with the consequences.

Looking at it another way, I could say that if I'd been raised by both parents, Dad may not have focused all his time and ambitions on me, and I may not have rebelled and applied for a random job to stake out my territory as an independent person. Which means I would never have heard of the Local Spoon Awards ceremony, much less attended it and taken an ill-considered dive towards a confectionery nightmare. And Ben would never have had the chance to practise his superhero skills or get to know me and ask me out.

I wash my bowl and wander back to my bedroom. Suzanna uses it as a study these days, which makes sense. This room was never large enough to be a proper bedroom. I wonder why I didn't notice that when I lived there.

I'm meeting Ben at ten o'clock outside Châtelet Métro station. I wonder how his meeting went yesterday. I know how anxious he's been to impress Julianne. I've only met her a couple of times. She seems focused and efficient, and Ben has mentioned a couple of times he enjoys working with her.

She would be wise to snap him up. He has a creative brain and a gift for writing in a clear and engaging way. It's not a common combination, as Julianne must know. Dad, too, although he's no longer involved with the minutiae of hiring. I've heard him complain a thousand times about woolly thinkers and interns who produce flowery prose that says nothing.

Even if *Whisk* don't take him on as a permanent member of staff, Ben is bound to find something equally good. But I hope they do. *Whisk* would benefit as much from having someone like him on staff as he would from working there.

I leave the apartment at nine o'clock and take the train to Châtelet. I arrive early and sit at a pavement cafe while I wait for Ben. The day is sunny and warm, and half of Paris seems to be out to enjoy it. It isn't just tourists, although there are plenty of those. There are also groups of office workers sitting together at cafe tables, talking and laughing.

I'm reminded yet again of the French ethos of working to live instead of the other way around. I wonder whether Isabella has French blood. She told me the other day her mother was born in Scotland, to which Isabella attributes her love of shortbread. But she would fit right in here. I can picture her sitting at a pavement cafe, sipping her café au lait and enjoying a croissant – or, knowing Isabella, several croissants – and finishing with an enormous helping of Tarte Bordaloue.

She owns her own cafe and can do something similar most days. In fact, that's exactly what she does. But I imagine she would particularly enjoy doing it in this particular setting. It seems an Isabella-y sort of place.

I don't know about Lily. I like her a lot, but I haven't got to know her quite so well. This isn't surprising as she has two young children to take care of. She and Jack seem to be rushed off their feet most of the time, even though they both have parents living locally. I see Angela Carson quite often. She comes into the bakery with Daisy and Ethan, and I'm always impressed by her endless patience and good humour.

Isabella is pretty busy too. She doesn't have children or a full-time partner, although she clearly has an active social life and an endless stream of dates. I've met a few of them when they've come into the bakery looking for her. They all seem nice, and several of them have been extremely good looking. But Isabella doesn't seem to want to settle down. She told me once she prefers to play the field because she can't imagine any one man holding her attention for more than a couple of months.

This is easy to believe. Isabella isn't one for routine or predictability. She finds something to divert her in the most uneventful things. She seems to consider the human race specifically designed for her own personal amusement – a sort of anthropological playground. Her life suits her, just as Lily's appears to work for her. They're both permanently busy and often exhausted. They also appear to be content with their life choices, which is an enviable thing.

I don't know whether I feel the same about my own life choices. I'm not doing what I originally planned with my life, which is disconcerting. But I'm doing what I love, which has to be a good thing. How long I can keep doing it is another issue. My contract with the bakery only lasts for a few more months, and I have nothing else lined up. But I knew that when I took the job, and I'm grateful to Lily and Isabella for giving me the opportunity to discover whether this is what I want to do long term.

I think it is. Perhaps not working in a small bakery in a tiny village, although there's a lot to be said for that. But my love of baking has only increased since I've been working at the Sugarloaf, and I can see myself staying in this line of work for quite a while. I'd like to gain more experience before taking my next step. I'd also like to get some more qualifications.

I'd like to take a course in working with chocolate. The hotel where I worked part time when I was a student had their own chocolatier, and it was fascinating to watch him at work making chocolate sculptures. I'd love to be able to do that one day. Although I may stay away from chocolate fountains even after I'm qualified.

A clock nearby chimes, and I realise it's later than I thought. I can't sit here daydreaming about my future plans. I'm meeting someone who is very much a part of my present plans, and I don't want to miss his arrival. He hasn't been to Paris before, and by his own admission he only speaks a few words of French.

I practically skip back towards the Métro station. I have to see Dad tonight, but that's a necessary evil and shouldn't take too long. I refuse to allow the thought of it to intrude before it has to. I'm in Paris, the city of love and/or pandas. The sun is shining, and there's a zing in the air. I'm off to meet the man I've been dating for several happy weeks, and we're about to take a tour of one of my favourite places in the whole world. Life doesn't get much better than this.

Chapter Twenty-Two

To my surprise, Ben is already waiting outside the station when I arrive. His face lights up when he sees me, and he pulls me in for a hug.

'I've missed you,' he murmurs into my ear before kissing me.

'You saw me the day before yesterday,' I remind him.

He kisses me again. 'Exactly. Let's never make it this long in the future.'

'That's quite a commitment,' I say. 'What if one of us is invited to an audience at the palace without a plus one?'

'We'll tell the King to make it snappy.'

'Fair enough. How about if I need to go to the hospital?'

'I'll be there at your bedside,' he promises.

'What if it's an infectious disease and I'm not allowed visitors?'

'I'll bribe the matron.'

'Aren't they all called managers now?'

He sighs. 'Fine, then I'll find the nearest NHS manager and bribe them.'

I consider this. 'What if there's a zombie apocalypse in Honeywell and Isabella makes me drive away with all our cakes to prevent them being stolen by the zombies?'

He holds me away from him. 'You're ruining the moment.'

I tiptoe up to kiss him. 'I'm sorry. I promise I won't do it again. You're right. We're here now. Let's not spoil our day discussing hospitals and royal invitations.'

'You're the one who started talking about your imminent trip to Buckingham Palace, followed by an admission to a plague hospital,' he says. 'I don't understand how your mind can run on such things on a glorious day like this.'

I take his arm. 'We'll argue about it later. Meanwhile, have you come prepared for your mystery day out?'

He points to his backpack. 'Your refusal to tell me what we're doing today has created quite the packing challenge. I've brought sunscreen, a water bottle, several chocolate bars, insect repellent, and a full change of clothes just in case.'

'You won't need any of that. Except perhaps the water and the sun cream. It's a hot day, and we'll be outside.'

'I'm glad to hear it,' he says. 'I imagined a whirlwind tour of Paris would include lots of stuffy museums and galleries, and me learning more about the history of the city than I currently feel up to.'

'No museums,' I promise. 'And no pictures. You can see them on the internet any time you like. What you can't see is what the city feels and smells like and how the light changes throughout the day.'

'What does the city smell like?' he asks. 'Cheese? I mean *fromage*. Have you booked us on a cheese-tasting expedition? Is it too late to swap it for a wine-tasting tour?'

'We can do that some other time,' I promise. 'I'd love to go to the south of France one day for a wine-tasting course. It would expand my culinary education.'

'That could be an excellent excuse for doing quite a few things,' he says.

'Who says you can't mix business with pleasure? You could do the same thing, particularly now you're a food writer. It's essential for you to have a wide understanding of every part of the food and drink creation process. You can expand that to cover anything you'd like to do – visiting a chocolate factory, spending the night in a distillery, or whatever.'

'I knew there was a reason I pursued this career,' he says. 'Ok, lead on to whatever mysterious activity you've arranged for me.'

'It isn't that mysterious,' I say, starting to walk with him towards the meeting place.

I feel a sudden stab of apprehension. Why didn't I think to ask him about this before making the booking?

'I assume you can ride a bike?' I ask.

'I'm afraid not. I was frightened by a bike salesman as a child. Apparently, I didn't talk for three months afterwards. I vowed then never to go near one of those monstrosities as long as I lived.'

I blow out my cheeks in frustration. 'I can't believe it! I assumed you'd be fine with cycling.'

'Not only am I not fine with it,' he says, dropping my hand, 'but my childhood experience left me with such a velocipedal phobia that I can't be anywhere in the vicinity of a metal monster without breaking out in hives. If I get too close to one, my throat swells up and I need urgent medical attention. So, if you notice any of those horrible things while we're here, please warn me immediately.'

I glance at him and see his lips are twitching.

'I might have known it,' I say. 'You're having me on. So, you can ride a bike?'

He puffs out his chest. 'Ride one? I won the all-England under-twelve cycling obstacle course when I was a boy. I appeared on Newsnight and was invited to give an interview to our local newspaper. I believe it was that which inspired my ambition to enter the noble profession of journalism.'

'All I need is a simple yes or no.'

He grins down at me. 'I'm sorry. Yes, I can ride a bike, although I'm not sure why it's so desperately important to you. Why have you developed this sudden obsession with my grasp of basic life skills?'

I point to where a young man is standing outside a hotel, talking to a small group of people wearing shorts and T shirts. 'Because we're taking a tour of the city on bikes.'

Ben studies the group. 'Are you sure? Those people look more like beachcombers to me.'

'Perfectly sure. We leave in fifteen minutes.'

'Couldn't we take a boat tour instead?' he suggests. 'Far less strenuous.'

'It's too late for that. I've already paid. You'll cycle around the city with me and like it.'

'Fine,' he says. 'But if I pass out with heat stroke or get my trousers tangled in the wheel, I hope you'll stop and rescue me.'

'Not a hope,' I say callously. 'I don't want to miss any of the sights.'

He sighs. 'I knew you were single-minded, but I didn't realise quite how much. If something happens to me, will you promise to inform my employers I won't be in to work again? My password is *Narnia* if they need to retrieve my files.'

'I'll do that. In turn, please apologise to Isabella for me missing Danish pastry day.'

We arrive at the meeting place and are greeted by the young man.

'This tour, it will be in both English and French,' he informs us in charmingly accented English. 'My name is Michel. Please ask me as many questions as you wish.'

'If I have enough breath left,' murmurs Ben. 'It's been a while since I rode one of these.'

We both choose a bike and adjust our helmets. The last few stragglers arrive, and we set off for Le Marais. I haven't ridden a bike for years, but after a couple of minutes I find my balance. I speed up, and Ben follows, wobbling slightly as we round a curve in the road.

'I thought you were the under-twelve champion,' I say.

He gives me a pained look. 'That competition took place in a local car park, not on the mean streets of Paris. Also, I know you're mathematically challenged because I've seen you attempt to give out change in the bakery, but it doesn't take a mathematician to work out that was sixteen years ago. A lot can happen in sixteen years. Or even six weeks, which is how long I've known you.'

'Have you been counting?'

He nods. 'Six weeks, six days, and fifteen hours – or sixteen if you allow for the time difference between the UK and France. But who's counting?'

'Obviously not you. Any regrets?'

He stretches out a hand to take mine, gives a perilous wobble, and grabs his handlebar again. 'This is neither the time nor the place for emotional conversations.'

'The more I see you in action, the less I believe in your childhood achievement,' I say. 'It's the kind of thing people put on their resumes, knowing it's unlikely anyone will take the time to check it out. I'll do a search this evening.'

'There's no point,' he says. 'The internet hadn't been invented back then. Or not to any great extent. People didn't think to upload things like my bicycling triumph. You'll have to take it on trust.'

'I don't enjoy taking things on trust,' I warn him. 'I prefer to check them out for myself. Your spectacular win should be in the Internet Archive somewhere.'

'Unless my parents requested my anonymity was preserved,' he says. 'Which, now I think of it, I'm sure they did. Let's not waste any more time thinking about that. We appear to have arrived at Le Marais, and I for one am most interested in what our guide has to tell us about it.'

Chapter Twenty-Three

Michel starts to talk, and I listen with half an ear as he explains about this area of the city during the medieval period. I've been here several times, and I've read up on it. I'm more interested in watching Ben and his reaction to everything he's told.

When you know something well, like a wonderful film or a favourite book, you often feel a pang of envy when you see someone enjoying it for the first time, knowing you can never do that again. It's the same with places you've grown to love. You can revisit them, and each time you find something new and exciting to appreciate. But you can never again see them for the very first time. Something has been lost forever, no matter what else has been gained.

I've been looking forward all week to watching Ben enjoying Paris. I've been hoping to re-live my own experience again through his eyes, even if it's only a second-hand experience. I'm not disappointed. I watch his eyes roam around the buildings, taking in their intricate designs and appreciating their history. It's a privilege to experience this with him.

He turns his head and catches my eye. His smile makes my heart turn over. I've never felt this connection with anyone else. A little voice tells me I never will again. But little voices can tell you all sorts of things, not all of them true. I don't listen to anything else it may have to say but concentrate on immersing myself in the moment. I want to fix this all in my head so I can look back on it whenever I want – the feel of the warm sun on my cheeks, the languages being spoken around me, and the look on Ben's face as he listens to Michel and allows his eyes to wander around the scene, absorbing one of life's firsts.

I mustn't get too emotional about this. Ben and I have hundreds of firsts ahead of us – maybe separately, maybe together. Only time will tell. One particular experience doesn't define our lives. But some experiences stay with us for longer and make a deeper impression. I suspect this will be one of them.

The guide finishes talking and takes a few questions before we all clamber back onto our bikes and set off towards the Place des Vosges, where we stop again to listen to more of the area's history. Ben doesn't appear to be concentrating as intensely as during our first stop. Maybe he's saddle-sore. I hope not because we have a fair way to go.

We move on to the Hôtel de Sens and hear all about the Archbishops being deposed. Our guide invites us to admire the gothic architecture.

'I assume this is something like your flat in Christchurch?' I whisper to Ben.

'You've been to my flat,' he murmurs back.

I feign surprise. 'The place where you cooked me dinner last week? I assumed that was some tiny hovel you were renting while you waited for your servants to finalise repairs on your real accommodation.'

'I'm afraid not.' He gives me a look of anxious enquiry. 'Does that change the way you feel about me?'

'It's too early to tell. Let's discuss it when we get home. It would be a pity to spoil this lovely day by breaking up.'

He slips an arm around me. 'My sentiments entirely. How about you? I know you're staying in Eleanor's house while you're working at the bakery, but I assume you have something far grander in London to which you can return?'

I walked into that one. I could tell him that I grew up in a seven-bedroom house on Hampstead Heath, but I'd prefer not to. It would involve a level of detail and explanation I'm not currently prepared for. I console myself with the reflection that it isn't my house. It's Dad's. He could choose to sell it or gamble it away in a game of poker at any time, and there's nothing I could do about it. If he ever visits Honeywell, he's quite likely to lose it to the members of the poker club. Those women play for keeps.

Ben looks at me in surprise. 'One minute you were here with me, and the next you'd disappeared somewhere else entirely. Where did you go?'

'I was wondering how long it was until lunch,' I say at random.

His puzzled expression clears. 'Now, that I can believe. Someone in your line of work must be constantly thinking of pastries, cakes, and pies.'

'You have me confused with Isabella,' I say. 'I'm not hungry yet, but I will be when this is over. I'd like to take you to one of my favourite places for lunch if you don't have other plans. It's a bistro on the edge of the Luxembourg gardens, which is the last place we'll visit on this tour. Suzanna and I used to go there whenever we could afford it. I'd like to see it again.'

'I'm entirely in your hands,' he says, picking up his bike and climbing back onto it with a slight wince. 'Or I will be in a couple of hours. In the meantime, we're in Michel's hands, and he seems to want us to follow him to whatever's next on the itinerary.'

'The Conciergerie,' I say, getting onto my own bike. 'The place where Louis the Sixteenth and Marie Antoinette were sentenced to death.'

'You're full of cheerful facts, aren't you?' he says as we set off behind our fellow cyclists.

I swerve to avoid a taxi. 'History isn't all roses and pretty dresses.'

'I've never been much interested in history,' he says. 'I prefer to think about the future. That's the only thing within our control.'

'And not always that. All we can do is play the hand we're dealt and hope it's a winning one.'

'Are we talking about your bakery's poker club?' he asks. 'It sounds a lot of fun. Would they allow me to join in sometime?'

'I have no idea. I should warn you they take it extremely seriously. If you get involved with them and lose, you have to be prepared to pay for your body weight in cake and stump up for several gallons of tea. I advise staying away from them. They're a formidable group.'

'I'm not scared,' he says. 'I'm about to visit the place where the King and Marie Antoinette met their fate. Your poker club holds no terrors for me.'

I throw up a hand before remembering where I am and clutching my handlebars again. 'You've been warned. There's nothing else I can do.'

The Conciergerie is as beautiful as most places in Paris, but I feel the usual shiver run down my spine as I consider how the royal couple must have felt on that fateful day. They may not have been the most sympathetic characters, but no one deserves that.

Michel recounts the apocryphal story of Marie Antoinette telling the starving populace to eat cake, and my mind drifts back to Isabella. She often gives very similar advice, although, to be fair to her, in a rather different context.

I hardly hear anything else of what Michel says and only realise the group is moving on when Ben touches my arm. 'We've lost you again. Where were you this time?'

'At the Sugarloaf,' I say truthfully. 'I was thinking about Isabella.'

His face flashes in instant comprehension. 'You mean the *Let them eat cake* thing?'

I nod, and he laughs. 'I should have known. It's an obvious connection. But you'll have to think about it another time. If we don't hurry up, everyone will be out of sight, and we'll be left to cycle around the city, lost and alone and no nearer to getting our lunch than the French population were during the eighteenth century.'

I reluctantly pick up my bike and follow him in the direction he indicates.

'Next stop is the Pont Neuf,' Michel calls back over his shoulder, and I speed up. Of all the many beautiful bridges in Paris, this is my favourite. Not just because it's the oldest, but because it's iconic yet unassuming. It's world famous and appears in so much art and in hundreds of movies. Yet it sits peacefully in the sunshine, ignoring all the fuss, watching the river flow gently past underneath its grey stone arches.

We lean against the balustrade, admiring the spectacular views of the Seine. A *bateau mouche* approaches, and I lean forward to take a look. I love watching people who aren't watching me. It's fun to speculate on who they are and what combination of events has combined to bring them to this particular place at this particular moment.

I wonder whether any of them are doing the same thing to us – gazing up at the group of people leaning over the parapet to admire the view. What would they make of me and Ben, standing close together admiring the city skyline with the sun on our faces and our hair tangled and blowing in the breeze off the water? Would they see at a glance that we're together? Not just together on a bike tour but together in the sense of people who've been looking for each other for a long time and have finally found each other?

They're probably just thinking about the buildings they're passing and the lunch they plan to enjoy afterwards. Ben and I are nothing more than a part of the landscape to them, unobserved and unimportant. I can live with that. We all have our own lives to live, and right now mine feels as close to perfection as anyone could get.

Chapter Twenty-Four

I would happily stay here forever, but Michel has other ideas.

'Next we will ride to St Germaine,' he tells us. 'Which is not only a football club.'

Several people laugh, including Ben.

'Do you follow football?' I ask him.

It strikes me that I simultaneously know very little and quite a lot about him. It's always like that when you meet someone with whom you have a connection. It's never a linear thing. You open up about various areas in your life in random ways. It's like a river that flows at different speeds and contains varying depths. You set off along it together and spend random periods of time in the back waters, discussing the most surprising things. At other times, you're whirled along by the current with barely time to appreciate any of the scenes you pass.

It doesn't really matter. You're both heading towards the same destination, and the route you take to get there will never be the same as the route anyone else takes. I've heard a fair amount about Ben's family and the difficulties his parents encountered during their early lives and how grateful he is to them for all their encouragement and sacrifice on his behalf. But I haven't heard much about what he does in his spare time or whether he supports a particular football team or has a favourite song.

'I watch the odd game when the team's schedules coincide with mine,' he says. 'My Dad has always supported Liverpool because that's where his family came from originally. So, if they're playing, I root for them. But it's not really a passion. How about you?'

I don't tell him that Dad has season tickets for Arsenal. I'm not sure why not. They're nothing to do with me, except that Dad used to take me when I was living at home. It's probably the fact they're an annual gift from one of our advertisers. It's easier not to mention them in case Ben asks further questions.

I'm not terribly keen on football, but I've always enjoyed going along with Dad. It feels like a tiny connection with him, and I feel a pang to think it may be lost forever. I wouldn't mind sitting through even the longest match in the pouring rain if it meant he was still keen to spend time with me. But, much like the French revolution, that's firmly in the past now. There's no point in thinking about it and making myself unhappy on such a lovely day.

Ben touches my arm. 'You've left me again.'

I try to focus on what we were talking about. 'I'm sorry. What were you saying?'

'I asked whether you enjoy watching football. It didn't seem a question that merited this level of consideration. But perhaps it's a major part of your life, in which case, I apologise.'

'I used to quite like it,' I say. 'Not so much nowadays.'

He tucks my arm into his. 'I'm glad we've cleared that up. If you're ready, shall we climb aboard for the final leg of the tour? I fear neither of us will be awarded the yellow jersey this time. That belongs to Eric.'

He nods to the elderly man wearing a Hawaiian shirt, who's pedalling next to Michel and chatting away about something that appears to interest them both.

'I hope Michel doesn't write a report on us when we get back,' I say. 'I used to get the most dreadful PE reports when I was at school. My favourite comment was *Meghan rarely stirs.*'

Ben gives a shout of laughter. 'I wish I'd seen you. So, it isn't just football you aren't keen on?'

'No, I was a great disappointment to all my games teachers. They spent the best part of seven years trying to convince me of the joys of hockey. It must have been a thankless task.'

'Whereas I was the star fly half on our school rugby team,' he says proudly. 'I broke my collarbone twice.'

My eyes fly to his shoulders, which show no sign of permanent damage. Still, it's another brick for me to put into the structure that is Ben Davies.

'I'd have guessed you were a rugby player even if you hadn't told me the first time we met,' I say. 'You tackled me so professionally. Your teachers would have been proud.'

He tries and fails to look modest. 'I like to think so, but we'll have to postpone discussing my athletic prowess until another time. The rest of our group has almost disappeared over the horizon.'

I sigh. 'Would it be worth the fine just to dump our bikes here and send Michel a text to say we've given up and gone home?'

Ben picks up my bike. 'If there's one thing I'm not, it's a quitter. And I don't believe at heart you are either. Besides, you're the one who booked this tour. The least you can do is finish it. Then we'll go and have this lunch you promised me. My only condition is that you don't order me snails or frogs' legs.'

'Calf brains, it is,' I promise and cycle off at top speed before he has time to expostulate.

We catch up with the rest of the group before anyone notices we're missing and sends out a search party to find us. We take a quick tour of St Germaine, then pedal off toward the Luxembourg Gardens. I'm glad we've saved this for last. I love these gardens. Suzanna and I used to come here on Sunday afternoons and wander around looking at the flowers and watch the children sailing their model boats on fine days. Even in wet weather, the gardens are worth a visit, and today they should be at their absolute best.

We lock our bikes and follow Michel up and down the walkways while he tells us about the history of the gardens.

Ben's attention appears to wander. I nudge him. 'You can't fall asleep here. We have to take our bikes back to the hotel when the tour's over.'

'I'm not falling asleep,' he says. 'I've heard every word he's said. Flowers, an assassination, something about Olympic history.'

'That's a little vague. What exactly did he say about the assassination?'

He frowns. 'No one told me there would be a written test before I was allowed to leave.'

'Not written,' I reassure him. 'Simply a quick verbal recap of every single thing our guide has told us. If you fail, it's a quick trip to the Bastille.'

'They're a bloodthirsty lot over here,' he grumbles. 'Someone should have warned me. Fine, you can tell me who was assassinated if you've been listening so carefully.'

'I'm not here to do your homework for you. Look it up for yourself. Better still, ask Michel.'

'I knew it!' he says triumphantly. 'You have no idea either.'

'It was something to do with one of their kings,' I say with fake confidence.

'That doesn't narrow it down. From everything we've heard today, that could apply to almost any of them.'

'I was looking at the flowers,' I defend myself. 'No one can be expected to concentrate when there are so many beautiful roses around.'

I point to a climbing rose, and he takes a step towards it. 'You should have said so! I'll get you one.'

'Don't you dare! I don't want you to be arrested before I've had the chance to eat my lunch. I won't come and bail you out.'

He appears undecided. 'I'm sure they'd give me something to eat while we waited for you to appear.'

'Mouldy bread and water. I don't recommend it while I'm sitting at Chalet de Roses eating their signature duck confit.'

'I thought you were ordering brains,' he says.

'Only for you. It's a delicacy every first time visitor to Paris has to try. But those of us who know the place better can order whatever we like.'

Michel glances over at us. 'Did you hear all that I said?'

Ben gives him a guilty smile. 'I'm afraid I was distracted for a few moments by my companion here. She insisted on talking about the flowers.'

'You're the one who was distracted!' I say. 'That's how this conversation started.'

'I was looking at the ponies,' says Ben. 'There's a place over there where you can have a pony ride.'

Michel smiles. 'It is for the children only. Someone as large as you can only watch.'

I poke Ben in the ribs. 'Quite right too. Have you no regard for the ponies' welfare?'

'There's no harm in asking,' he says. 'They may let me ride one if I keep my feet on the ground and help the pony along.'

'I do not think so,' says Michel. 'In any case, we are to leave now. We must return to the hotel in time for the next tour. Please join the group again.'

We follow the tour group to the main gates and unlock our bikes.

'You wouldn't like to push our bikes back to the hotel for us?' Ben asks Michel. 'There's a couple of Euros in it for you if you do.'

Michel shakes his head. 'I do not think so. It is better for the ponies if I do not leave you here unaccompanied. And possibly for the rest of the visitors too.'

'What a cheek,' says Ben when Michel is out of earshot. 'Anyone would think we hadn't behaved well on this tour. Whereas we've been model cyclists and upheld the prestige of our country at all times. I even said *Bonjour* when I met him. What more does he want?'

'Actually, you said *Bonsoir.* It's a little different, but I'm sure he appreciated you making the effort.'

We set off towards the hotel. As we turn a corner, a small dog comes running out of nowhere and hurtles towards us. I brake sharply. Ben, who's riding just behind, crashes into me, tipping both of us into the gutter. We land in a tangle of limbs, and Ben's bike falls on top of us. Mine lands on the sidewalk. We hear a screech of brakes as a car swerves to miss us, and the driver shouts something out of the window as he passes.

'What did he say?' gasps Ben.

'I'm not sure. I was too shaken to notice.'

'I expect it was something nice,' he says. 'He was probably saying what heroes we were to avoid the dog. Speaking of which …'

He looks around in time to see a man running towards us. He's holding a lead in one hand and gesticulating wildly with the other.

He breaks into a flood of French as he reaches us. Ben stares at him blankly.

'He's thanking us for not hitting his dog,' I say, pushing Ben's bike to one side and climbing stiffly to my feet.

'Are you sure?' Ben asks dubiously. 'He sounds angry.'

'That's how the French sound when they're excited,' I tell him.

The man takes my arm and enquires whether I'm hurt. I assure him I'm not, and he turns to help Ben.

'*Vous êtes blessé?*' he asks anxiously.

'He wants to know whether you're hurt,' I tell Ben.

'Just a couple of scratches. Is the dog ok?'

The dog in question runs over to us and gives Ben an apologetic lick. The man snatches its collar and clips the lead back on.

'I am most sorry,' he says in English. 'He pulled … pull … I cannot hold him.'

He points to the clip on the dog's lead. 'I must make it …'

'Fix it,' supplies Ben, and the man nods.

'It's fine,' I say. 'As long as no one's hurt.'

Michel has realised something is wrong and is cycling back towards us. He must be regretting taking our booking. No one else has caused any trouble today.

He looks from us to the man and breaks into rapid French. The man gestures to us, then to the dog, and Michel nods in comprehension.

'I'm afraid my bike wheel is a little the worse for wear,' says Ben apologetically. 'I'll pay for the damage.'

Michel runs his eyes over the bike. 'I can straighten that out. This man tells me it was not your fault. You were protecting his dog.'

'Trying to, at any rate,' I tell him. 'We all had a lucky escape.'

Ben grins. 'I'll bet you're wishing you'd let me stay at the gardens and have a pony ride now.'

Michel shakes his head. 'Me, I am like Édith Piaf. I regret nothing.'

Ben raises an eyebrow. 'If we're referencing the entertainment business, I'd like to channel Frank Sinatra and say I did it my way.'

'I must return to the group,' says Michel. 'Can you follow when you are ready?'

Ben helps me onto my bike. To my surprise, and no little embarrassment, the dog's owner grasps me by the shoulders and plants a kiss on each of my cheeks.

'*Merci beaucoup*. Louis, he says thank you also.'

I wave at the little terrier, who's wagging his tail and laughing up at us. 'He's very welcome. I know a dog just like him, and I'd hate to think of anything happening to him.'

The man grasps Ben's shoulders and kisses him too. To Ben's credit, he doesn't pull away or look embarrassed.

He nods to the man. '*Au revoir, mon amour.*'

The man looks startled but nods and smiles. Ben and I cycle off in the direction Michel went.

'Are you aware you called him your love?' I ask as we turn onto the Rue d'École.

Ben gives a snort of laughter. 'Is that right? I blame my school. Why couldn't they have taught us a few useful things for everyday situations? All we got was *My gardener has been taken ill* or *Unfortunately, the milliner's shop is closed every second Wednesday.* It would have been far more helpful if they'd taught us how to say, *I am delighted to have saved your canine friend from an untimely fate.* Still, I'm sure that man knew what I meant.'

'Maybe leave speaking French to me in future,' I advise him. 'I'm getting hungrier by the minute, and I don't fancy the idea of you getting carried away and ordering us both raw pigs' trotters when we finally reach the restaurant.'

Chapter Twenty-Five

We arrive back at the hotel where we started without further mishap. We say goodbye to Michel and the rest of our tour group, making sure to leave a generous tip, then take a taxi to the restaurant. My legs and back are aching, and I'm starving.

It feels as though we've cycled a hundred miles this morning. It's probably closer to six miles, which doesn't sound quite as impressive. I remember they measure distances in kilometres on the continent, which makes the overall number sound higher. I'm not sure of the exact conversion rate from miles to kilometres, but I expect it makes our trip today much closer to one hundred. Ben may have been right when he commented on my lack of maths skills.

'Have you eaten at this place often?' Ben asks as we arrive at the bistro.

'Loads of times. I spent a year in Paris between school and university.'

'That's where you learned to cook?'

'Yes. I didn't intend to, but I saw the course advertised when I arrived, and it looked interesting.'

'What did you plan to do when you came over here?' he asks.

'I didn't have a plan for the year. I wasn't sure how long I would stay. My friend Suzanna was living out here, and I thought it would be fun to spend some time with her. We decided to rent a flat together. She couldn't afford anywhere by herself, but with the two of us it was different. We rented a place in the sixth arrondissement. It wasn't luxurious, but we were hardly ever there. I stayed there last night and was surprised by how small it was. I didn't notice it at the time.'

'But how did you afford it if you weren't working during your year off?' he asks.

I don't answer. Dad was happy to pay, but I don't want to mention him.

'Sorry,' he says. 'That's none of my business.'

'I had some savings,' I say at last. 'My mum left me some money. And my father helped me too.'

'I wish I'd taken a year off to travel,' he says. 'But it was tough enough facing all that student debt without adding to it.'

Now is definitely not the time to mention that Dad not only paid my course fees but provided me with accommodation while I was at university. I'm very grateful for his help, but I might not have taken it if I'd realised it came with a set of implied obligations.

'Here we are!' I say, opening the door to the restaurant. 'You're going to love this place.'

Lunch at Chalet de Roses is as good as I remember. I was worried it might have changed hands or gone downhill since I lived here, but it hasn't. The maître d' greets us and shows us to my favourite table. It's next to the window with a view of the gardens. He doesn't appear to recognise me, but that's hardly a surprise. I haven't been here for years, and it's a popular place.

'Would you like me to translate the menu?' I ask when our server has left.

'I think I'll manage,' says Ben, scanning it with a frown. 'My rule of thumb is never to order anything you don't recognise or that Google Translate has difficulties with.'

'That isn't very adventurous of you. As a food writer, I would have thought you'd take every opportunity to dive into something new and different.'

'Which shows what you know about the subject,' he counters. 'Rule number one of culinary journalism is that you live to tell the tale. Or write the tale. They taught us that on the first day of our course.'

'But you didn't know you were going to become a food writer,' I say. 'You told me you expected to go into travel writing or political reporting.'

He grins. 'That was before I realised the number of free meals I could get by going into this line of business. Once I realised that, I forgot all about other kinds of journalism.'

The meal is everything I've dreamed of, from the duck confit and fricassée de poulet to the tarte tatin. We linger over it for a long time.

'What would you like to do next?' asks Ben when we've finished.

'Lie down and sleep for several hours.'

'You'll have to save that for another time. We can't waste our brief stay in this beautiful city having a siesta.'

'That's Spanish,' I say. 'You mean a *sieste*.'

'I'll take your word for it. You still aren't having one. You can sleep tonight.'

I yawn. 'I can curl up in the corner while you go sightseeing by yourself. You don't need a chaperone.'

'Yes, I do. I hardly speak any French. The residents will take advantage of my ignorance to sell me onions and berets and striped sweaters at a hugely inflated cost.'

'Only if you let them. Just say *non!*

He pulls me to my feet. 'Come on. We have lots to do before you meet your friend tonight. Don't you want to work up an appetite for your dinner?'

I follow him to the door, still grumbling. 'Not really. French people don't eat much for dinner – barely more than a glass of water and a crust of bread. They're famed for it.'

'My readers will be horrified to hear that. I'm under strict instructions from my editor to keep a record of all my meals this weekend and include them in an upcoming article.'

'It will be a short article,' I say. 'I promise you no one here eats more than a few crumbs in the evening.'

'Is that what you'll be having?'

I'm not sure how to answer this. I'm supposed to be meeting Dad at his favourite restaurant near to the Louvre. He and I have eaten there a thousand times together. Apparently, they do the best langoustines in France. Dad loves them. I usually have the Quiche Lorraine. Although, after ploughing through five courses at lunch with Ben, I may stick to a garden salad.

'I don't know what we'll be having,' I say at last.

He nods. 'Whatever it is, you'd be doing me a great favour if you took notes. And maybe photos too if your dinner companion doesn't mind. You could stand on the table to get the best angles. You won't mind doing that for me in the interests of great food journalism?'

'Not a hope,' I say. 'But feel free to do that next time you come into the bakery. I'm sure Isabella and Lily will be delighted.'

We set off towards the park gates, walking slowly because we're too full to run anywhere.

'I'd like to walk down and see the roses again,' I say. 'And, of course, the lake. Although I'm not taking you anywhere near the ponies, so don't bother suggesting it.'

'You know this city well,' he says.

'Only the tourist parts of it. I lived here for a year, but I was at the cookery school for most of that time. Some days, I barely even saw daylight.'

'What about the nightlife?'

'I was too tired. Or I had assignments to write up for the following day. Spending a year in Paris isn't as glamorous as it sounds.'

'It sounds pretty cool to me,' he says. 'Do you still come here for your holidays?'

'I've spent the occasional weekend here. It's lovely to catch up with Suzanna, and it's such a simple trip on the Eurostar.'

'I'll book that the next time I visit,' he says. 'It will be fun to watch all the fish as the train speeds by.'

I look at his face to see whether he's joking. His expression doesn't flicker, but I'm learning to read his tells.

'It was particularly magical this time,' I say. 'A shark swam past almost close enough for me to touch it. I almost opened the train window to get a better look, but you never know when those glass walls will spring a leak.'

He raises an eyebrow. 'Maybe I'll stick to flying.'

'Coward!' I taunt him.

He lifts a hand in defence. 'Not at all. But I'm not a strong swimmer.'

I link my arm through his. 'Have we run out of jokes about the Channel Tunnel?'

He draws me closer. 'I imagine the operators have heard them all before.'

'If you've got them out of your system, shall we try the gardens again?'

'It's the only reason I got out of bed this morning,' he assures me. 'That and the prospect of a long bike ride. How long do we have?'

'All afternoon. I'm not meeting my … dinner companion until seven thirty.'

'Where are you meeting?'

'Why do you want to know?' I ask. 'Are you planning to stalk me there?'

'That wasn't on the agenda. I haven't yet decided what I'm doing this evening. I was planning on visiting the Moulin Rouge, but a travel writer friend informed me it was both overpriced and underwhelming.'

'They were right,' I say. 'At least, that's what Suzanna and I thought when we visited it.'

'If you don't tell me where you're having dinner, you only have yourself to blame if I turn up there,' he says.

'I think I'm safe. We're eating somewhere my … the person I'm meeting always likes to go when they're in Paris. It's way off the beaten track and most tourists don't know anything about it. Very few locals do either. It's pretty exclusive.'

'So, you aren't eating at Pizza Hut?' he says.

'If that's what you consider fine French dining, I'd stick to writing about British food,' I advise him. 'You're good at that.'

He slips an arm around my shoulders. 'I'm not sure whether to be flattered you've said that or insulted you think I'm so provincial.'

'A bit of both,' I say, laughing back at him.

He drops a kiss on the top of my head. 'I can always rely on you to keep me humble.'

The laughter dies on my lips, and I freeze. The man walking towards us along the lake looks horribly familiar. If it weren't for the fact I know he isn't arriving in Paris until late afternoon, I might almost think –

The man catches sight of us, and his face jolts in shock. Either he's offended by my old jeans and non-Parisian top, or he recognises me.

I dart a look around, searching for a crowd to melt into or a small alleyway I can dive down. But it's no good. The park is distressingly free of both.

'Are you ok?' Ben asks me. 'You look as though you've seen a ghost.'

My brain unfreezes long enough to realise where I am and what's going on.

'You're my French boyfriend!' I hiss, and he grins.

'You drank too much wine at lunch. But one out of two isn't bad.'

'You don't understand!' I hiss more urgently.

'I'm glad we're finally putting a label on it,' he says.

'I don't mean that,' I mutter, trying not to move my mouth in case the man approaching us has unexpected lip-reading abilities.

Ben looks confused. 'You mean I'm not your boyfriend? What would you prefer me to call myself – your side-piece, your fancy man, your paramour? Whatever you choose is fine with me.'

The man has almost reached us. I subdue an urge to break free of Ben's arm and turn and run as fast as I can, leaving him to answer any inconvenient questions. That would be the cowardly thing to do. More importantly, there's no time. My few seconds' delay has cost me dearly.

'Call yourself what you like,' I say in an urgent undertone. 'But you're French, all right? We met when I moved over here, and we've been seeing each other ever since.'

There's no time to check whether he's understood my directions. The man stops next to us, looking at me with a quizzical expression.

'I didn't expect to meet you here,' he says. 'What a lovely surprise.'

His eyes flick towards Ben, then back to me, and one eyebrow lifts.

I take a deep breath and give him the most unconcerned smile I can muster. 'Hi, Dad! What an amazing coincidence.'

I grab Ben's hand and turn to face my father. 'I'd like to introduce you to my boyfriend, Jean-Luc Gaultier.'

Chapter Twenty-Six

Ben's hand twitches in mine, and I give it a reassuring squeeze.

Dad's other eyebrow shoots up as he studies Ben. 'Pleased to meet you, Jean-Luc.'

I hold my breath, waiting for Ben to answer, wondering whether he understood what I was telling him. I needn't have worried. He rises to the occasion superbly.

He holds out his hand to Dad. '*Bonjour.* I am vaiiry plizzed to meet you.'

Dad takes his hand equally solemnly. '*Bonjour,* Jean-Luc. Would you prefer us to speak in French? I'm a little rusty, but I could probably manage.'

I feel Ben's shoulders shake slightly, but I ignore it.

'Jean-Luc and I prefer to speak in English,' I say. 'He's keen to practise, and I love his accent.'

'I see,' says Dad. 'Shall we find somewhere more convenient to talk? We appear to be holding up the passers-by.'

It occurs to me I haven't properly greeted him. I should have hugged him when we first met, but I was too busy thinking about how to deal with the situation.

I let go of Ben's hand, take an awkward step towards Dad, and give him a brief hug. 'It's nice to see you.'

'And you,' he says in a formal tone.

I give a mental sigh. Will things ever return to how they were before we fell out over my choice of career? It doesn't look like it.

Ben touches my sleeve. 'Should I greet your *papa* as ze French do?'

I freeze him with a look. 'There's no need. English people don't kiss each other when they first meet.'

He spreads his hands and gives a Gallic shrug. 'I am laairning zo much!'

Dad settles himself on a nearby bench, and we sit too. I take care to put Ben on the far side of me in case he's overcome by a wish to show exactly how French he is by making a lunge at Dad and embracing him.

'You didn't tell me you had a boyfriend,' says Dad.

'I was planning to mention it when I saw you tonight,' I say untruthfully.

'How long have you two been together?' he asks.

'A few weeks,' I say at the same time as Ben says, 'Mainy, mainy month.'

I quell him with a glance. 'I haven't been in Paris for many months.'

He gives me a soulful look. '*Mais, cherie,* it feels az though I 'ave known you for much longer. Love, eet eez like that.'

'How romantic,' says Dad mildly.

'Isn't it?' I say, turning my back on Ben so he'll have to lean right around me to address Dad. If I'd had more time to think about it, I would have instructed him to be a mime artist. If it comes to that, why did I decide to make him French at all? It's all rather hazy, but I believe I had some idea that having a French boyfriend would reinforce my story that I'm a current resident of Paris.

Ben shifts slightly, and I lean forward to block him from view.

'I thought your flight wasn't arriving for a few hours,' I say to Dad.

'I took an earlier one. It occurred to me that I wasn't leaving myself time for all the things I needed to get done before meeting you. So, Cheryl called the airline and got me a seat on the eleven o'clock flight. I had lunch at my hotel before deciding to take a stroll in the park. I had no idea I would be lucky enough to bump into you.'

I force a smile. 'What a lovely coincidence.'

Dad gives me a considering look before peering around me at Ben. 'Are you comfortable there, Jean-Luc? You look as though you're falling off the end.'

'He's fine,' I say, nudging Ben to tell him not to talk. His French accent wouldn't be out of place in a Pink Panther movie. And, whatever else he may be, Dad isn't stupid.

'I am … 'ow you say … *très amusant*,' says Ben, leaning forward and giving Dad a pleasant smile.

'*Amusant?*' enquires Dad, surprised.

'It's slang,' I improvise. 'You know how words change. Young people in Paris now use *amuser* in a completely different sense. It means to be fine or comfortable. Just like young people in the UK talk about things being sick or lit or …'

I trail off, trying to think of further examples. I seem to be sadly out of touch with current youth culture. Maybe it hasn't yet reached Honeywell.

'Or gnarly!' I add with a triumphant smile, remembering one of the village school children describing our chocolate brownies as gnarly. I'm not sure why.

'Gnarly?' says Dad.

'It means extreme. Just like *amusant* means fine. Language changes. You know that.'

'Of course,' he says. 'Well, now we've sorted that out, why don't you tell me more about how the two of you met and what Jean-Luc does?'

I feel Ben lean forward again. I shift my bodyweight so my shoulder is pressing into his chest, forcing him back against the seat. Hopefully, it will look as though I'm snuggling up to him. I hear him gasp as his head jerks back. To my relief, he doesn't say anything.

'There isn't much to tell,' I say. 'We met at a party.'

'Art gallery,' comes a voice behind me and I grit my teeth. Hasn't he got the message that his contributions to this conversation are both unnecessary and unwelcome?

Dad looks confused. 'Which one was it?'

I dig my elbow into Ben's ribs. 'It was both. It was a party at an art gallery.'

'And what were you doing there?' Dad asks Ben, who, for some inexplicable reason, has leaned forward again.

Ben waves his hands. 'I am … 'ow do you say, an *artiste*.'

'How interesting,' says Dad. 'What sort of art?'

'He doesn't like to talk about it,' I say. 'He always tells me his art is a very private thing, and I respect that.'

'I am a painter,' says Ben. 'I like to paint ze peectures.'

'But he doesn't like to talk about them,' I repeat. 'So, it's best not to ask.'

'*Au contraire*,' says Ben. 'It eez of all things my favourite subject.'

'Do you paint on canvas?' asks Dad.

'Canvas?' says Ben with an air of polite bewilderment.

'*Toile*,' I say shortly.

He waves his hands in apparent comprehension. '*Mais oui!* The canvases, I do not use them.'

'Then where do you paint?' asks Dad.

Ben gestures around the park. 'Wherever I am inspired to. On ze sidewalks, ze walls, ze underpass.'

'So, you're a graffiti artist?' says Dad.

'Of course not!' I say with a light laugh. 'Jean-Luc works on commission only.'

'Eet eez truc,' confirms Ben. 'I wait until ze council eenvites me to create my art. It is not often, but when they do …'

He circles his arms enthusiastically, almost knocking the hat off an elderly man walking past.

'One zousand pardons,' he says to the man, who glares at him.

'*Qu'est-ce que vous avez dit?*'

Ben looks wildly at me, and I stifle a laugh. '*Il est très désolé, monsieur.*'

The man frowns but moves away.

I give Dad a cheerful smile. 'Jean-Luc talks to me so much these days that he sometimes forgets which language he's supposed to be speaking.'

'So I observe,' he says. 'And what do you do, Jean-Luc, when you're not meeting my daughter at art galleries or waiting for the *conseil municipal* to call on you to beautify their infrastructure in the manner of a Parisian Banksy?'

'He spends most of his spare time with me,' I say.

'Is that so?'

It's difficult to tell what Dad is thinking at the best of times. Today, it's impossible. Maybe it's because I'm feeling tense. Maybe it's because he doesn't want me to know. Either way, I feel increasingly uncomfortable.

'I work in the publishing industry,' he tells Ben. 'I expect Meghan has told you that.'

Ben gives me a politely uncomprehending glance.

'Dad publishes magazines,' I say, hoping Ben won't ask for details.

'Our best known one is *Whisk*,' says Dad, and I feel Ben's leg jump.

'But none of us wants to discuss work at a time like this,' I say. 'It's such a lovely afternoon. Why don't we sit here without talking and enjoy the flowers and the beautiful lake?'

'I started that magazine from scratch,' Dad goes on as though he hasn't heard me. 'It was something I'd always dreamed of doing. Meghan's mother and I worked together to make it a reality.'

Ben doesn't speak. I don't dare look at him. Why did Dad have to mention the name of the magazine? I was hoping Ben would think Dad published magazines about cars or windmills or ancient thatched buildings. Anything but food. I wait for him to burst into speech, but he doesn't.

'Meghan is coming to work with us after she's had her holiday in Paris,' Dad goes on. 'I'm counting the days.'

'Wait a minute,' I say, but he carries on without appearing to notice.

'I'm sure you know she's interested in cookery, Jean-Luc. But did you also know she has a journalism degree?'

'I must have mentioned it at some point,' I chip in. 'But now isn't the time –'

'It's perfect for our magazine,' says Dad. 'Our food writer retired a few months ago. I hoped Meghan would start with us straight away, but she had other ideas. She wanted some time off after university, which was understandable. So, we gave the job to someone else while we were waiting for her to return.'

For one moment, I feel a flash of hope that Ben hasn't understood this. Dad speaks quickly, and he's made no effort to simplify his vocabulary. Too late, I realise the idea of Ben being French is a figment of my imagination. He'll have understood every word Dad said. How can he and I discuss this without letting Dad know I've been playing a stupid game with him for the past half hour?

I make an elaborate show of looking at my watch. 'Goodness, is that the time?'

I jump to my feet. 'I'm afraid we have to go. We have somewhere we need to be.'

Dad stands too. 'What a pity. But I'll be seeing you this evening. We can catch up then. Will Jean-Luc be joining us?'

'He's busy!' I say at once. 'He's going to … er … be somewhere else. But thanks for the offer.'

I hold out my hand to Ben. 'We ought to be going if we don't want to be late.'

He doesn't move. He stares up at Dad with a blank expression. 'You're David Blake Taylor?'

'That's right,' says Dad, resuming his seat.

I try to sit down again in an attempt to separate the pair of them, but it's no use. Ben has shifted along the bench towards Dad and is staring at him as though he can't believe his eyes. 'You're the guy who owns *Whisk*?'

'That's right,' says Dad again. He doesn't seem to have noticed Ben's sudden miraculous grasp of the English language.

Ben glances up at me, then drops his gaze back to Dad. 'Did I understand you to say you've hired someone temporarily to fill the position of food writer?'

Dad nods. 'We have. But only on a six-month contract. I made sure of that. Apparently, this new man is doing well, which is good. We'll give him an excellent reference, which should help him find a place somewhere else.'

'So,' says Ben slowly, 'there was never any chance of you extending his contract, no matter how good he was at his job or how many extra hours he put in?'

Dad frowns. 'It's quite common in our industry to take people on as temporary hires. In our case, we had an excellent reason for that. We're keeping the post open for Meghan here. She'll do an excellent job. She's been writing pieces for us since she was fifteen.'

Ben stands abruptly, not meeting my eyes. 'I'm glad I've met you, David. And I'm glad to have heard your plans. Allow me to tell you they stink. It's bad enough that you're hiring your own daughter for the position. But you might at least have had the decency to inform her unwitting stopgap where he stood instead of allowing him to believe he had a chance of getting the job on his own merits.'

Comprehension is dawning on Dad's face, mixed with bewilderment. I can't entirely blame him. It isn't every day you set off for a walk through a Parisian park and bump into not only your partially estranged daughter but also her so-called French boyfriend, who morphs without warning into one of your temporary employees. And that's without the one-hour time difference to further confuse your brain.

'Are you saying …?' Dad begins, looking from my flushed face to Ben's white one.

'That's exactly what I'm saying,' Ben says in an icy tone. 'I'm the young nobody you deigned to get in to cover the food writing desk while you were waiting for your real pick to be ready to take over.'

'Ben!' I say urgently.

'That's a rather exaggerated version of affairs,' says Dad.

'I don't think so,' says Ben. 'Well, I'm pleased we've had this conversation. And I'm pleased we're doing this face to face. It saves me the trouble of writing my resignation letter. Please consider this as a notice of my intention to vacate the post at once. Either you'll have to con some other poor mug into taking it for a few months or your real choice will have to step up and start work rather sooner than she thought.'

'Ben!' I say again in a despairing tone, but he shakes his head.

'There's nothing else for us to say. I'll leave you both to it. See you around, Meghan.'

He swings his bag onto his shoulder and strides away without a backward glance.

Chapter Twenty-Seven

I start to run after him, then stop. He and I need to talk, but I also need to talk to Dad. I'm not sure with which of them to begin.

Dad makes up my mind for me. 'Well, this is a turn up for the books.'

His voice is calmer than I expected, but that feels worse than anger. It tips me over the edge.

'What made you say that to Ben?' I almost shout.

He looks confused. 'Say what?'

'The thing about only employing him while you were waiting for me?'

He shakes his head as though trying to order his thoughts. 'I'm not sure I understand what's happening here. Why don't you start at the beginning and tell me what's going on?'

I sink down onto the bench. I'm blindingly angry with Dad, but I don't know why. He wasn't to know who Ben was. He rarely goes into the office these days, and I doubt he was there for Ben's interview.

'I don't have time for that now,' I say at last. 'I have to find Ben and explain.'

'If I were you, I'd give him some time to himself,' he says.

I round on him, relieved to have found a legitimate vent for my anger. 'Don't tell me what he needs or doesn't need! You don't know the first thing about him.'

'Apparently not,' he says in an ironic tone that only makes me more angry.

I stare at my feet, fighting for control. 'I don't know where to start.'

He smiles. 'The beginning is the traditional place. Didn't you learn anything at journalism school?'

'Don't turn this into a joke!' I snap. 'There's nothing amusing about what just happened.'

The corners of his mouth twitch. 'I'm not sure I agree with you. But I can see you're upset, and I'm sorry for that.'

'Of course, I'm upset! And it's all your fault.'

His look of amusement disappears. 'I'd like to hear your justification for that.'

I throw up my hands. 'That's easy enough. You told one of your employees you only employed him because you were waiting for someone else to be free to take over his job.'

'I don't think I quite put it like that,' he says. 'But why not? We issued him with a six-month contract. We didn't pretend it was anything more.'

'Maybe not. But you didn't tell him it definitely wouldn't turn into anything more.'

'Why should we?' he asks with a puzzled frown. 'I'm sure if Ben had asked her, Julianne would have told him there was no possibility of the contract being extended. Did he ask?'

'I don't know. But that isn't the point. There's a vast difference between being given a short-term contract and finding out you were only ever second-best.'

'No one said that!' he expostulates.

'You didn't need to. You told him I was about to take his job, the job he loves and has worked hard at in order to prove himself to you.'

Dad stops smiling. 'In my defence, I had no idea who he was when I said that. If I'd known –'

'What?' I demand. 'You wouldn't have told him a thumping great lie?'

He looks shocked. 'That's an unfair accusation. I would have been more tactful in my phrasing, but I told him nothing that wasn't true.'

'Yes, you did! You announced I was coming to work for you.'

There's a long pause as he takes in the implications of what I've said. Finally, he asks, 'Is that no longer the case?'

'That was never the case! As you're well aware.'

I expect him to snap back at me, but he doesn't. Instead, he looks bewildered. 'But we had an agreement.'

I exhale sharply. 'No, we didn't! You know perfectly well I have no intention of working with you. I made that clear the last time we saw each other. That's the reason you barely speak to me these days.'

His shoulders jolt in shock. 'That isn't true! You're the one who chooses not to have a relationship with me. I'm not sure why, but I've done my best to respect that and give you some space.'

It's my turn to feel bewildered. 'The reason I wanted space was because I knew you were upset with me when I told you I didn't want to come and work at *Whisk*. You may not have said much, but I know you pretty well. I thought it would be a good idea to take some time away and allow you to get used to the idea. I never imagined it would take you this long, but that's your prerogative.'

Dad lets out a very long sigh. 'I don't understand you, Meghan.'

'Perhaps you never did.'

He brushes this aside. 'I mean literally. As far as I'm concerned, you and I had a conversation after you graduated, during which you told me you weren't yet ready to work at the magazine. You wanted a few months off before you started with us.'

'I said nothing of the kind! I made it clear I didn't want to work with you. I told you if that ever changed, I would let you know.'

'You said you'd get back to me,' he tells me. 'I assumed that meant when you were ready to talk about starting work. Anyone would have assumed the same.'

'No, they wouldn't. They would have realised it meant I wasn't coming back at all. It's standard brush-off protocol. "Don't call us. We'll call you." You've done it a thousand times over the years.'

'Perhaps,' he concedes. 'But never to my daughter. And it wouldn't have crossed my mind she would do that to me. What prevented you from telling me clearly that you didn't want the job I was offering?'

'I did!' I protest. 'I could ask in my turn what prevented you from hearing it?'

'Touché. But, however the misunderstanding arose –'

'Not a misunderstanding on my part,' I mutter.

Thankfully, he ignores me. 'However it arose, we are where we now are. The question is, where do we go from here?'

'Nowhere. At least, it's all out in the open now.'

He considers this. 'Not entirely.'

'What do you mean?'

'Brushing aside the question of whether or not you wish to work at *Whisk*, it seems to me there are several other things we should discuss. The first being why you and my employee saw fit to inform me he was your French boyfriend.'

I feel my face flame. 'It was half true.'

'Indeed? May I ask which half?'

I give an exasperated sigh. 'You must know Ben isn't French.'

His mouth quirks. 'I did wonder.'

'Was it the *amuse* thing or the graffiti artist thing?'

'Call it intuition,' he says. 'So, I take it the boyfriend part was correct?'

'Kind of.'

'Why didn't you tell me who he was and introduce us properly?'

'Because I'm not actually living in Paris. If you'd asked him what he did, and he'd told you the truth, it wouldn't have taken a genius to work out I couldn't have been dating him from a different country.'

'It could have been a long-distance relationship,' he says.

'I only realised that once it was too late,' I admit. 'I panicked when I saw you walking towards us, and I went with the first thing I could think of. Obviously, I wouldn't have done that if I'd known you were about to announce you were his employer.'

'Ex-employer,' says Dad. 'But I understand what you mean.'

'I'm sorry I didn't tell you I wasn't living here,' I say.

He smiles. 'I already suspected that.'

My mouth falls open in shock. 'No, you didn't!'

'I'm afraid so. You may not have been in contact with me as much as I would have liked during these past few months, but that doesn't mean I've forgotten about you.

'Where did you think I was?' I ask, and he smiles.

'I cherished the hope you would contact me and tell me yourself.'

'You didn't ask Uncle Matt?'

'Does he know where you're currently living?' he asks, surprised.

I flush. 'Only because I asked him to be listed as my next of kin for my new job. I'm working in a bakery in the New Forest.'

Dad nods. 'I see.'

'I'm sorry,' I say awkwardly. 'I asked him not to mention it to you because I didn't know how to tell you. I'd only just told you I didn't want to work with you. I couldn't make things worse by saying I'd taken a job somewhere you'd absolutely hate.'

He looks worried. 'Somewhere I'd absolutely hate? Meghan, are you all right? Do you need money? Because, if so –'

I cut him off. 'I don't mean that sort of thing. But I knew you wouldn't like me pursuing a career you'd already told me was a dead end. Let's not worry about that now. The main thing is that I intended to come to Paris. I really did. Then I saw a job advertised somewhere else, and I applied for it. I didn't expect to get it, but when I did, I changed my mind about Paris.'

'I see,' he says again. I can tell he's hurt, but he doesn't press the matter.

He appears to be choosing his words carefully. 'I can't say I wasn't disappointed you didn't tell me what you were up to. But I told myself that was your business. I hoped you would let me know what you were doing in your own time. I'm more disappointed you've chosen not to take up the job opportunity that's been handed to you.'

'That's exactly the point!' I flash. 'Who wants something that's been handed to them?'

'I don't understand,' he says. 'You've always known you were scheduled to take over the business when I retired. Until recently, you were happy with that. I don't know what's changed.'

This is how it always is with Dad. It's his way or nothing. I'm beyond frustrated with him, but there's no way to explain this. He always has to know best what everyone should do, by which I mean me. He's inflexible and tunnel-visioned and stubborn. He'll never change. Which means that he and I will never have a proper relationship. Maybe it's time I accepted that and moved on. Something that's more difficult to do in real life than it is in a book.

'I don't want to discuss it anymore,' I say. 'I have more important things I need to be doing.'

'Such as?'

I pick up my bag. 'Finding Ben, for starters. I should have gone after him right away instead of wasting my time talking to you. I ought to have learned by now there's no point in trying to do that. You'll never change. You've always thought you knew best, and you always will. We'll both have to live with that.'

He tries to speak, but I lift a hand. 'Don't bother. It will only make things worse.'

He looks shell-shocked. 'Will I see you tonight?'

I snort. 'Only you could ask a thing like that. Obviously, you haven't been listening to a word I've said. I don't know why that surprises me. Why change the habit of a lifetime?'

I don't wait for him to speak but turn on my heel and stride off in the same direction Ben took. I doubt I'll catch up with him, but I know I have to try.

Chapter Twenty-Eight

I pull out my phone and call Ben as I run towards the park exit. He doesn't answer. I send him a text, but I have no way of knowing whether he sees it. What am I doing, running after someone who clearly doesn't want to speak to me? But I can't give up. I have to find him, even if it means searching every street in Paris.

Perhaps not every street. Paris is a large city, and it would take years to search every corner of it. But Ben can't have got far. I was only talking to Dad for a few minutes, so there's no need for me to panic.

What would I do if I'd had a row with someone and stormed off? I'd probably put some distance between us, then go in search of caffeine. There are several cafes in the direction in which Ben was heading. I'll start with those.

Sure enough, I spot him sitting outside the third one I pass. There's a cup on the table in front of him, but he isn't drinking, just staring out over the Seine with a blank expression.

I give a gasp of relief and wave frantically, but he doesn't respond. Has he seen me?

I wave again. 'Ben! Over here!'

He nods but doesn't speak as I arrive at his table, breathless and panting.

'I've been searching for you everywhere!' I gasp. 'I'd almost given up when I caught sight of you here. May I join you?'

'I was about to leave.' His voice is flat, and he avoids looking at me.

I drop into the chair opposite him. 'I know you're upset, but I can explain.'

'There's no need.'

'Yes, there is!' I insist. 'I understand what it looked like back there, but you've got it all wrong.'

A flash of annoyance passes over his face. 'Is that right? So, that man isn't really your father?'

'Yes, he is.'

'And he didn't tell me he only took me on at his magazine because he couldn't get anyone better?'

'No! He said he gave you a six-month contract. That's entirely different.'

'Is it?' he asks. 'Because from where I'm sitting, it feels like the same thing.'

'But it isn't! You know it isn't. I can understand why you're upset, but you don't have any reason to be.'

'With all due respect, I don't think you're in a position to say that.'

I hate it when people start a sentence with, 'With all due respect'. Everyone knows what they actually mean is, 'With absolutely no respect at all,' but they don't have the guts to say it. I keep myself in check, reminding myself that Ben has had a shock.

'Please let me explain,' I say as calmly as possible. 'I know it doesn't look good, but my father has got it all wrong.'

His smile doesn't reach his eyes. 'Unless you're telling me he's a confused elderly citizen who wrongly believed you were his daughter, and you decided to play along, I don't think that's likely.

He seemed quite sure of what he was saying. It all makes sense when you come to think of it. Apparently, you're his actual daughter. As it turns out, you're also a journalist. I'm surprised you didn't mention that earlier. It seems the sort of thing that might have come up in conversation.'

I feel my cheeks heat. 'I was planning to tell you. Of course, I was. I just hadn't found the right moment.'

He raises an eyebrow. 'That's what you say when you tell someone they have three months to live. How difficult is to mention in passing that you possess the same qualifications as the person you're dating, and that you intend to use your family connections to leapfrog over your fellow journalists and crush the competition?'

'That isn't what I'm trying to do!' I say hotly. 'If you could stop talking for one minute, I might be able to explain.'

He shrugs. 'Go ahead.'

A server appears, and I order a café au lait. Ben hasn't invited me to share his table but I'm doing it anyway. If things go badly, I'll ask for my coffee to go. If things go extremely badly, I can tip it over Ben's head. It's always good to have options.

'I'm sorry I didn't tell you who my father was,' I begin. 'I didn't think it was relevant.'

'Don't give me that!' he interrupts. 'Of course it was relevant. Are you telling me that at no point during our … during the time we've spent together did it cross your mind to say, "By the way, my father's the person who writes your pay cheque, so you should be nice to me or you might find yourself suddenly unemployed?"'

I'm glad my coffee hasn't yet arrived. I might be tempted to give him a caffeine shampoo sooner rather than later.

I take a deep breath and try to control my temper. 'It did occur to me as a matter of fact, but not in the way you say it. There was no connection between what I felt for you and the person who wrote your pay cheque. Or made a bank transfer, seeing that we live in the 21st century rather than the dark ages and move money electronically these days. The point is that my father was keen for me to work with him, but I told him that wasn't happening.'

'Really?'

'Yes, really. Is it so hard to believe I wanted something else for my life?'

He takes a sip of his coffee while he considers this. 'That doesn't fit with what your father said in the park. He seemed pretty sure of his facts.'

'That's the point,' I insist. 'They were his facts, not mine.'

'He seems like a smart guy. He must be or he wouldn't have succeeded in business. Are you saying you told him no under all circumstances, but he heard that as delighted acceptance?'

'You're twisting things around,' I say. 'It's no secret that he expected me to work at *Whisk* after I'd finished university. It makes sense that a parent would want their only child to follow them into the family business. But that isn't what I wanted. I once thought it was, but I was wrong. I graduated last year, and Dad assumed I'd be starting work at *Whisk*. I told him that wasn't happening.'

'Ever?' he asks.

'Maybe not in so many words. I didn't want to upset him. He seemed so hurt when I said I didn't think journalism was for me. And he was distinctly unimpressed when I told him I wanted to go into hospitality. He thought catering was great as a part time job while I was studying journalism, but I should want something more for myself when that was finished.'

Is that a flash of sympathy in his eyes? If so, it's gone in a moment.

'So, you didn't say a final no?' he asks.

'I said I'd get back to him if I ever decided to work for him.'

'*If* you decided to work for him, or when? It's an important distinction.'

'You were offered a short-term contract,' I say, exasperated. 'And you accepted it. Isn't that all that matters?'

'No, it isn't. I told you I was hoping to do well at my job and get that contract extended. You, of all people, knew how hard I was trying, and yet you encouraged me to keep hoping.'

I let out a squeak of frustration. 'That was because I had no idea he seriously expected me to take the job. I have no intention of doing so.'

His eyes darken. 'Nice of you to let me know. It's a great comfort to hear you've decided I can keep my employment because you don't want it after all. I can rest easy now. Unless, of course, you change your mind and decide it's too good an opportunity to pass up. Would you tell me in person, or do you and your father have minions to do that sort of thing for you?'

I glare back at him. 'Thousands of them. We keep them for all our dirty work.'

He lets out a laugh and seems to relax. 'Sorry. That was below the belt. No one can help their family's circumstances. It has nothing to do with who they are.'

'That isn't what you've been implying. You seem to have a problem with who my father is.'

'Not at all,' he says. 'And I have no problem with you taking over the family business. It happens all the time. I do, however, have a problem with you lying to me about it.'

He sees my shocked face and relents. 'Not lying, exactly. But you didn't tell me the truth, which comes to the same thing.'

'No, it doesn't! No one tells everyone all the tiny details of their lives. Everyone's entitled to their privacy.'

'They are,' he says. 'But that isn't what we're talking about here. I hesitate to say anyone owes other people anything. But if they ever do, I think you owed me at least a part of the truth. The part that concerned me. Do you have any idea how humiliating it is to discover I've been telling you all my plans and hopes, and you've been laughing at me behind my back all along?'

Tears fill my eyes, and I angrily brush them away. 'I have never laughed at you behind your back, Ben, and I never would.

If you don't know that much about me, we'd better call it quits right now and go our separate ways.'

'Perhaps you didn't laugh at me,' he says. 'But you made no effort to be honest with me. You held all the power here, and I didn't know it. That doesn't make for an equal relationship.'

'But I didn't!' I burst out. 'If anything, you held the power. From the moment I met you and realised where you worked, I was terrified you'd give me away to my father. As far as I knew, my father had no idea I wasn't in Paris. I was panic-stricken that night I met you at the awards. That's why I left so quickly afterwards. I thought I'd got away with it because I believed you'd returned to London. I was horrified when I saw you walking along the high street the following morning.'

He frowns. 'When I came to look around the bakery?'

'That's right. I was sure you'd left the area, but suddenly there you were.'

'But you weren't in the bakery,' he says. 'I would have remembered that. It's a small place. I remember talking to Lily, then Isabella showing me around the kitchen. There was no sign of you. Did you rush out of the back door?'

'There wasn't time. I hid in the kitchen. First behind a table, and then between the fridge and the wall.'

His lips twitch. 'You hid behind the fridge rather than face me?'

'Not behind it. I was sort of squashed in next to it.'

He gives a short laugh. 'I've had people try to avoid me before, but I don't think anyone's ever gone to those lengths.'

'You wouldn't know that unless they told you,' I point out.

'True.' The smile disappears from his face. 'Fascinating as that is, it isn't relevant to what we're talking about.'

'Yes, it is. I'm saying I was far more frightened of what you could do to me than you could have been about anything I could do to you.'

He's silent for a minute. I try to read his expression, but it's no good. I still don't know him well enough to tell what he's thinking.

'My family was so proud of me when I got my place at university,' he says at last. 'I was the first one of us to go into higher education. My parents were great, but they both grew up poor, and they didn't have the opportunities I had.'

'I get that,' I say, but he shakes his head.

'No, you don't. How could you? You were born into opportunity. I know you lost your mum, which must have been terrible for you and your father. But your future was still secure. You had the privilege of studying what you wanted. I won't ask whether you have any student debt because it's none of my business. But I suspect not. And you had the opportunity to turn down a job many people would give their eye teeth for, while knowing it would always be open for you if you wanted. Either you don't realise your privilege or you don't value it.'

'I realise it!' I cut in before he can say anything else. I can't bear to hear any more of this. He's saying all the things I've secretly worried about for years and hoped no one else was thinking about me.

'I'm not sure you do,' he says. 'Or you would have found it in yourself to be honest with me.'

I can't answer him. How do you tell the man you've recently started dating that you're terrified of losing him? How do you explain it takes you longer than most people to allow someone into your life in case they don't stay? Yes, I should have been honest with Ben right from the start. But I couldn't risk him turning on his heel and disappearing.

He gives me a curt nod. 'It's as well for us to find out now how incompatible we are. You and I come from such different backgrounds, Meghan. We've led such different lives. It would have been a miracle if we'd found enough common ground to make this work.'

My throat is too tight for me to say anything. I stare down at the checked table cloth, fighting fresh tears. Have I ruined everything for no reason? If I'd told him who I was from the start, would we be sitting here right now, unable to meet each other's eyes, with me feeling as though my world has ended?

He drops a hand onto my shoulder. 'Don't look like that. We gave it a try, and it didn't work out.'

I force myself to speak. 'It did work out! This is all a stupid misunderstanding. We can figure this out. We can find Dad and tell him again that I never want the job. I'm sure he'd be happy to give you a chance.'

I break off, seeing the look on his face. 'I didn't mean it like that.'

'I know you didn't. But it shows yet again how little we understand each other. I have to go. Will you be all right getting back to the apartment?'

I nod, knowing that if I try to speak I'll break down and humiliate myself in front of all the interested onlookers.

He squeezes my shoulder. 'Good. Well, I'll see you around, Meghan.'

He strides away towards the Métro station. I watch him go, feeling as though something has broken inside me. Something I'm not sure can be fixed. I have the stupidest impulse to run back to the park and see whether Dad is still sitting on the bench. But what's the point? Even if he's there, he and I have nothing to say to each other. Maybe we never have. Maybe the only thing keeping our relationship intact has been our shared belief that he knew what was best for me and would do everything he could to make that come true.

If so, there's no point in talking to him again. No point in trying to explain that I want to be my own person and follow my own path while remaining a part of his life. I couldn't bear to hear that isn't what Dad wants and to have it confirmed once and for all that he and I were never anything more than an illusion.

He and I need to have that conversation at some point, but not now. I've lost Ben, the man I was starting to allow into my life, the man I believed liked me for what I was and not who I was. I can't bear to lose Dad on top of that, even if it's only losing the illusion of what he and I had rather than the reality.

I catch the server's eye. He looks sympathetic. '*Vouz avez besoin de quelque chose?*'

I shake my head. There are many things I need right now, but I suspect he's referring to a *café au lait* or an *apéritif.* What would he do if I threw my arms around him, laid my head on his shoulder, and burst into a flood of tears? He's French, so he might surprise me by taking it in his stride. But I'd prefer not to make the experiment. All I want to do is to collect my bags and take a taxi back to Gare du Nord.

Once I'm back in Honeywell, all this may seem like a bad dream. I hope so. Even a bad dream is preferable to a bad reality. The longer I stay in Paris, the worse I'll feel. I don't want to share a city with the two men with whom I most wanted to share my life and now realise I never can. I'll leave them to enjoy it in their own separate ways while I get back as quickly as I can to what is starting, somewhat to my surprise, to feel like the home I never had.

Chapter Twenty-Nine

Isabella bursts into the bakery at ten past nine on Monday morning. She sticks her head around the kitchen door.

'You're back! I had a bet with Lily you'd stay in Paris. Now I'll have to clean the coffee machine for an entire week.'

'Why would I stay in Paris?' I ask, confused.

'Oh, you know. It's the city of love, and all that. I thought you and Ben might have decided to stay there permanently.'

'Leaving you in the lurch?' I say in as light a tone as possible to avoid giving myself away. I can get through the rest of this day if no one asks me about my 'romantic' trip to Paris. If Isabella digs for details, I know I'll break down and start howling into the dough.

'We'd have managed,' she says. 'We could have called Mabel in to cover for you while we were looking for a replacement. I'm glad we don't have to. You always make madeleines on Mondays. It's the only thing that gets me out of bed after the weekend.'

'I'm mixing the second batch now,' I say, pointing to the bowl. 'The first batch will be ready in twenty minutes. I'll call you when it is.'

I turn away and stir the batter. I expect to hear the kitchen door close as Isabella reluctantly returns to the shop, but I don't.

I concentrate on mixing while I wait for her to leave. I hear light footsteps coming towards me and feel the touch of her hand on my shoulder. 'Meghan? Are you all right?'

'Fine,' I say in a muffled tone. 'I'm behind with my work, that's all.'

She gently turns me to face her. 'You aren't fine. You're crying.'

I look around to see where the onions are. I could claim I've been chopping them for the lunchtime soup. But they're in the vegetable rack near the door, which is annoying of them.

'Allergies,' I say, wiping my eyes on my sleeve. 'I always get them at this time of year.'

'You mean, like hay fever?'

I'm about to agree when I realise it's the middle of August. Not a lot of plants are currently shooting out pollen to hijack the unwary passer-by.

'Not hay fever,' I say, taking another quick look around the kitchen in an effort to identify a possible culprit. 'I think it must be the flour.'

Isabella gives me an innocent smile. 'You've developed an intolerance to flour?'

'That's right. It seems to have come on quite suddenly. I expect a dose of antihistamines will take care of it.'

'I hope so,' she says. 'Or your fledgling career as a pastry chef will come to an abrupt end. In the meantime, and before you book an appointment with our overworked local GP, why don't you tell me what's really going on?'

'I told you. It's the flour.'

'I hate to be a cynic, but in the interests of full disclosure I have to say I'm not convinced. You may say that's my problem, and I expect you'd be right. But I hope you don't. I feel we've become friends over these past few months. I don't like thinking my friends can't talk to me when something's wrong.'

She's right. She and Lily have become my friends since I moved here. And friends don't shut each other out.

'I can't …' I begin, then stop, horrified to feel more tears slipping down my cheeks.

She pulls me towards her and hugs me. 'It's ok, Meghan. Everything's going to be fine.'

I give a choking sob. 'No, it isn't! Nothing is ok.'

I burst into tears as I say this, and we stand together while I cry until there are no more tears left.

Isabella strokes my hair. 'Come and sit down in the cafe while I get you something to drink.'

'I can't! The customers will see me.'

She claps a hand to her forehead. 'I forgot to open up!'

'How can you have forgotten? It's past nine o'clock.'

'I know,' she says, unperturbed. 'You'd think I would remember by now. I've been doing it every day for years. That's not quite true. Lily used to arrive before me. Then she had Daisy and Ethan, and everything seemed to fly out of her head. I can't imagine why. They're both such sweethearts and no work at all.'

'Go and open up the shop!' I say. 'You'll have customers lined up down the street. You mustn't alienate your clientele.'

'There was no one outside when I arrived. And no wonder. It's pouring with rain. No one with any sense would be outdoors today if they didn't have to be.'

'That isn't the point,' I insist. 'People need to know the Sugarloaf is open, even if they don't plan to use it at this precise moment.'

'I respectfully disagree,' she says. 'This business is a two-way thing. We need the customers to keep us afloat financially, but they need us to provide for all their bakery-related needs. It's what the scientists call symbiosis.'

I'm not convinced. But it's her bakery, after all.

'Could you bring me a coffee in here?' I suggest. 'That way, I can get on with the madeleines.'

'I'd forgotten about those!' she exclaims. 'Don't tell me they're burned?'

'The timer hasn't gone off,' I reassure her.

'Thank goodness for that. Fine, I'll make us both a cup of coffee, and we'll drink it in here while we wait for the madeleines to achieve madeleine-esque perfection.'

She disappears into the shop. I hear the bakery door open, followed by a murmur of voices. I'm glad she's seen sense and opened up after all. I don't want to be the cause of her and Lily's business going under.

Isabella reappears, clutching two mugs. 'Here we are. Lily's arrived now, so the ravening hordes won't have to wait in the rain after all. How long until the madeleines are done?'

The timer pings, and she beams. 'Perfect timing! It's as though the universe wanted us to be here at this particular moment. Where are the oven gloves?'

'I'll do it,' I say. 'I don't want you getting over-excited and burning your hands.'

'I've only done that twice,' she says with an injured air.

I put the cakes on the rack to cool and frown at Isabella as she tries to grab one. 'What did I just tell you about the cakes being hot?'

She pulls a face. 'Spoilsport. All right, you win. Tell me what's happened while we wait for them to cool down.'

'On second thoughts,' I say, 'you're welcome to burn your hands.'

'Don't change the subject. Come on, Meghan. You know you'll feel better if you talk about it.'

I'm not convinced. But I couldn't feel much worse, so I decide to give it a try.

I launch into an account of my weekend. I start with my trip over to Paris, describe the time Ben and I spent together, move onto meeting Dad, and finish with the disastrous conversation Ben and I had outside the cafe. Isabella is a good listener. She doesn't look horrified or interject with tales of her own similar experiences. She listens in silence until I've finished.

'Now you know everything,' I say. 'Although I can't say I feel much better.'

She squeezes my hand. 'That's because you haven't had your breakfast yet.'

'How do you know that?'

'No one eats breakfast after they've had their heart broken. It's a well-known trope. Except for me. I find heartbreak only increases my appetite.'

'Of course it does. Is there anything that doesn't?'

'Nothing springs to mind,' she says. 'I once had to skip breakfast when I had my tonsils out as a child. That was a bad day. I'd rather not talk about it.'

I give her a reluctant smile. 'I want to say Eleanor cooked me a full English breakfast this morning, but it wouldn't be true. I'm ashamed to say I'm one of your tropey females. I haven't eaten anything since yesterday lunchtime.'

'I should run classes,' she says. '*How not to lose your appetite when your love life takes a hit.* I could make millions.'

She eyes the tray of madeleines. 'Are they cool yet?'

'I expect so.'

She picks up two plates and loads the cakes onto them. 'Half for us, and half for our non-existent customers. That seems fair.'

I don't attempt to argue. I'm too tired, and no one has ever got the better of Isabella when it comes to the subject of cake.

I eat the madeleine she hands me, but only because I'm too tired to protest. And I have a vague hope that forcing Isabella to share might prevent her blood sugar from skyrocketing to such an extent that she spontaneously combusts.

She finishes her second cake. 'What will you do next?'

'What I was going to do before all this happened – finish my contract here, then look around for something else to do.'

'Such as?'

'I have no idea. I already knew I couldn't work for my dad, and this weekend has only confirmed that. I doubt he'd want me now anyway. He doesn't like people telling him he's wrong about things. Especially me. He's always believed he knows what's best for me, and he hasn't been shy about telling me so. As long as I hadn't positively decided against working at the magazine, he was ok with me. Now I've told him it's never happening, and he won't like that.'

'Do you wish you'd told him earlier?' she asks.

'I did tell him earlier. He didn't listen.'

I think about this some more. 'Maybe I could have been clearer with him, but that wasn't entirely my fault. My father doesn't make it easy for people to tell him what he doesn't want to hear. That may be why he's successful at business. He has all the answers. And he raised me not to argue with him.'

'Family businesses can be difficult,' she agrees sympathetically. 'I work part time for ours, and it isn't all smooth sailing. My uncle sounds a lot like your father. He's friendly and charming, but he's used to getting his own way.'

'I can't imagine anyone making you do anything you didn't want to do,' I say, regarding her with some amusement.

'You'd be surprised. I never expected to work for him. After I finished my accountancy qualifications, I planned to move to London and find a job with a big company. But my uncle was having trouble finding someone to suit him, so he persuaded me to work for him on a temporary basis while he was recruiting. Weeks turned into months, until he came to see me in the office one day and said we may as well make my job permanent. It took me a while to agree, but I could see the sense in it. It was a shock to wake up one morning and realise I'd been working for him for more than four years.'

'You could still have given in your notice and gone to London,' I say.

'I could,' she agrees. 'But I found I didn't want to. I enjoyed what I did, and I enjoyed living in the countryside. I'm not a city girl at heart. I prefer to live where I can get to know the people around me. I was grateful when I realised what my uncle had done.'

'I'm not sure what the point of this story is supposed to be. Are you telling me my father knows what's good for me after all? Because if so –'

'Goodness, no!' she exclaims. 'You should do exactly what you want with your life. Everyone should. I'm saying that things can work out in ways we didn't plan for, and we can find ourselves being happy in unexpected ways. I never thought I'd co-own a bakery, and look how well that's turned out.'

'That's a very different case. Talk about a match made in heaven! The only thing I can't understand is how the idea didn't occur to you sooner.'

'It's a mystery to everyone,' she agrees. 'All I can think of is that sometimes we don't see things in a particular way until we're ready to do so. I learned a lot working for my uncle. It came in useful when I started a business of my own.'

'How about delivering sheep?' I ask. 'I seem to remember you telling me that was an essential part of your duties when you worked on the farm. How did that prepare you for running a bakery?'

'It helped me to cope with unexpected situations,' she says. 'But that was something I did for fun. I'm sure my uncle could have found someone to take over lambing if I'd wanted him to, but it was one of the things I most enjoyed about working for him.'

She sees my expression and laughs. 'I mean it! Not the lying on my back in the middle of a waterlogged field trying to deliver twins. But it's a huge thrill when they're born, and you realise the mother and babies are both safe and well due to you. You should come out with me sometime and have a go yourself.'

'I would, of course, but aren't lambs born in the spring? I won't be here by then. You'll have to persuade Abby to come along with you instead.'

'Don't think I haven't tried!' she says. 'Lily too. And everyone else who's worked here since we took over. But no one has yet taken me up on the offer. I can't understand it.'

'One of life's great mysteries,' I say. 'Returning to the original topic, I'm not sure where that leaves me.'

'Wherever you want it to leave you. Your future is in your hands, whether that involves delivering baby animals or buying a run-down bakery. You have to decide your future for yourself rather than leaving it up to someone else to decide it for you.'

'Which is what I've been trying to do,' I say. 'It isn't my fault my father wouldn't take no for an answer.'

She considers this. 'It sounds as though you didn't say *no* as much as *maybe*.'

'I didn't want to hurt him by being too blunt. But he would have got the idea if he'd been prepared to listen.'

'It sounds as though he's got the message now,' she says. 'So, all's well that ends well.'

I bite my lip to stop myself from bursting into fresh tears. I was all cried out, but the coffee has rehydrated me enough to be able to start again if need be.

Isabella blows out a sigh. 'I'm sorry, Meghan. That was insensitive of me. I wasn't talking about Ben.'

'I know you weren't. And there's no point in thinking about him. Whatever happened between us is well and truly over now.'

'Are you sure it's over?' she asks. 'Once you've both had time to cool down –'

I shake my head. 'Trust me, it's over. He's right. I wasn't straight with him. When you've broken someone's trust like that, there's no going back. Even if I apologised and promised never to do it again, it would always be there between us. I wish now that I'd trusted him enough to tell him the truth when I had the opportunity. But I didn't, and we are where we are. I doubt I'll ever see him again.'

'What about the article he's writing?' she asks.

'He's left the magazine, remember? I don't know whether the material he's gathered belongs to him or *Whisk*. If it belongs to the magazine, Julianne will ask someone else to write the article.'

I give my eyes a final wipe and pull on my overall. 'There's nothing more to be gained by us meeting. It's better that we both go our separate ways and forget this whole ridiculous episode. And now I have to ask you to leave my kitchen or there won't be any more cookies today. Then your customers really will have something to complain about.'

Chapter Thirty

I don't have time to think about Ben during the following week. That isn't entirely true. I do my best not to think about him. There's no point. He and I are over, which is probably for the best. Things were becoming complicated. Our relationship started with a lie – at least it started with me withholding things from him. And it went downhill from there.

It felt as though the closer I got to Ben, the less able I was to tell him the truth. I told myself it didn't matter. It was the sort of unimportant detail anyone could have omitted to mention to the person they were dating. But I knew that wasn't true. When I tried to hide where I came from, I was hiding an essential part of who I was.

Worse than that, I was telling Ben I didn't trust him. He was good enough for me to date, but not good enough to deserve my honesty. No wonder he was upset when he found out the truth.

And what a way for him to find out! If I'd searched for a way to tell him the truth in a manner that would cause him the maximum possible pain and humiliation, I couldn't have done a better job of it.

I can't imagine what Ben thinks of me at the moment. Always supposing he's thinking of me at all. Maybe he isn't. Maybe he's out every night with a different woman, giving profound thanks to have been released from such a ridiculous entanglement. He may be getting on with his life, happy to be no longer mixed up in such a bizarre situation.

A person like him deserves a lot better than to be with someone like me. I've been concealing my identity from him as though I've imagined myself to be some famous movie star or long-lost descendant of the Romanovs hiding from the frenzied speculation and attention the revelation of my true self would bring. Whereas, in real life, I'm not an interesting person at all. I'm just someone who's unable to maintain lasting relationships and be honest about herself.

I'm trying not to think of the flip side of all this, but it's difficult. Have I been so desperate to conceal my identity because I'm not sure who I really am? If so, I have no business dating anyone. If I can't tell my own father who I am, what makes me think I can maintain a healthy relationship with someone else?

I get along with my bosses all right, but that's a somewhat forced partnership on both sides. I have to be cordial and accommodating with them because my livelihood depends on them. And they have to be pleasant to me because, if they aren't, they may be left without a pastry chef.

It's the same with Eleanor. She and I enjoy a friendly relationship, but it's a financial one, so it doesn't count. The customers are nice enough to me, but why wouldn't they be? I'm serving them cake. Who's daft enough to be unpleasant to the person providing them with one of life's essentials?

That may not be one hundred percent true. This Wendy woman I hear so much about never seems to be satisfied with us, no matter what we do. And she has no qualms about broadcasting that fact far and wide. But she's the exception that proves the rule. The rest of our customers have the good sense to know on which side their scones are buttered.

I'm roused from my pity party by Isabella coming into the kitchen asking whether I've finalised the plans for Friday afternoon. I've arranged for my pupils to come to the bakery to showcase their business ideas to the Silver Surfers, who have apparently been offering them all sorts of suggestions and advice over the past few weeks.

'It will be the event of the year!' Isabella says with a confident smile.

I move quickly to dampen down her optimism. 'It's a minor event at the end of the working week. Most people won't know it's happening.'

'They will when they find we've closed the bakery.'

'We're only closing it an hour earlier than usual,' I say. 'Hardly anyone comes in at four o'clock on a Friday. They're too busy trying to sneak off work early and get home to start their weekend.'

She shrugs. 'If they sneak past our bakery, hoping for a quick pick-me-up after a difficult week, they'll be out of luck. Serves them right for cheating their employers out of an honest day's work.'

'Whereas I will be working extra hours that day,' I remind her.

'You've mentioned that quite a lot this week. I'm a little hurt you don't see it as an honour to be requested to spend more time at such a lovely place as this.'

'I'll be taking an hour in lieu on a day of my choosing,' I tell her. 'Lily agreed that, so it's too late for you to refuse.'

'I'm disappointed. You'd think any employee of mine would want to put in as much extra time as possible just for the love of it.'

'It's unfathomable,' I say. 'I can't understand myself. To return to your question, yes, I have everything sorted out. Each person will give their presentation and hand out free samples. The Silver Surfers will do the taste testing and make suggestions. When everyone has had their turn, I'll present the certificates and rosettes. It isn't a competition, so we don't need to pick a winner. But I'd like to mark the fact they've completed the course, if only to acknowledge the fact they've put up with me for all these weeks.'

'Are you still feeling down?' she asks. 'You shouldn't. Things will work out in the end. They always do.'

'You've obviously never read any Russian literature. Or, for that matter, Thomas Hardy. Would you have told Tess of the D'Urbervilles everything works out in the end?'

'I don't know,' she says. 'I avoid reading Thomas Hardy as far as possible. I prefer optimistic, upbeat novelists. What happened to this Tess woman?'

'You don't want to know. Let's just say matters wouldn't have been greatly improved by a plate of cakes.'

'Now I know you're joking,' she says. 'There's nothing that can't be improved by the judicious application of cream buns. Even a broken heart. A well-timed doughnut may not mend it entirely, but you'll feel better while you're processing what's happened.'

She brightens. 'Shall we make the experiment right now? We'll sit down and eat a plate of doughnuts, and you can tell me whether you feel better afterwards.'

'I'll watch you eat a plate of doughnuts,' I offer.

'I'm not sure it works like that,' she says dubiously. 'But I'm willing to put it to the test. It's your break now, isn't it? Come on through, and I'll make you a drink while we try the great doughnut experiment.'

Lily is cleaning the tables when we arrive in the shop.

'All ok with the preparations for Friday?' she asks when she sees me.

'That's what we've been talking about,' says Isabella. 'Meghan assures me everything is sorted, but I'm worried about her. She doesn't seem as cheerful as she should be. I'm going to try the age-old remedy of applying doughnuts to see whether that improves matters.'

'Like a poultice?' says Lily.

Isabella grins. 'That would be a waste of good doughnuts. I was planning to go down the more traditional route and apply them internally.'

Lily laughs. 'The question is, to whom?'

I switch on the coffee machine. 'I think you can guess the answer to that one. Isabella seems to believe it will make a great spectator sport for us – like watching the gladiators enter the arena. Only, instead of lions, the contestant will battle doughnuts.'

Lily tosses her cloth into the sink. 'I don't need to stay and watch. I've seen a similar spectacle many, many times. All I can say is that it would be unwise to bet against Isabella.'

'I wouldn't dream of it,' I say. 'I'm only here to keep score and apply the Heimlich manoeuvre in case of an emergency.'

Isabella gives us both a scornful smile. 'Anyone would think this was my first rodeo.'

'Don't you mean tournament?' says Lily. She looks thoughtfully at me. 'Are you ok, Meghan? You look tired.'

'She isn't ok, but she will be,' says Isabella. 'Who could fail to cheer up while observing a doughnut-eating contest?'

'Is it a contest when there's only one of you?' asks Lily. 'Seriously, Meghan. Why don't you go home early today? That's what I'm about to do. It's been a quiet afternoon. Isabella can close up.'

'It isn't what I envisaged when I set out to improve your spirits,' says Isabella. 'But I suppose that could work. Fine, off you both pop. I'll stay here to hold the fort and keep the business running. Can you imagine how either of you would cope if I weren't here to organise everything for you?'

Chapter Thirty-One

I arrive at the bakery on Friday morning to find Isabella already waiting for me.

'Did your alarm go off unexpectedly this morning?' I ask sympathetically. 'How awful for you.'

She gives me a hurt look. 'Are you saying it's not like me to be early for work?'

'I don't have to. You've just said it yourself.'

She frowns. 'I think that's sass, but it's too early for me to work it out. I'll have you know I've come into work early before.'

Lily comes out of the office holding a stack of papers. 'It's true. Isabella comes in early once a year – the weekend the clocks go back.'

'It's true,' says Isabella. 'I can never remember what the time is meant to be doing. But I balance it out by being an hour late when the clocks go forward.'

'It's the first of September,' I point out. 'The clocks don't change for ages.'

'Maybe I'm practising. You must realise what a conscientious member of this business I am. I leave nothing to chance.'

'And maybe I called this morning and woke her,' says Lily. 'I'm sorry about that. I assumed you kept your phone on silent while you were asleep.'

'I do,' says Isabella. 'But you're a starred contact. My goddaughter may need me at any time. I wouldn't like to think I was unobtainable.'

'I've told you repeatedly that Daisy doesn't have a mobile phone,' says Lily patiently. She sees the look on Isabella's face. 'And neither will she until she's at high school, so don't even think about it.'

Isabella pouts. 'I want to play Candy Crush with her. And we could message each other every night after she's gone to bed. Just think how it would improve her spelling and vocabulary. She'd be top of the class from day one.'

'Not if we allowed her to stay up all night texting her godmother,' says Lily. 'You both need your beauty sleep. Neither of you is good at getting up in the morning as it is.'

'It's a thankless task being a godmother,' Isabella tells me mournfully. 'I do my best to fulfil my duties, but it's hard going with all the road blocks put in my way. Even Jack, who was always much more fun than my business partner, is boring and unimaginative now he's become a father.'

'I'm sorry we can't provide someone for you to play with twenty-four hours a day,' says Lily. 'You'll have to have one of your own. Then you can stay up all night playing with them and reap the consequences in the morning.'

'You see what I'm talking about?' Isabella asks me. 'Dull and unimaginative. I shouldn't need to have a baby of my own. I have Daisy. And Ethan too, when he's not busy yelling his head off to be fed or falling asleep in his highchair. You should check with your health visitor whether that's normal, Lily. I'm sure I never fell asleep as a child when there was food on offer.'

'I don't doubt it,' says Lily. 'If you've finished talking about food, can we run through this afternoon's event? I want to make sure we have everything sorted in case Ben –'

She shoots me a guilty look and stops.

'In case Ben turns up?' I ask. 'It's highly unlikely now he no longer works for *Whisk*. If they still plan to run this article, they may decide to send his replacement to report on it. I hope they do. It would be a pity for the article to be spiked because one of their reporters has left.'

'Of course,' says Lily, not meeting my eyes.

I hate this. It's bad enough that Ben and I have broken up. It makes things ten times worse when my employers tiptoe around the fact. I wish everyone would pretend it never happened. Denial is not only a river in Egypt. In this particular case, it's the obvious way forward. But I know Lily is trying to be tactful because she cares about me, so I don't say any of this.

Instead, I pull out my phone and make a show of checking my notes. 'Certificates written and signed. Afternoon tea prepared. Rosettes purchased. Guest list prepared.'

'That sounds great,' says Lily. 'You've done a stellar job with this, Meghan. We're particularly grateful because none of this was in your original job description.'

'It will be in all our future employees' job descriptions,' says Isabella. 'I've learned a valuable lesson about contract writing this year. From now on, I won't be drafting any contracts unless they contain loopholes through which you can drive a coach and horses.'

'I believe you,' I say, laughing. 'Don't worry about me, Lily. I enjoyed taking these classes. They were nowhere near as daunting as I imagined.'

'They've been a great success,' she says. 'We'll definitely be running more of them in the future. It's a pity you won't be here to lead them.'

'But Abby will. She's far more qualified and experienced than I am. She'll be able to offer proper cookery lessons.'

Lily glances at Isabella. 'You should take a look at Abby's contract before she gets back. She may refuse to get involved.'

'Not if she wants to stay in my good books,' says Isabella. 'As a matter of fact, I checked her contract last week. It's annoyingly specific in some areas, but there's some wording in there that seems ambiguous enough for me to make my case. Especially if I threaten to contact Meghan and ask her to run the next lot of classes for us at an extremely competitive rate of pay.'

Lily gives her a startled look. 'Isabella! We can't afford to —'

'But Abby doesn't know that,' says Isabella.

'What about me?' I say in a hurt tone. 'You've just offered me attractively renumerated employment and then rescinded the offer. That isn't just unkind. It falls under breach of verbal contract law. And I have a witness.'

'Goodness!' says Isabella. 'I hope you're wrong.'

She brightens. 'But your witness is Lily. She'd be willing to lie herself blue in the face on the witness stand if you took us to court. Game, set, and match to the Sugarloaf!'

'Don't look so worried,' I tell Lily. 'I have no intention of suing the bakery for anything. You're the ones writing my reference.'

'We'll be writing you an excellent one,' she promises. 'I wish we didn't have to lose you, Meghan. It's been a lot of fun having you here.'

'Likewise,' I say. 'But I don't want to think about that today. I'd prefer to concentrate on this afternoon's presentation. All my pupils have worked so hard. I want everything to run smoothly for them.'

'This is a Sugarloaf Bakery event,' says Isabella. 'Smooth running is our watchword.'

Lily flashes me a grin and sits down to go through her paperwork.

'How many people do you think will come?' I ask Isabella.

'I have no idea. The Silver Surfers will be out in force. We've reserved the largest two tables for them. Then there are your six pupils —'

'Five,' I say. 'Ben won't be here.'

She gives me an apologetic look. 'Sorry, I never could count correctly. It comes from having an accountancy degree.'

'And from allowing yourself to be distracted by cake whenever you sit down at your computer,' puts in Lily.

'Cakeonomics is an up-and-coming discipline,' says Isabella. 'It won't be long before they're teaching it at all the best universities. Then you'll have to eat your words.'

'We'll have my five pupils,' I say before she can lapse into a pastry-filled trance.

She appears to come back to reality with a jerk. 'And several other people from the village have expressed an interest. With any luck, there will be too many for the bakery to hold. We'll be turning them away at the door.'

'With any luck?' I ask.

'That's right. It always looks good when there are queues of people snaking around the block trying to gain access to an event. It makes us look exclusive. We should have sold tickets. I can't think why Lily always overlooks these basic business opportunities. We'll know for next time. If there are too many people trying to get in, we'll allow them inside in five-minute shifts on the understanding they all buy something.'

'Let's not get carried away,' I say. 'I imagine most people have better things to do on a Friday afternoon than to stand around watching amateurs display their food products.'

'Hey!' she says indignantly. 'Oh, you mean your pupils.'

'Well, I think my side of things is sorted,' I say. 'If you don't need me for anything else, I should get on with my actual contracted job. I plan to make some eclairs if I have time after I've finished the first batch of bread.'

Isabella waves towards the kitchen. 'A worthy goal! Don't let me stop you. Could you also make some custard slices?'

I work right through lunchtime. Lily tries to persuade me to take a proper break, but I wave away the suggestion.

'You could bring me a chicken pie if we have any left,' I say. 'I can eat it on the run. I'm behind as it is, and my pupils will be arriving in an hour.'

'Can I help you with anything?' she asks.

I wipe the dough from my hands. 'Can you keep Isabella out of the kitchen for the next hour? She's been popping in every ten minutes "wondering" how long the eclairs will be. I almost tipped her head-first into the bread mixer the last time she appeared.'

'I'll chain her to the coffee machine if I have to,' promises Lily. 'Call if you need me.'

I work as quickly as I can, calculating timings in my head. I check the time – three o'clock.

The kitchen door opens, and I give an exasperated sigh. 'I thought you were manacled to the coffee machine. Take one step into my kitchen and I'll jam you down the side of the fridge and see how funny you find that.'

There's no answer. I drop a cloth over the dough and swing around. 'I mean it, Isabella! I've had just about enough of –'

The man standing in the kitchen doorway looks as unlike Isabella as possible. He's wearing a neat grey suit and shiny black shoes, and his thinning hair is neatly combed behind his ears.

Neither of us speaks as we study each other. I swallow hard, hoping my voice doesn't betray the shock I feel at seeing him again so unexpectedly.

'Hello, Dad. What are you doing here?'

Chapter Thirty-Two

He doesn't move. 'Hello, Meghan. How are you?'

Only my father could ask such a ridiculous question at a moment like this. How does he think I am? I toy with answering honestly. I could tell him I'm heartbroken and still have no idea what I want to do with my future. But what's the point?

Luckily for both of us, my intrinsic Britishness kicks in. 'I'm fine, thank you.'

I almost add some remark about the weather but stop myself in time. It's possible he's come all the way to Honeywell to talk about the effects of this summer's lower-than-average precipitation on the crops, but it's highly unlikely.

'That's good,' he says. 'May I come in?'

'To the kitchen?' I ask, and he nods.

'You're supposed to have a certificate. We don't allow just anyone in here without a good reason.'

His face flickers, and I feel a pang of guilt. That was unnecessary.

'We could sit in the bakery for a few minutes,' I say. 'I can make you a cup of coffee while you tell me what's brought you here. I don't have long, though. We have a thing happening later, and I have a lot to do.'

'I know you do,' he says. 'That's why I'm here.'

I frown, unsure what he means. 'I assumed you were here to see me? I was talking about something completely different.'

I pull off my overall and point him towards the cafe. 'Find yourself somewhere to sit while I make you a drink.'

Isabella is standing behind the counter looking suspiciously innocent. I narrow my eyes at her as I pass, but she only smiles in an abstracted manner.

Lily is serving a few late lunches. 'I'll do that, Meghan,' she says when she sees me. 'What would you both like?'

'I'll have a latte,' I say. 'And my … he'll have a filter coffee without milk.'

I look to Dad for confirmation, but he's staring out of the window, apparently engrossed in studying the precise layout of the high street.

'Coming right up,' says Lily.

I sit down facing Dad. 'You're the last person I expected to see here today.'

'I might say the same thing to you.'

I don't have time to play stupid games. Neither do I have the inclination.

'Are you telling me you happened to be in the area and wandered into our bakery for a nourishing snack? Because, if so, I may as well tell you straightaway that I don't believe you.'

His eyes crinkle in that way I remember clearly from my childhood. 'Of all the bakeries, in all the towns, in all the world, he walks into mine?'

'Well, yes. Except we aren't in North Africa, and you aren't Humphrey Bogart.'

'Of course, I didn't end up here by accident,' he says. 'I came to see you.'

'I understand that,' I say patiently. 'What I don't understand is how you knew exactly where to find me. If Uncle Matt didn't tell you where I was, who did?'

'I saw it on your bakery website.'

I sit with this for a moment before asking, 'How did you know what to search for? Do you make it a habit to trawl through hundreds of websites each day just to see what every single UK small business is up to?'

'Not as a general rule,' he says. 'But I was intrigued to read about the Local Spoon Awards back in May. I read the article when Ben wrote it and looked at some of the business websites. Imagine my surprise when I found my daughter's picture staring out at me from the front page of The Sugarloaf Bakery's website under the caption *Temporary New Member of Staff.*'

I dart a glance at Isabella, who's busying herself with counting the remaining macarons and making ostentatious notes about them in the notebook we keep next to the till.

'It was all the more surprising,' Dad goes on, 'since up until then I had been labouring under the impression my daughter was living in Paris. I gave the matter some consideration and came to the conclusion that either you had perfected the art of teleportation or, for reasons of your own, you had decided not to move abroad and had come here instead.'

'About that,' I begin, but he lifts a hand.

'I have said I was surprised, but that was not my primary emotion.'

'I know,' I say. 'You were angry.'

His head jerks up and his eyes widen. 'Of course not! What was there to be angry about?'

'Your only daughter lying to you about her whereabouts? And not just a ten-mile lie. One that included an entirely different country.'

He smiles. 'I'm not sure the exact number of miles was the issue uppermost in my mind.'

'Then what was?'

He eyes me steadily. 'That my daughter felt unable to tell me the truth about where she was and what she was doing. It felt as though someone had hit me.'

Whatever I'd expected him to say, this wasn't it. It knocks the breath out of me, and I can't speak for a full minute.

I clear my throat at last. 'I'm sorry, Dad. I shouldn't have done that. I've been regretting it for months. I should have told you the truth and faced the consequences. That would have been the courageous thing to do. But I ran away and hid instead of facing my problems head on.'

He gives his head a bewildered shake. 'I'm not blaming you. I was angry at myself.'

'But why? You weren't the one telling lies to cover up what you were doing.'

'I was angry with myself for being someone you didn't feel you could talk to. The fact you could tell your Uncle Matthew where you were and not me is a huge indictment on me. I can assure you I feel it very strongly.'

I stretch out an impulsive hand to take his. 'Don't say that! I'm the one to blame here. I thought I didn't have any choice, but I've come to realise that wasn't true. We all have choices to make, and we need the courage to own them. I didn't do that. I wasn't sure how to talk to you about what I was doing, so I avoided it. To be honest, I didn't think you'd care.'

His face freezes in shock. 'You didn't think I would care what my daughter was doing, or whether she was safe and happy?'

'I knew you'd care whether I was safe. That's why I allowed you to believe I was going to Paris. I assumed that, as long as you knew where I was, you wouldn't give it another thought.'

He closes his eyes, and I'm shocked to see the look of pain on his face.

'I'm sorry, Dad,' I say quietly. 'I take it I was wrong?'

He nods without speaking, and I realise I've been telling myself a story about him to appease my conscience and shield myself from having to own the consequences of my decisions.

We don't speak for a long time. Lily places our mugs in front of us, returns with a plate of scones, then disappears as quietly as she arrived. There are several customers in the bakery, but I barely notice them. It's as though Dad and I are the only two people here, neither of us daring to look at each other properly for fear of what we might see.

I break the silence. 'I've known for a while that I needed to come and talk to you. I was busy gathering the courage to do that when we … I bumped into you in Paris, and we had that disastrous conversation. That sent everything back to square one. All I could think about was how angry you were that I'd lied to you and was refusing to work with you. And how you would never forgive me. There didn't seem much point in trying to contact you after that.'

'Why did you think I was angry?' he asks.

'Because you were! Don't try to pretend you weren't. You've always wanted me to work with you. You've always told me you expected me to take over the business when you retired. For a long time, I accepted that. It was only after my year off before university that I started to question it. When I took my journalism course and realised I was enjoying my evening job far more than my studies, I tried to discuss it with you, but you told me I was being ridiculous. You said no one enjoys the hard work of getting a qualification, but everyone has to go through it to get to the place they want to be.'

I take a deep breath. 'And that's when I realised *Whisk* wasn't the place I wanted to be. I tried to ignore the tiny voice telling me I was looking for something completely different. But the more I tried to tell myself I needed to be the person you wanted me to be, the more stressed and miserable I became. In the end, all I could think of was to run away.'

'But why didn't you tell me all this?' he asks, looking more confused than ever.

'How could I? It's what you've been dreaming of for me since I was a little girl. You and Mum, both. You told me so many times how proud you were that I was following in your footsteps, and how happy you were to think the family business was safe in my hands. How do you turn around and tell the most important person in your life you don't want what they're offering? I didn't know how to do that.'

I break off and stare at my coffee cup, feeling the treacherous tears pricking the back of my eyes. I seem to have cried more since I came to work at this bakery than the whole of my previous life. I must remember to mention that to Isabella sometime.

Dad reaches over and takes my hand. I don't pull it away.

'There's no point in trying to pretend any longer,' I say. 'I've been doing that for years and look where it's got me.'

He sighs. 'I'm not sure where to begin. For one thing, your mother never expected you to follow in our footsteps. She and I built something together because we enjoyed it. If at any point we had stopped enjoying it, we would have let it go and done something different.'

'I can't imagine you doing anything different,' I say. 'You've been the face of *Whisk* for as long as I can remember. You've built up the circulation and established the brand, with everyone looking up to you and using you as an example of how to succeed in the publishing business. They even talked about you in our journalism course. I wanted the floor to open up and swallow me when they mentioned your name.'

'Because you were ashamed of what I did?' he asks.

'Not at all. But it's the reason why I applied for my course under Mum's name. The last thing I wanted was for people to connect me with you and think I was only there because you'd got me a place. I was determined to succeed on my own terms or not at all.'

'I would never have interfered to get you a place on any course,' he interrupts. 'I doubt I could have done so even if I'd wanted to. Either you were good enough or you weren't. There would have been no point in me prolonging the inevitable if you weren't. But you were good enough. You always got excellent grades at school, and you graduated from university with a first. You could hardly have doubted yourself after that.'

'It wasn't that I was doubting myself,' I say. 'And it wasn't because I was worried about being able to do the job. But I was no longer sure it was what I wanted to do. You say you wouldn't have interfered to get me into university. But I've always been aware I had advantages others on my course didn't – all those contacts in your address book offering me work experience whenever I wanted it, and your knowledge of the industry. It gave me an unfair leg up.

'Is that what this is about?' he asks. 'You wanting to prove yourself?'

'Partly, but not entirely. I can admire what you've built, and I can recognise the talent and hard work that went into building it. But that doesn't mean I want to do it too. I spent my time at university becoming more and more aware that I would never be my own person if I walked a path someone else had cut out for me.'

'You could have applied to work for another publication,' he says.

'That's what I'm trying to tell you. I don't want to work in journalism at all. It isn't me. I'm not sure what I'll end up doing, but it will be culinary-related in some way. I've been thinking about applying for a chocolatier course when I leave here. I'd like to extend my skills.'

He nods. 'I think you'd be very good at that.'

'Really?' I say, taken aback.

'Definitely. You did very well at your course in Paris before university. It's obvious you haven't lost interest in it during the intervening years. And here you are, working for a bakery and by all accounts doing an excellent job. I'm so proud of you, Meghan.'

I want to ask why he thinks I'm doing a good job here. He's only just arrived at the bakery. Isabella, fluent talker though she is, hasn't had time to talk to him about what I've been doing here, let alone how well I've done it. But that isn't important. Dad can't really know much about my life here. The main thing is that he's expressing an interest in it. For the first time in years, it feels as though he's trying to see me.

'Thanks, Dad,' I say awkwardly, and he gives me a half smile.

'So, is that why you're here today?' I ask. 'You saw this event on our website?'

He hesitates. 'I heard about it and decided to come down here to support you – if you allowed me to do so. I half expected you to throw me out on my ear the moment you laid eyes on me, or else command your redoubtable boss to do it for you.'

I catch Isabella's eye and see she's grinning at us.

'I haven't ruled it out,' I tell him.

He raises an eyebrow. 'Your new profession seems to have taught you a certain amount of assertiveness.'

I suppose it has. No one can deal with customers without learning to be firm yet pleasant. More importantly, Dad has referred to what I do here as my profession. It may seem like a small thing, but to me it's a huge step forward.

'I should have learned to speak up for myself much earlier,' I say. 'It would have saved us both a lot of time.'

'I blame myself,' he says. 'I didn't realise until I saw you in Paris that you felt smothered by me and believed I didn't want you to be yourself. That was never my intention, Meghan, although I can appreciate it came across in that way. I've done a lot of soul searching since I saw you. I've realised how unfair it was for me to assume you would want to follow in my footsteps in any way.'

'That isn't quite true,' I say awkwardly. 'There are plenty of ways in which I'd like nothing better than to resemble you. Your work ethic, for instance. And your passion for communicating. And how you really care about your employees. I've watched you over the years carrying out small acts of kindness with no recognition. I'd hate you to think I hadn't learned from you or that I'm ungrateful for everything you've done for me and tried to do for me. It's just that –'

'I understand,' he says. 'You don't want me living your life for you. Nor should you. You're a remarkable person, and I'm proud of you no matter what you choose to do. You're smart and caring and loyal. And you make me laugh more than anyone I've ever known. I've missed that.'

'Me too,' I admit. 'I'm sorry we haven't spent much time with each other this past year. I hope we can make up for that now.'

His eyes are suspiciously bright. 'I would like nothing more. I'm sorry, Meghan. I know I got it wrong when I tried to bring you into the company. I always intended it to be a gift, not a burden.'

I put my arms around him and hug him, feeling the roughness of his jacket against my face, smelling his familiar aftershave. Some things never change, and I'm glad about that. I don't want to lose everything about my past. I just want to have some control over my future.

'They're here!' says Isabella's voice, bringing me back to reality.

I release Dad and take a step back. 'My pupils are arriving for what my boss patronisingly refers to as their "show and tell".'

'I'm looking forward to it,' he says. 'I can't wait to see what a great job my daughter is doing.'

The bakery door opens, and Ellie comes in, looking even more nervous than usual. She's followed by Greg and Bethany, who also look unaccustomedly serious.

'Welcome to The Sugarloaf Bakery –' I begin.

I break off abruptly as I see Ben standing on the pavement, wearing an inscrutable expression and carrying a small cardboard box.

Chapter Thirty-Three

Lily doesn't seem to notice my confusion as she steps forward and opens the door for him. 'You seem to have your hands full. Nice to see you again, Ben.'

He gives her a brief smile. 'Hi, Lily.'

He steps inside the bakery and looks around. My mind flashes to my various options, decides there aren't any, and goes numb.

Ben catches sight of me and gives me a questioning look. I have no idea what he's trying to ask, and I don't much care. For all I know, he's here to order eight dozen wholemeal rolls. He'd better not ask me to make them for him.

He doesn't seem surprised to see Dad standing next to me. For one moment, I feel a flash of hope they won't recognise each other. They've only met once, and that was in a foreign country. It's always difficult to recognise someone when they're away from their usual surroundings.

This hope is dashed when Dad holds out his hand. 'Jean-Luc, if I remember correctly.'

Ben grins as he shakes it. 'Only when I'm in Paris.'

I look from one to the other, frowning. Why are they so cheerful? The last time I saw them, they were two seconds away from challenging each other to a duel.

I don't have time to think about this as Isabella claps her hands for silence. I dart her a questioning look. Has she taken it upon herself to interfere yet again? She smiles at me and gives the tiniest shake of her head.

'What are you doing here?' I ask Ben in an undertone. I'd prefer to ask it in an extremely loud tone, but this is neither the time nor the place. We're here to celebrate the achievements of my pupils, not to start World War Three.

'I'm giving my presentation,' he says calmly.

'I'm delighted you were all able to be here this afternoon,' says Isabella. 'Thank you to the Silver Surfers and the rest of our customers who've made a special effort to be here with us today. This is the first time we've run an event like this, but I hope it won't be the last. As you know, Meghan chose the theme of local food, and it's an excellent one. There's no need to fly in ingredients from all over the world when they're available right here on our doorstep. So, without more ado, over to you, Meghan.'

I return to reality with a crash. 'I'm sorry. I lost focus for a while.'

'Understandable,' she says. 'But I wouldn't like to cheat your pupils of their chance to shine, to say nothing of everyone who's made the effort to come here to support them.'

'Of course not.' I pull myself together and wave to the group sitting together at a window table. 'Are you all ready?'

'We've been ready for a while,' says Greg. 'We've been waiting for you.'

I muster my remaining shreds of dignity. 'I'm ready now. Who wants to go first?'

'And,' continues Greg as though he hasn't heard me, 'Ben shouldn't get any ideas about preferential treatment just because he's dating you.'

'Actually, he isn't,' I say. 'Also, this isn't a competition. It's a presentation. No one is getting preferential treatment. That's not what this afternoon is about. It's about showing how much you've learned and what you've achieved by working together as a group. And we're giving your potential customers the chance to offer valuable feedback. This was a course for local businesses. Everyone here today lives locally and knows everything there is to know about the area.'

Greg gives me his trademark grin. 'I'm winding you up, Meghan. Ben's one of us.'

'Then let's get started,' I say. 'Would you like to go first?'

Greg jumps to his feet. 'Ladies and Gentlemen, I present to you Greg's Gourmet Popcorn!'

He hands around the bags of popcorn and explains how the idea first came to him. He talks about the business plan he and his father have drawn up and shows us their projections and ideas for advertising. There's a spontaneous round of applause as he finishes.

'That was amazing,' I tell him. 'It must have taken you a long time to prepare, but you've done a great job. What does our audience think? Would you buy Greg's popcorn?'

'I'd have to check first whether it's safe for dogs to eat,' says Mrs Ogilvie. 'I wouldn't want Bernie choking on it.'

Greg looks confused. 'Is Bernie a dog? This is a product for humans, not for pets.'

'Don't bother,' advises Mabel. 'You'll wear yourself out talking to her, and the upshot will be that she'll still feed it to him if her vet doesn't expressly forbid it.'

'I'd buy it,' says Ivy. 'It would be great for our girls' nights out. Mavis and Mary and Barb and I leave our husbands at home every couple of weeks and go out on the town to catch up on the latest films and theatre productions. Your popcorn will make a welcome change from Mavis' boring Werther's Originals.'

Greg looks pleased. 'Maybe we could set up a regular film night in the village hall? Greg's Gourmet Goodies could be the official sponsor.'

'And my chocolates,' interrupts Bethany. 'You can't watch a film without eating chocolate. We could donate part of our profits to charity.'

Everyone breaks into a spirited discussion about the films they'd like to see and which night would be best. Mrs Ogilvie's protests that dogs can't eat chocolate are lost in the hubbub.

I hold up a hand for silence. 'It's a great idea, but maybe you can all discuss it afterwards? We have four more presentations to get through.'

The bakery falls silent, or as silent as it ever does when it's filled with a group of over-excited and opinionated customers.

Ellie goes next and presents her ideas for Ellie's Jellies. She's brought a box of samples in tiny glass jars, which she passes around to everyone along with individual packets of crackers.

'Lavender and Lime,' announces Mabel, peering at the label on hers. 'With any luck, the mutt has a citrus allergy.'

She catches her sister's eye. 'Just kidding.'

Ellie's presentation covers everything from social media marketing to press releases and sustainable packaging. The audience obviously approves. Ellie sits down at last, blushing madly but looking delighted with the reception her product has received. I remember how nervous she was the evening she had to present her ideas to us. Seeing her confident demeanour today makes it all worthwhile.

Bethany goes next and presents her idea for handmade chocolates. She too hands out samples to everyone and receives an enthusiastic reception. Mrs Ogilvie forgets her worries about Bernie and tries an orange creme and a hazelnut praline. Mabel finishes the rest of the samples in record time and gives Bethany a thumbs up.

Sue goes out to the kitchen to fetch her ice cream samples. She returns with a tray of miniature tubs.

'Was anyone hiding behind the freezer?' asks Isabella.

'Behind the freezer?' says Sue, confused. 'Was there supposed to be?'

Isabella winks at me. 'Not as a general rule, but it has been known. Lily and I think the bakery is haunted. The ghost of one of our pastry chefs appears in the most unexpected places.'

'Don't let the samples melt,' I say before Isabella can get too carried away.

Sue hands out the cups, and everyone tastes the various flavours while she outlines her ideas for selling her product at local fairs and parties and offering ice-cream-making workshops as part of the school holiday club programme.

'Only the school?' asks Mabel, disappointed.

'To begin with,' says Sue. 'But I'll offer the classes more widely if they're a success.'

'Bernie is very fond of strawberry ice cream,' says Mrs Ogilvie, ignoring Mabel's derisive snort.

We finish with Charlie's presentation. He tells us about his idea to promote his craft beers at local pubs and festivals. There's a medieval fair twice a year near Harfield, and everyone agrees he would make a killing there if he ran a stall.

I'm glad he's only brought small samples of beer for the customers to taste. Things are already lively, and I don't want them to descend into chaos. The Silver Surfers knock back their samples with such practised ease that I don't like to think how rowdy things might become if Charlie started handing out pints of the stuff. Besides, I'm not sure where we stand on the subject of licensing laws. The bakery is closed, and we aren't selling the beer, but it's as well not to risk the local constabulary descending on us. Isabella could probably talk them out of prosecuting us by stuffing them with as much cake as they could eat, but I'd prefer not to make the experiment.

Charlie finishes at last and sits down, pleased with the enthusiastic reception his business idea has received.

'That was excellent,' I say. 'All of your presentations were most impressive. You've done a fantastic job and should all be proud of yourselves. I look forward to hearing how your businesses are doing after I've left Honeywell.

Isabella picks up a pair of tongs and performs a drum roll on the countertop. 'And now for the moment of truth. Will the judges hold up their score cards?'

'What score cards?' I ask.

'Don't be so literal,' she says. 'I was speaking metaphorically. I'm trying to increase the tension. Are we asking the audience to vote or are you assuming dictatorship?'

'I was planning to ask the audience for feedback,' I say. 'I've already told you we aren't deciding on a winner.'

Everyone starts to talk loudly, offering their opinions on the best overall product without listening to a word anyone else is saying. Ivy and Mabel look as though they're about to come to blows over the best flavour of jam, while Mrs Ogilvie is arguing vociferously with Mavis about the wisdom of offering dogs a bowl of ice cream on a hot day. They beckon Sue over to settle their argument, and she gives me an imploring look which makes me laugh.

Things are descending into chaos, and I don't know how to rescue them. Who knew an innocent show-and-tell would threaten to destabilise the entire village in this way? It's always been such a peaceful, friendly place. Have I ruined that? Will this event cause a schism from which Honeywell will never recover, with families being split down the middle and long-standing friendships destroyed? The Montagues and Capulets have nothing on what's happening here.

I wave my hands for silence and raise my voice to be heard over the mutterings still coming from Mavis Sotherby's table.

'Thank you so much for your input. It's nice to know you all feel passionate about what we're trying to do here. Perhaps the best thing would be to postpone some of these discussions until later and proceed with handing out the certificates.'

'Who's handing them out?' asks Mabel. 'I'm happy to step up in my capacity of professional chef. I'm not sure why you didn't ask me in the first place.'

'Professional chef!' scoffs Ivy. 'You once washed up a few dishes in some back-street Melbourne dive. That's if we can believe any of your stories. No one was there to prove or disprove it.'

Mrs Ogilvie turns pink. She turns to Ivy, her mouth tight. 'Don't you speak about my sister like that. If she says she worked in a restaurant, that's what she did. She's an excellent cook. She makes chicken casserole exactly as Bernie likes it.'

Mabel jabs her in the ribs. 'Do you want to ruin my reputation forever? I told you I'd stop making it for him if word ever got out.'

Bernie grins at her and licks her hand. She gives his head an exasperated pat. 'If you weren't too daft to know what's going on, I'd sell you to the first person who offered for you.'

'That's all very well,' says Barb. 'But it doesn't qualify you to hand out the prizes as though you think you're the Queen of Australia! I think Mavis should do it.'

I catch Mabel's eye, and she winks at me.

'If you paid any attention at all to world events,' she tells Barb loftily, 'you'd know that Australia has an Emperor. Don't display your ignorance all over Honeywell.'

I shoot one last despairing glance at Lily, who's bright red in the face. For a moment I think she's upset, then I realise she's struggling not to laugh. Either way, she won't be any help. I look over at Ben, whose face gives nothing away.

Ivy stands and points at Mabel. 'And another thing –'

The solution strikes me like a bolt of lightning. I spin around and catch Dad's eye. 'Is there any chance …?'

He also seems to be trying not to laugh, but to my relief he nods.

I turn back to the angry mob. 'If I could have your attention, Ladies and Gentlemen. How many of you have heard of the magazine *Whisk*?'

Isabella's hand shoots up at once, and Lily gives a choke of laughter.

'Anyone else?' I say. It will be awful if no one raises their hand. Dad couldn't fail to take it personally. I should have checked before starting off down this rabbit hole.

'You mean the food magazine?' asks Mavis. 'I read it whenever I see it.'

'Me too,' says Ivy. 'It's the only good thing about visiting the dentist. He always has a copy of it in the waiting room.'

'I'm glad to hear so many of you are enthusiastic about the publication,' I say. 'What you may not know is that the founder of *Whisk*, and the current chief editor, is with us today. I'd like to introduce David Blake-Taylor, who has kindly agreed to hand out the rosettes.'

Mabel gives Dad a hard stare. 'If that's the case, why didn't you mention it earlier? I was about to arm wrestle Mavis Sotherby for the honour.'

Dad gives her a charming smile. 'It's a great honour for me to be invited to hand out the rosettes.'

'Well, of course it is,' she says. 'Is that all you have to say for yourself? I could give a better speech than that.'

'I'm desperate for another cup of tea,' puts in Ivy. 'But I know I won't get one until you've finished, so you'd better hurry up.'

Dad ignores this as he smiles around at my group of pupils. 'Everything I have seen here today is of a very high standard. The five of you appear to have done your research and come up with a host of creative ideas.'

Sue raises her hand. 'I'm sorry to interrupt, but what about Ben? He said he was giving a presentation too.'

'I think Ben was joking,' I say.

'No, I wasn't,' says Ben. 'I told you I'd prepared a presentation, and I have. I wasn't sure you'd allow me to give it, but I brought it just in case.'

He gestures to the box he was carrying when he came in. 'What do you say, Meghan?'

'Never mind what she says!' interrupts Ivy. 'We're the customers, and we want to hear it.'

'Fine,' I say, bewildered. 'But I thought you were a journalist, not a small businessman.'

'I can always make time for something extra,' says Ben. 'I never do any more work than I have to, and I cut corners wherever possible. Some days, I barely achieve anything.'

'You can't imagine how delighted I am to hear that,' says Dad. 'Did you mention this during your initial interview at *Whisk*?'

'Of course not,' says Ben. 'They might not have offered me the job if I had.'

Dad laughs. 'I can see we'll have our hands full with you. But I'm afraid I will have to disqualify you from this particular event. I'm sorry, Meghan, but Ben has a strong conflict of interest in making this presentation.'

I feel my cheeks heat. 'Not because of … because he and I used to … because that wouldn't be fair.'

'Not because of that,' he says. 'Your personal life is your own business. I cannot allow Ben to make a pitch for his new business today because he is one of my employees.'

'No, he isn't!' I say in exasperation. 'He gave in his notice when we were in Paris. Don't say you weren't listening. That's typical of you.'

'I'm afraid you're out of date,' says Dad. 'I'm delighted to say that Ben is the newest permanent member of staff in the food writing department at *Whisk*.'

Chapter Thirty-Four

I look at Ben, who's regarding me with some amusement.

'Is this true?' I ask.

'I'm afraid it is.'

I glance back at Dad, who's looking as imperturbable as usual. 'When did this happen?'

'Shortly after I met you both in Paris.'

'That can't be right,' I say. 'When Ben and I met you there, he told you he was quitting. I distinctly remember him saying so.'

Dad glances at Ben, who grins.

'I remember it too,' Ben says. 'And I meant it. I was pretty upset at the time.'

'I know you were. You told Dad his plans stink.'

Dad's lips twitch. 'I have chosen not to remember that part of our conversation.'

The anger is rising inside me. I have no idea what's happening. All I know is that Ben and Dad both hurt me, and neither of them seems to be taking it seriously. They seem more amused than anything.

'I have no idea what's going on,' I say. 'Obviously, the pair of you have some private joke you don't want to share with me. But that has nothing to do with what we're doing here today. So, shall we move past that and get on with the thing we all came here to do?'

I turn to Ben, who's leaning against the counter, watching me closely.

'There's no point in you being here any longer,' I say. 'If what you and Dad say is true, you don't need to give any kind of presentation, so you'll want to get going. I'm sure you have things to do.'

He straightens up. 'Not really. I wanted to talk to you. That's the only reason I'm here.'

I do my best to look indifferent. 'I can't think what you have to talk to me about, but now is not the time. Shall we get on with this award ceremony?'

His face doesn't change. 'If that's what you want.'

It is, in fact, the last thing I want. But I have no intention of letting him know that and allowing him to hurt me any further. What I really want is for Ben and me never to have gone to Paris and met my father, and for the whole stupid falling out thing not to have happened.

I try to keep my voice steady. 'I think it's best, don't you?'

I hand Lily the list, and she calls out everybody's name. Dad shakes their hands and gives them their certificates and rosettes.

'And that concludes the afternoon's proceedings,' says Isabella when everyone has been congratulated. 'I think we can all agree it's been a great success. Meghan has done a sterling job with her business lessons. Lily and I have agreed to offer similar lessons again in the future, either before Meghan leaves or after Abby comes back.'

'That's right,' agrees Lily. 'And now it's time for refreshments. The first drink is on the bakery, and we will provide you all with cookies. We hope you enjoy them.'

She and Isabella carry plates of cookies around to each table. I expect everyone to dive in at once. My experience of our customers is that most of them are able to eat their bodyweight in baked goods given half a chance. To my surprise, no one moves.

'Is everything all right?' asks Isabella.

'Fine,' says Mabel. 'But I think I speak for everyone when I say this afternoon isn't yet over.'

Ivy nods. 'I agree. Not by a long shot.'

'Is there something wrong with the cookies?' asks Lily. 'Meghan only made them this morning.'

'There's nothing wrong with the cookies,' says Mavis Sotherby impatiently. 'But we haven't yet heard what that young man has to say.'

'Which young man?' asks Lily. Her gaze falls on Ben, and her eyebrows shoot up. 'Do you mean Ben?'

'Of course, we do. He told us he had come here especially to say something. We want to hear what it was.'

Lily gives a snuffle of laughter. 'I think he was talking to Meghan.'

Mary waves an impatient hand. 'We know that. But he's here now, so he can get on with it. None of us is going anywhere until he does. Besides, Meghan is one of us. We want to make sure she's all right.'

I'm very touched they think I'm a part of the village. It's good to feel as though my time here hasn't been for nothing.

Ben's eyes are alight with laughter. 'I'm glad you think so much of Meghan. But Lily is right. I came to talk to Meghan in private.'

'You don't know Honeywell very well, do you?' interrupts Mabel. 'Nothing is private here. You might think it is, but word gets around somehow. You may as well cut out the middleman and say what you want to say in front of us all.'

Ben gives me a hunted look, and I stifle a laugh.

'Could I talk to you outside?' he asks me.

I shake my head. 'Mabel's right. Whatever you have to say to me can be said in front of everyone.'

I force myself to meet his eyes. 'You're the one who was so upset about me keeping secrets. It seems you've been keeping a few of your own. You don't have to tell me if you don't want to. But if you do, now's the time.'

He sighs. 'Remember this was your idea, not mine.'

'I think it was Mabel's. But let's not quibble about details.'

He takes a step towards me. 'I wanted to tell you I'm sorry.'

I study his face. 'For what?'

'For what happened in Paris. But not only that. I understand why you didn't want to tell me who you were when we first met. And I understand why you needed time to know whether you could trust me before you told me more about yourself.'

'What else do you think you understand?' I ask.

He glances at Dad. 'That you lost someone important when you were very young, and you have difficulty trusting that people will be there for you no matter what.'

He draws a painful breath. 'I didn't do anything to help. I walked away as soon as things went wrong. That's entirely on me. I wouldn't blame you if you didn't want to see me again. But I hope you'll give me a chance to try again and do things better this time around.'

I turn to look at Dad. 'Did you tell him all that?'

He hesitates, then nods. 'You gave me a lot to think about when we met in Paris. You and Ben both did. I contacted Ben as soon as I got home and asked him to come and see me. I'm glad he agreed. We had a long talk, during which he told me what he'd said to you and asked how he could persuade you to talk to him. Apparently, you had blocked his number.'

He takes a deep breath. 'I told Ben he needed to respect your decision. But I also explained to him how difficult it was for you to open up to people. In his turn, he told me how I've been making you feel by assuming you wanted to follow in my footsteps. He said you didn't feel as though you were loved for who you were, just for what you chose to do. And that you felt I looked down on your life choices.'

He clears his throat. 'That wasn't easy for me to hear, but I appreciated Ben's honesty. I also realised how badly we had been treating him by holding his job open for someone else. I apologised to him for that. Thankfully, he accepted my apology and agreed to become a permanent member of the *Whisk* team. So, if you're cherishing hopes we will allow you to change your mind, I should inform you the position is no longer open.'

He smiles. 'I think you are far better suited to what you have chosen to do. It has been wonderful to be here this afternoon and see some of what you've been doing and hear how highly everyone thinks of you. I can't tell you how proud I am of you, Meghan, even if I'm no longer prepared to work with you.'

My eyes fill with tears. 'Thanks, Dad,' I say in a choked tone. 'You don't know how much that means to me.'

He gives me a quick hug. 'I'm just glad to have you back in my life.'

I wipe my eyes. 'Me too.'

Mabel leans forward. 'What about Ben?'

Ben takes another step towards me. 'Yes, I've been wondering that.'

He meets my eyes, and my heart gives an unaccountable thud.

He takes my hand. 'Can we start again, Meghan? I'd do anything to make that happen.'

I consider this. 'Would you dive into a chocolate fountain for me?'

'In a heartbeat!'

'Would you take another bike tour around Paris?'

'Without a second thought.'

'Would you ride another mechanical bull?'

'Ten times over,' he says. 'Is it enough?'

'For now,' I say.

He looks as though he's unable to believe what I've just said. 'So, that's a yes?'

'Don't you mean, that's a *oui*?'

He gives a crack of laughter. 'You're quite right. I need to brush up on my French if I want to keep up with you.'

He slips his arms around me, and I lift my face to his. The feel of his lips on mine, the smell of his aftershave, and the solid warmth of his body is so familiar I want to cry. I never thought I'd see him again. Yet here he is, telling me he still wants me, not caring that half the village is here, watching us with interest.

Mabel gives a loud whoop, and we pull away from each other. I'm half laughing and half crying.

'What a dreadful noise!' Mrs Ogilvie tells her reprovingly. 'Bernie was quite shocked.'

'He'll get over it the minute you tell him he can have another dog biscuit,' says Mabel. 'In fact, I wouldn't be surprised if he pretended to have a fit of the vapours especially to get one.'

She eyes me and Ben. 'If the hound doesn't like what's going on, he can jolly well mind his own business.'

Ben wraps his arms around me again. 'I completely agree. And if anyone else doesn't like it, they can wait outside with Bernie until I've kissed Meghan again.'

Chapter Thirty-Five

I pull away at last and look around, embarrassed. The Silver Surfers are watching us with interest. Dad is staring out of the window as though once more fascinated by Honeywell high street. Isabella catches my eye and winks at me. Lily looks delighted with the way things have turned out.

'Well, thank goodness for that,' says Isabella when no one speaks.

'Did you know Ben was coming today?' I ask her.

'I thought he might. But I wasn't sure.'

'I hoped we would see you again,' Lily tells Ben.

He slips an arm around me. 'Thank you. I missed Meghan's Eccles cakes. And her lattes.'

'I knew there was some reason you couldn't keep away,' I say, resting my head on his shoulder.

'I had another motive too,' he says, pulling me closer. 'I've missed you, Meghan.'

'I've had no time to miss you,' I say. 'I've been far too busy organising this presentation.'

'Don't listen to a word she says,' advises Isabella. 'She's been moping around the place like a wet weekend ever since she came back from Paris.'

'The less said about that trip the better,' I tell her.

I turn to Dad. 'Don't pretend you aren't listening to every word. The litter blowing up the high street can't be that enthralling.'

He turns his head to look at us. 'I'm doing my best not to intrude.'

'That ship has pretty much sailed,' I say. 'I hope you don't mind too much that I won't be working for *Whisk*?'

He shakes his head. 'I've had the chance to consider the matter more carefully, and I realise it was never the best idea.'

'It wasn't,' I agree. 'Ben will do a far better job than I ever could. But I should have been more direct with you. I've spent the past few months hiding how I felt, and it hasn't worked. All it did was make me unsure about who I really was. And that's what I intend to find out from now on.'

Dad smiles at me in the way he used to before the pair of us got our wires so hopelessly crossed it appeared we would never untangle them.

'Who you are has always been more than enough for me, Meghan. It always will be. Your mother and I knew how lucky we were when you came along.'

My eyes are suddenly wet. I blink hard and give him a watery smile. 'Thanks, Dad. I don't want to lose you from my life. I never have. I should have realised you didn't want that either.'

'I could have made it clearer,' he says. 'I'll try to do better in the future.'

I slip free of Ben's arms and hug Dad. I can't imagine how I could have considered letting him wander out of my life.

'We still haven't seen this presentation everyone's talking about,' Mabel says impatiently.

'Keep up!' says Ivy. 'He doesn't really have one. It was all a ruse to get Meghan to let him into the bakery.'

'That's not entirely true,' says Ben. 'I have, in fact, prepared a presentation. I was trying to think of something original – something that would do our esteemed leader credit.'

He nods towards me. 'That's you, Meghan.'

'I'm aware of that,' I say. 'But I'm not sure I want to see what's inside that box.'

'Of course, you do.'

He hands it to me. 'I'm afraid I didn't have time to make samples for everyone. Also, I'm not interested in anyone else's opinion. I only care about what Meghan thinks.'

'What's the business idea?' demands Mabel.

'It's difficult to describe,' says Ben. 'I was thinking of marketing it to men who've messed up their relationships but would really like the chance to try again.'

'I can't imagine there's much of a market for that,' she says. 'I've rarely met a man who would admit to being wrong about anything. But go ahead!'

'Thank you,' he says gravely. 'In your own time, Meghan.'

I open the box and pull out a bar of chocolate and a box of matches.

'It's a make-your-own chocolate fountain,' he says. 'It was the best I could do at short notice.'

I pick up a small, white tin. 'What's this?'

'It's a puncture repair kit. I'm hoping to take many more bike tours with you in the future, and it's as well to be prepared. I've also included a first aid kit in case of any stray dogs.'

I reach into the box again and pull out a packet of earplugs.

'For the next time you're forced to listen to a long and boring presentation,' he tells me.

'A surprisingly useful gift,' I say. 'Thank you.'

Next comes a pocket-sized book titled *Essential phrases for your holiday in France*.

I glance at Ben, who grins. 'It tells you exactly when you should and shouldn't use the word *amusant*. Among other things.'

'And this?' I ask, waving a false moustache at him.

'All the best French boyfriends are wearing them this season,' he says. 'And they're tricky to grow at short notice. You'll notice I've also included a tiny watercolour kit. Essential for all fake boyfriends. At least, the ones pretending to be artists.'

'In Jean Luc's case, a can of paint spray might have been more appropriate,' I say. 'And bail money.'

I delve back into the box and find a sheriff's badge with the words Calamity Meg enamelled on it.

'You earned it,' he says. 'That mechanical bull didn't quite finish me off, but Dead-Eye Derek would have done so if it hadn't been for your timely intervention.'

At the bottom of the box is a single dried rose. For a moment, I can't think where it's come from. When has Ben ever sent me roses?

'It's from the Luxembourg Gardens,' he says. 'I went back and picked it after I left you that day.'

'But why? You'd just told me you didn't want to see me again.'

'Don't remind me,' he says ruefully. 'I regretted it almost immediately.'

He smiles. 'I almost got kicked out by one of the gardeners after I'd picked that rose. I had to make a run for it.'

'I wish I'd been there to see it. You should have jumped onto one of the ponies to make your daring escape.'

'Cattle rustling isn't my thing,' he says. 'You saw me on that mechanical bull. What are the chances I'd have stayed on a pony for long enough to get out of the gardens?'

'Not good. But thank you very much for the rose. I'll treasure it forever.'

'I'll pick you another one the next time we go to Paris,' he promises. 'Maybe I'll buy you a bunch of them. It might be safer.'

I look up and meet his eyes. 'Do you think your apology boxes will sell?'

'You're my target demographic,' he says. 'You tell me.'

I look at all the things he's put together just for me. 'I'd buy it.'

His face lights up. 'Really?'

'Yes. I can't guarantee you'll get it funded if you take it to Dragon's Den. But as far as I'm concerned, it's perfect.'

Isabella peers over my shoulder. 'That chocolate looks delicious.'

'You can't have it,' I say. 'Ben put it in there for me.'

'I did,' he says. 'This box is just the start. We've only known each other for a short while, Meghan. We haven't had time to make many memories, so I did the best with what I had. I'm hoping we'll make plenty more memories together, and our box of strange and bizarre experiences will fill up over the years.'

'Me too,' I say. 'Thank you, Ben. It's perfect.'

Isabella claps her hands. 'We have a winner!'

'I thought this wasn't a competition,' says Greg.

'It isn't,' I reassure him. 'But I didn't expect to see Ben here today, so I don't have a rosette for him.'

'I'm way ahead of you,' says Isabella. 'I realised as soon as he arrived that you hadn't made provision for him. So, I took the liberty of slipping into the supply closet and fashioning a makeshift one in case it was needed.'

She hands me a pink striped paper rosette. 'I tore up one of our gift bags, sprinkled on some of that edible food colouring, and finished it with a twist tie. I knew all my years of watching children's television would pay off one day.'

I take the rosette from her and hold it out to Ben. 'I spoke too soon. I can't give you the same one we gave everyone else because your product isn't yet ready for the wider market. But I'd like to award you this for creativity, persistence, and general all-round shamelessness. Will you pin it on or shall I do it?'

'You, please,' he says. 'Is this where I make a speech about my journey so far and all my future hopes and dreams?'

'It is not. You know my opinion of pompous presenters with their over-inflated egos.'

He takes my hands and looks down at me with an expression that takes my breath away. 'The first time I met you, you were doing your best to take a racing dive into a chocolate fountain. Since then, you've hidden behind a fridge, rescued me from a would-be gold thief, knocked me off my bike into a Parisian gutter, and tried to pass me off as your French boyfriend. And every single thing you've done has made me realise you're the person I want to spend all my time with.'

I'm laughing and crying at the same time. 'The first time I saw you, you were boring everyone senseless talking about food awards. Since then, you've forced me to hide behind a fridge, taken me to an extremely dodgy nineteenth-century saloon, pretended very unconvincingly to be a French artist, almost collided with an innocent dog, and gate-crashed an important presentation. And every single thing you've done has made me feel exactly the same way about you.'

He pulls me into his arms again and kisses me as though we're the only two people in the room.

I emerge at last, breathless and laughing. 'This is neither the time nor the place.'

His eyes are darker than ever as he looks into mine. 'I hesitate to contradict you, but in my opinion it's both.'

Isabella gestures towards the kitchen door. 'Let's split the difference. We have a perfectly good kitchen where you can continue this discussion. In the meantime, who would like some more cookies?'

'I think Bernie is a little peckish,' says Mrs Ogilvie, and Bernie gives a hopeful bark.

'That dog is a lot of things,' says Mabel darkly. 'Hungry is very rarely one of them.'

Mrs Ogilvie bristles. 'You've never been fair to Bernie.'

'You've been fair enough for the both of us!' retorts Mabel.

Several people join in to express their opinions, and Bernie adds his mite to the discussion. Amid the hubbub, Ben takes my hand and leads me through the crowd towards the kitchen.

'There isn't a chocolate fountain in there,' he says. 'But there's a very large fridge for you to hide behind if the mood takes you.'

He pushes open the kitchen door and gestures me inside. 'I was curious about that back door the first time I was in here. I think we should open it and step outside to see what happens.'

'Good idea,' I say. 'It probably won't lead to a magical world, but I don't care.'

He wraps his arms around me and pulls me close. 'I couldn't agree more. You and I are the luckiest people in the world, Meghan. We may not have Narnia, but we'll always have Paris.'

I hope you enjoyed this book. If you did, please consider leaving a review on Amazon. It helps new readers find my books, and I really appreciate it.

Join my mailing list to receive a free story about a reluctant bridesmaid and be the first to be notified about my upcoming books.

rosemarywhittaker.com/signup

A Sugarloaf Valentine

When the ingredients for love turn into a recipe for disaster…

Lily's world is turned upside down when her ex-boyfriend Stephen walks into her bakery, hoping to buy Valentine's cookies for his new girlfriend. To make matters worse, he wants Lily to decorate them with a message of love.

Determined not to let him see her heartbroken, Lily tells him she has met someone else too and has never been happier. It's a risky deception, but luckily, she knows just the man to help her out.

She doesn't count on ending up on a double date with Stephen and his new girlfriend. Nor does she expect her fake boyfriend to have a secret of his own.

As Valentine's Day approaches, and Lily struggles to create the perfect cookies, she wonders whether the recipe for happiness has been in front of her all along.

With a cast of charming characters, and a dash of sweet romance, A Sugarloaf Valentine is a delightful read that will have you falling in love with love all over again.

Available now in paperback and Kindle ebook

A Tale of Two Christmases

Annie never comes home for Christmas. There's too much chance of running into Alex. He broke her heart, and she never wants to speak to him again.

Alex always comes home for Christmas. He's desperate to talk to Annie about what went wrong between them.

Faced with a family crisis, Annie reluctantly agrees to spend the holidays with her parents. It shouldn't be too difficult to avoid Alex for just one week.

But she didn't expect to arrive in the middle of the wedding of the year. The entire village will be there, and no one will be able to avoid anyone else.

It's a battle of two Christmases, and only one can win.

Snuggle up in front of a roaring fire with a mug of hot chocolate and enjoy this sparkling Christmas romance.

Available now in paperback and Kindle ebook

The Cinnamon Snail

She's found the love of her life. He just hasn't realised it …

When Christian moves from Copenhagen to London, Kate quickly tumbles into love. He's the most handsome and charismatic man she's ever met, and she's all set for her Happily Ever After.

Until he announces that he's returning to Copenhagen, and he doesn't want her to go with him. Nothing Kate can say will change his mind. All she can do is plan a new future without him. And if that future happens to be in Denmark, that's entirely her own business.

She gets a job at The Cinnamon Snail Cafe and sets out to win Christian back. His new girlfriend is a slight problem – but when true love is on the line, anything goes.

Kate has a year to prove she can settle into a new country and persuade the love of her life she means business. A piece of cake!

A delightful new story of Danish pastries, romance, and lots and lots of hygge.

Available now in paperback and Kindle ebook

About the author

Rosemary Whittaker wanted to be an author as soon as she was old enough to hold a book the right way up. From that moment on, she was the despair of her teachers, who attempted to impart the basics of an education while she stared out of the window, making up characters and situations.

Having accidentally absorbed enough to graduate and become a teacher, she spent the next few decades moving around the world with her husband, children, and menagerie of unexpected pets.

She accidentally found herself in Australia some years back and intends to stay there for a very long time. She currently spends her time writing, sourcing English marmite and salad cream and wrangling her two determinedly destructive house bunnies – Pumpkin and Midway.

Rosemary has written several light-hearted romance novels set in the different countries in which she has lived. She also writes children's books as R J Whittaker – in particular a series of books about a recalcitrant monkey named Pom Pom, who is not in any way, shape or form based on her experience of raising her own four boys.

Printed in Great Britain
by Amazon

45845076R00145